Praise for *Captain Cut-throat*:

"Only John Dickson Carr, the master of suspense novels, could write this whodunit."
—*Chicago Sunday Tribune*

"An old and professional hand at murder and suspense chillers, John Dickson Carr has once more added a dash of history to his formula of quick deaths cleverly solved." —*New York Times*

"Tension, terror and swashbuckling action by one of the all-time masters." —*Chicago Daily News*

Other John Dickson Carr mysteries
available from Carroll & Graf:

Bride of Newgate
The Curse of the Bronze Lamp
Dark of the Moon
The Devil in Velvet
The Emperor's Snuff-Box
Fire, Burn!
Nine Wrong Answers
Papa Là-Bas

John Dickson Carr
Captain Cut-Throat

Carroll & Graf Publishers, Inc.
New York

Published by arrangement with Harold Ober Associates, Inc.

First Carroll & Graf edition 1988
Second edition 1998

Carroll & Graf Publishers, Inc.
19 West 21st Street
New York, NY 10010

ISBN: 0-7867-0547-7

Manufactured in the United States of America

Contents

John Dickson Carr
Captain Cut-Throat

Let us be masters of the Straits for six hours, and we shall be masters of the world.

— NAPOLEON BONAPARTE, *to Admiral Latouche Treville*

Chapter I

Thunder Over Boulogne

Along the whole length of the Iron Coast, from Alprech Point to Cape Gris-Nez, five out of seven corps of the Grand Army breathed the salt air of the English Channel.

The shadow of the new Emperor lay long across Europe. Behind massed guns, fevered to impatience, the camps stirred with a hundred and fifty thousand infantry, ninety thousand cavalry. Their centre was the Odre cliff at Boulogne, where the boss's grey pavilion looked out across a grey-green Channel towards the cliffs of Dover.

Restless, restless, restless! The four camps, from Ambleteuse and Wimereux to Outreau and Le Portel, echoed to two thousand drums which were seldom still. By day you heard the low, thick roll or the spring-rattle tap; the stamp, clink, and snuffle of horses; over all, a crawling growl of voices talking at once. By night, when it was quieter and a cold wind tore across chalky, light-brown headlands, rose the quarter-hour shout from the quays along the harbour below.

"Sentinels, attention!"

The inner harbour, crammed with shallops and flat-bottomed barges, was guarded by sentries at only fifteen paces apart. Back floated a mournful chorus farther out, amid broken light-reflections, from sailors in the ship-tops.

"Good watch! Good watch!"

It was ghostly when you contrasted this, by day, with the cursing or the laughter of embarkation-exercises on the beaches. All waited for the boss, though in early days the boss was seldom there. Sometimes he would dash from Paris in his six-seater coach, for a surprise visit which was not often a surprise either to Admiral Bruix or to Marshal Soult, the Commander-in-Chief.

If he brought with him the handsome, full-blown Empress amid her laughing ladies-in-waiting, they stayed at the château in the village of Pont-de-Briques, nearly a league away on the Paris road. Only the boss himself stayed at the pavilion, with his valet and his bodyguard. There he would peer through his great telescope, or sit for hours gesticulating in the council-room while everybody else had to stand up. Outside it, his grey riding-coat was all over the place: never still.

And yet, as the summer of 1805 waxed towards its hottest, that piled-up welter of men had gradually drawn towards an edge of nerves from too long inaction, from too much crowding, from too few women.

If all the artillery of the Iron Coast cut loose at once, from the battery of monsters on the Odre cliff to the guns of the two forts in the outer harbour, they said its noise would have thundered in Kentish hopfields. But to some French officers, gnawing at the undersides of their moustaches, it would have seemed less loud in imagination than words cried at once from so many throats:

"This pains my back! Why won't the boss get a move on and invade England?"

And now, the news had been creeping out, there was something much worse.

The night was a bad time, an eerie time for sentry-go. With an unknown murderer loose in the Boulogne Camp —appearing from nowhere, stabbing sentries, and then vanishing like a ghost—it might be a spark to powder.

Captain Cut-throat.

Late on the afternoon of August 20th, under the greasy shimmer of a heat-haze, a horseman in the uniform of the Hussars of Bercy galloped out of the high-town of Boulogne by the Porte Neuve and the route de Calais, along the roundabout way which led towards the Emperor's pavilion.

He rode like the devil, his dolman and busby-feather streaming out, a half-image in moving dust. He had a mission, but there was something else very much on his mind. As he drew near the middle of the camp, all those acres of wood and mud-walled houses arranged neatly in streets and avenues, the horseman sought someone, anyone, with whom he could speak.

The only person in sight was a common soldier of nondescript dress. He was a burly man, past his first youth, with a heavy moustache and shaggy dark hair. He wore no tunic; his breeches, waistcoat, and high-buttoned gaiters were all of a dingy white. Standing in the trim, tiny front-garden of one of the thatched-roof houses, built to shelter fifteen men, he was sprinkling flowers from a watering-pot.

The officer of hussars reined in, amid settling dust.

"Hoy! You! Grandpa!"

For a moment the burly man did not glance up. The watering-pot, painted bright blue, looked like a toy in his hands.

"Did you hear me, Grandpa?"

Grandpa raised his head, and slowly surveyed the man on the horse. Then he spat, in a majestic arc from under his moustache. But he spoke without heat.

"Shut that," he said, from deep in his throat. "Wipe the mother's milk off your moustache, my brat!"

A half-pleased, wicked smile tightened down the horse-man's mouth over the brass links in the chin-strap of his high busby. Though he spoke French like an Alsatian, he had actually been born in Prussia. He was a blond young man with a long, bony jaw and a nose of high arrogance; dust-stains whitened the freckles against the sweat of his long face.

"I am an officer, look," he explained. His voice also was young, cold, poised. "Perhaps you have heard of me. I am Lieutenant Schneider, of the Hussars of Bercy."

Grandpa spat again.

"And I," he said, "am Jules Dupont, a grenadier of the Imperial Guard. So what?"

Some distance away, a howitzer whacked from the direction of the harbour. Lieutenant Schneider, savouring the lesson he meant to administer, glanced in that direction. Over so many acres of thatched-roof houses there was little to be seen except the tall flag-staff between the Emperor's pavilion and the smaller pavilion of Admiral Bruix.

A strong wind, always raking those cliffs, whipped out flags run up as signals to the ships. From the beaches below, the wind rolled a faint, vast, struggling noise of troops at embarkation exercises.

"Clumsy damned louts! The English will make you eat musket-balls if you fall in the water like that!"

"So-and-so to you!"

Lieutenant Schneider, with a cold and poised sneer, naturally could not hear what was said. But, whoever had

3

called the men clumsy louts, that officer remained discreetly silent before the far-from-whispered reply.

For it was a regrettable fact that the French had little fondness for discipline of the more formal sort. Too many of them could remember the Revolution, comparatively few years ago, when the arrogant of this earth had fallen under the guillotine-knife and sneezed into the bran-basket. Even the boss himself, crowned Emperor only since last December, occupied a still-shaky throne undermined from within by both republicans and royalists alike.

"How dull it will be!" had sighed one of the pretty ladies, during the candle-lit coronation-ceremony at Notre Dame, when the weight of the boss's robes nearly pulled him over on his back like a beetle. "How dull it will be, now that we are all obliged to become Christians again!"

Only the boss could fully control that mighty but temperamental fighting-force known as the Grand Army. And even the boss himself could not always manage it. There had been no acts of open rebellion; but at such a time as this, with an unknown murderer roaming at night through the Boulogne Camp, a wise officer knew better than to shred frayed tempers too far.

Lieutenant Hans Schneider, of the Hussars of Bercy, held different views.

"Jules Dupont, grenadier of the Imperial Guard," he said, and committed the name to memory. Whereupon he sneered again. "Well, Grandpa. You made Syria, I suppose?"

The old-moustache looked back at him for an instant, and then went on sprinkling flowers out of the blue watering-pot.

"I have warned you once, Dupont. I won't warn you again.—You made Syria, I suppose?"

"Italy, Egypt, Syria . . . ah, bah! What does it matter?"

"That is a better tone, Dupont, though I mean to see it improved before I leave you. And aren't you at all curious, Grandpa? Don't you want to hear the news?"

"News?" growled the other, eyeing him. "Why should I guess what I can hear on sentry-go at Pont-de-Briques? The boss has been in Paris to see his Minister of Marine. Tonight," and Dupont's shaggy head jerked southwards, "he'll be back at the château with his women. Tomorrow he'll ride here to kick up a row about something, so you

4

run ahead to warn Soult. No, no, my gosling! You want to hear the news."

"I?"

"Hell, yes! The news of Captain Cut-throat."

Nowhere in that camp was the air very good. The complaint known as the itch had long been prevalent; and now, in the hotter weather, there was the added nuisance of fleas. Yet mention of that name, 'Captain Cut-throat,' made even unsavoury air grow poisoned.

"Yes, Captain Cut-Throat!" said Dupont of the Imperial Guard. "He stabbed another sentry last night. And two of Joyet's pals were looking on and saw it done, but didn't even see the whiskers of the man who did it."

Lieutenant Schneider's long, powerful legs seemed to grow longer as he stood up in his stirrups, above the saddle and the zebra-skin saddle-cloth. Though his light-blue tunic was dust-splashed, the greasy sun flashed back from arabesques of silver braid across his chest, and across the fur-trimmed blue dolman swung from his left shoulder.

"What are you singing there, Grandpa? That's impossible! You lie!"

"Lie do I?" yelled Dupont of the Imperial Guard. And the guardsman told the hussar officer exactly what he, Lieutenant Schneider, could do. "Now ride away and play, brat!"

From his right-hand saddle-holster Lieutenant Schneider took out the long flintlock pistol. Carefully, with deliberation, he fired straight at Dupont's heart and shot him through the left collar-bone instead.

Lieutenant Schneider's chestnut-coloured mare did not even blink at the unexpected powder-flare or bang of the shot. But it was as though the mare's hind hoofs had kicked Dupont spinning backwards, kicked him back on a sanded path decorated with a little trimming of sea-shells. The blue watering-pot flew wide, its contents gleaming under the sun, before it landed in a flower-bed.

Out of the house plunged and tumbled three more men of the Imperial Guard, all in undress. One, his face lathered, held a razor. Another was brushing the long-tailed uniform-coat, once dark blue with red facings and red shoulder-knots, which exposure to all weathers had turned muddy grey.

"Myself I'll report this to Marshal Soult," said Lieutenant Schneider, replacing the pistol. "You guardsmen, I fear, think you're the Emperor's pets. Learn better next time."

Flick went the wink of his spurs, lightly against the mare's flanks.

As the horse's hoofs thudded forward in dust along the street of thatched-roofed houses, a yell of rage went up from three sunburnt throats. Another guardsman, saying nothing, ran out of the house with a loaded musket. Flinging the stock to his shoulder, he would have put a ball into the retreating horseman if other men had not come hurrying out into the road to obstruct his aim. The strains of a flute, piping that old but still popular satirical tune, 'Nelson Played the Devil at Boulogne,' abruptly stopped.

"Stand aside! Stand aside!"

Again Lieutenant Schneider bent low and rode hard. His long jaws, framed in their wiry yellowish side-whiskers, appeared better pleased. He rode into the full reek of the camp, a travelling dust of cooking and horses and troops.

On his right stretched away the sun-baked earth of the parade-ground where, a year ago, the boss had reviewed his whole army under the eyes of the prowling English frigates in the Channel; and where, in four days' time, there was to be another grand review. Through dust bloomed uniforms: white-mantled Dragoons; the dark green of the Guides; the very dark blue, with orange facings and orange trouser-stripes, of the newly formed Imperial Marines. But Lieutenant Schneider did not draw rein until . . .

"Take care, I beg of you!" cried a youthful voice.

The road was partly blocked by a six-gun battery of Flying Artillery, which had no business to be there at all.

When one gun-team dropped the off-front wheel of an ammunition-wagon into a pot-hole, there had been an accident almost unheard-of; the axle broke but the powder-cart crashed down without further damage. Cynical artillerymen, who could endure much and spit far and were now wondering why they had not been blown to pieces, gathered round a young and nervous officer with a fluff of golden-brown moustache.

"That's done it, Lieutenant d'Albret," cheerfully said an old under-officer. "It's a good job the boss——"

"The Emperor! And stop scratching yourself!"

"Pardon, my lieutenant; I've got the itch. As I was saying, it's a good job the boss ain't here. If you'd seen us in the old days, when we hauled the guns over the Alps with lanterns in a snowstorm, we'd all have heard a thing or two about this."

Now the boss himself was only thirty-six, the oldest of his marshals no more than middle-aged. But they had measured time by so many battle-hours, they had marched in triumph through so many lands and under so many suns, that the line of lanterns crossing the Alps to Marengo seemed remote in history even though it was a scant five years ago.

So the very young Lieutenant Philippe d'Albret, immature face flushed, clearly born of old aristocrat stock now reconciled to the upstart Emperor, sat his horse in an agony of humiliation and good manners.

"A caisson-axle never breaks!" he said. "In any case, it shouldn't!"

"That's all right, now! Easily remedied," soothed the under-officer. Secretly he gave his companions a glare to back up their lieutenant, which they immediately did.

"An accident," cried Lieutenant d'Albret, "which could never have been foretold. Never! Is it worse, I ask you, than to have in the camp a murderer like a ghost, who can't be seen even when he walks in the light?"

D'Albret checked himself, and froze. Every man froze, hand on horse or gun-limber.

It was as though, into their midst had fallen a shell with a sputtering fuse. Every man was conscious of that shell, but not one would pretend to notice it until it exploded. They seemed to feel it in the very pores of the skin when Lieutenant d'Albret blurted out the unsayable: Captain Cut-throat.

A horse whinnied. Hans Schneider, who had been about to ride past the steaming gun-teams, again stood up in his stirrups. This time, ingratiatingly, he bared his teeth in an attempt at a polite smile.

"You, sir!" he called out to the too-young Lieutenant d'Albret. "I could not help hearing what you said about our murderer. I am Schneider, Hussars of Bercy. Perhaps my name or face may be familiar to you."

("Now who the devil," muttered the under-officer, as

Jules Dupont had wondered, "knows the name or face of a subaltern in the hussars?")

Schneider did not deign to notice this.

"I hear," he called, "there has been another killing: very well! But a fool of a grenadier says that other sentries were watching the victim and still saw nothing. You, sir. Is that true?"

Lieutenant d'Albret flushed and bit his lip like a girl.

"Yes, it's true! The sentry was attacked from in front: just like Saulomon of the 7th Light Infantry! But this man could have fired at anybody who came near; he was standing in full light for metres on every side of him. And yet two witnesses, who were looking straight at him, swear he was alone when he screamed and doubled up."

"So!"

"Here's General Savary," cried Lieutenant d'Albret in his clear, high voice, "the head of our Military Police. He had better find this assassin before, among weaker ones, there is mutiny. Nobody can talk of anything except Captain Cut-throat. But what, sir, does General Savary do? Nothing!"

"Savary is a fool. Everybody knows that."

"The general is a good soldier; he is not supposed to be intelligent. But at least he should try——"

"So?" enquired Schneider. "If they would really find this assassin, they must go much further for a man with wit enough to arrest him. They must go to Paris."

"To Paris?"

"To Fouché, the old fox! To Fouché, the red-headed skeleton! Most civilians, as you were about to say, are not worth the powder to blow them up; I agree. But Fouché, from what I have heard, knows how to keep dogs chained and the mob in its place."

The old under-officer, even while he glared at Schneider, could not help whistling loudly. Though the Grand Army professed to be careless or even contemptuous of the dreaded Minister of Police, who was said to keep five thousand spies in Paris alone, still Schneider could have mentioned no more potent name than that of Joseph Fouché.

"However!" he added, with an air of secret pleasure and a resumption of his former aloof manner. "That is no business of yours or mine. Who was killed last night? What regiment?"

"I don't know—officially! They won't announce it. But . . ."

"Continue, young man. I will tell you when I have heard enough."

"Well! Everybody knows it was Grenadier Joyet, of the Marine Guard."

"And in full light, you say? Where, in the night, could any sentry look about him in full light?"

"Come now," exclaimed Lieutenant d'Albret, flinging away all caution. "There could have been only one place for this murder. Don't you understand?"

"S-s-t!" the under-officer hissed warningly. "My lieutenant!"

Schneider stared back, his dust-caked lips framing some word they could not catch. Then he tossed his busby, and was off at so hard a gallop that within half a minute he had come near his destination.

Far behind him, and to his left, rose the slope of Boulogne high-town with the semaphore-arms on the tower of its town-hall. Just ahead, near the edge of the cliffs above the glittering waters of the Channel, was the Emperor's long wooden pavilion with its glass-enclosed front.

Night or day, occupied or empty, it was protected vigilantly by the Imperial Guard or the Imperial Marines, patrolling inside a head-high fence of wooden palings set back at some distance from the pavilion. Four grenadiers of the Guard paced there now, muskets shouldered and red plumes flying, in the high bearskin caps they wore on parade.

Schneider glanced at the pavilion, as though derisive yet faintly speculating. Then he looked past the flag-staff, past Admiral Bruix's smaller pavilion, to the little hut with the conical thatched roof where Marshal Soult lived half-underground like a savage.

He had started for there when Schneider, even Schneider, could not help jumping and flinging round his head at the sudden devastating roar of noise from below. Amid so many yells of execration, from men dancing with fury on the beaches, two voices clove through.

"The English ship! The same English ship!"

"Where?"

"There, you dummy! Look!"

"Always the same one? Are you sure?"

9

"Yes, very sure! Grand God, where is our artillery?"

In an instant he got his answer: noises half splitting the sky.

Some of the English cruisers, nose-thumbing, would run in under the batteries and loose a broadside for the devil of it. But this most insulting of all nose-thumbers, the forty-four-gun frigate *Medusa*, which never fired a shot . . .

In she stood, running before a fair breeze, straight on a line between the Crib Fort and the Wooden Fort.

Lieutenant Schneider galloped past the Emperor's pavilion to the edge of the cliff. For the third time he stood up in his stirrups above the zebra-skin saddle-cloth. The wind pounced at him, raking and stinging his eyes. But he could see clearly, against a grey-green Channel cut by the narrow edges of white-caps.

Though she was still far out, he could discern *Medusa's* rakish brown-and-red lines, and the sun-gleam on her two gun-decks. Up from the conical-roofed hut, ape-like, popped old Soult himself. He stood there with brass telescope raised, the gold oak-leaves gleaming against his marshal's tunic, and his great cocked hat printed black against the fiery sky. Through his telescope he could have seen the wrinkles in the face of the man on the quarter-deck, *Medusa's* captain, who had not yet troubled to raise his own glass.

"Closer yet! The so-and-so is coming closer! Have our gunners gone blind?"

"But they are seamen, these goddams! Admit it!"

"Put me peace to your treason! Hit her!—Ah!"

Now, without a telescope, they could all see the patches on the frigate's snowy canvas and her (literally) nose-thumbing crew. They could fancy if not hear the crack of canvas as her mizzen-topsails backed and filled. Then, as the frigate came round broadside, somebody in the Wooden Fort found the range.

A round-shot smashed and carried away her bowsprit, and howls of triumph from the beaches nearly drowned the gun-crashes. Momentarily the frigate staggered as though struck with a fist; French infantrymen went mad with joy and jumped in the water. But the frigate, despite flapping canvas and wrecked cordage, got away like a dancer and beat to windward under the fire of both forts.

Thick gunsmoke blew back above the sharp tang of

seaweed. Lieutenant Schneider, his eyes bitten by chalk-particles gouged there on the windy cliff-edge, lifted and shook his fist.

"That is insolence," he said aloud. "That is insolence we do not endure. Never to fire a shot, never to break out their colours, never to——"

"Gently, my friend!" struck in another voice.

Schneider, furious and flicking the reins with his wrist, had just escaped cannoning his chestnut-coloured mare into another horse, a fine dapple grey, whose rider was sitting motionless and looking at him.

The other cavalryman wore the green coat of the Mounted Guides: a dark green, its red collar and cuffs vivid against gold-buttoned white waistcoat. He was a young man of about Schneider's age, with a sun-tanned humorous face. Above a dark moustache his eyes and even his nose would have been mocking if the man himself, both by instinct and training, had not been polite to the point of indolence.

"Gently, my friend!" he repeated.

Guns still banged along the coast, though the shouts were fading into a resumed bark of officers. Schneider looked the newcomer up and down without favor.

"Be good enough," he said, "to move aside and not block my path. Perhaps you have heard of me. I am——"

"Yes. Yes, I know!" said the other cavalryman. "And I am called Mercier, Guy Mercier." He touched the single gold epaulet he wore. "A humble captain of the Guides, as you see. As for you, sir, in the past half-hour your name has been all but graven on my heart."

Whack! Whack! went a last salvo from the coast.

These two looked at each other, and something ran between them like light along a sabre-blade. Both horses shuddered and moved, but not from noise. From the left hip of each horseman, sabretache rattled against sabre.

"But I must apologize," continued Captain Mercier, in a deceptively innocent tone. "I have been following you, out of curiosity, ever since (quite properly, of course) you corrected that grenadier for his insolence. Then, when you began speaking of our ever-glorious Minister of Police, you really interested me. Are you acquainted with Joesph Fouché?"

11

"No. I am not. But I admire his methods. Why does it interest you?"

"Because," Mercier said musingly, "I am not sure you understand his methods at all. When I knew him . . ."

"You knew him?"

"I had that honor, yes. As a very young man, when I studied for the priesthood at Nantes, the then-hungry Fouché was my instructor in logic and mathematics."

"Come!" exploded Schneider, with a kind of sneering guffaw. "I did not know the Guides were honored by a man of your cloth."

"Alas! They are not," said Mercier in the same deprecating way. "I discovered, very early, I had no more call to the priesthood than prospective Father Fouché himself. Since then he has risen very high in the world: he has served Robespierre during the Revolution, and betrayed him; he has served Barras during the Directory, and betrayed him; now he serves the Emperor, and serves him well. He is quite untrustworthy and quite ruthless. But there is a certain likeable fascination about the old twister. If by any chance he were called into this affair, as in fact I have heard before . . ."

"I have heard he was to be called in," Schneider bared his teeth. "You would be good enough to approve it, Captain Mercier?"

"Approve it?" cried Mercier, with enthusiasm. "My friend, I cherish it as a romantic dream! The Minister of Police could not be here himself to find Captain Cutthroat; but he could send an agent. You know, I hope, that when possible he prefers to employ a woman?"

Schneider stared at him.

"A woman? A woman to trap Captain Cut-throat? A woman at the Boulogne Camp?"

On the edge of the windy cliff, above the green-glittering Channel and the smoke of the last firing, Mercier swept up his arm as though to invoke all the powers of the air.

"Why not two women?" he demanded. "Why not anything? When Joseph Fouché takes a hand in the game, the very cardsharps run and hide to escape his tricks. Where, I wonder, is the Minister of Police at this moment? What devious plot is he spinning now?"

Chapter II

The Blonde: With Satan at Home

The dreaded Minister of Police was at home. And at Paris, two nights later on the 22nd of August, he was receiving a guest.

From outside, his lair looked like a row of tall, dingy stone houses close-set along the whole length of the Quai des Augustins beside the Seine. Actually they had been turned into one house, a rabbit-warren of communicating doors, a hive of offices paper-crammed and stuffy in the heat.

At the extremity of one wing, in a room rather spacious though curtained and airless because Joseph Fouché had a weak throat, the Minister of Police sat behind his flat-topped desk, with a candle burning in a pewter candle-stick on either side of him, and smiled with genuine charm. Once upon a time, many years ago, the sister of Maximilien Robespierre would have married him instantly if he had asked her.

"You understand, my dear," he said to his present visitor, "that I am never surprised?"

"Yes, yes, of course I understand!" answered Madeleine, attempting to laugh. "All the same . . ."

Madeleine, blonde as a Grecian Venus, had a rich and warm laugh, an infectious laugh, when she could summon it up at all. At the moment, however, she was terrified and sick with foreboding. She knew she had done no wrong, but by this time she felt the whole world must be leagued against her.

The darkness was pierced only by those two burning points of the tapers, shining on Fouché's long emaciated cheeks and his dusty-looking red hair. In addition to everything else, the stifling heat of the office held a vague sour smell like that of illness; it made her nostrils twitch.

13

But the Minister of Police was not in the least ill. Pleasantly, disarmingly, he held up a bloodless hand.

"——and that, as I have explained," he went on, "was the situation as it existed two nights ago, when the Emperor arrived back at Boulogne and sent the order I have just read to you. Permit me to read it again."

His long hand, with its upstanding shiny knuckles and pale blue snake-veins, moved to his left and picked up a piece of paper. The movement of the hand made one candle-flame undulate slightly.

" 'Adopt what means you choose,' " he read, " 'but deliver this Captain Cut-throat to the military authorities within one week.' "

"One week?" cried Madeleine.

"Precisely."

"Commencing from when?"

"Presumably from two nights ago, the 20th, when I received this message by M. Chappe's semaphore."

The Minister of Police put down the paper at his left hand.

"Now that is characteristic," he added, almost admiringly. "For example! The cliffs below the Emperor's pavilion have a steep slope down to the harbour and the low-town. Long ago His Majesty discovered that he could scarcely climb down that goat-track, much less descend on horseback. 'Adopt what means you choose,' he said to his engineers, 'but I must be able to ride down that path in three days.' They said it could not be done.——Dear lady, it was done."

Fouché paused.

Tall and frail, rigid and high-shouldered, with a black muslin neckcloth wound round his long frail throat, he spoke as dispassionately as the schoolmaster he had once been. And then he smiled, showing bad teeth.

"Plots against the Empire or even the Emperor's own person? With these I can deal quite easily. If two persons in France come together to plot treason, one of these persons will be an agent in my own pay.

"But a solitary person? A madman, a royalist, a republican? Or, which is more probable, an assassin in the employ of William Pitt?" The name, as he pronounced it, sounded like Veeyam Peet. "That, I confess, is more difficult. But it must be done and shall be done.

14

"Now listen to me with care. Aside from one corps commanded by Bernadotte in the east, and another corps commanded by Augereau in the west, the entire Army is in the north. Everything waits, hangs, holds its breath, for the Emperor's thunderbolt-stroke against England. When will it come? I do not know. Where or how or by what strategy? None can say.

"But this much I tell you. One thing alone could destroy the Emperor's plan for invasion; and, more important, might destroy a raw new Empire as well. That is mutiny in his Grand Army. Already, according to General Savary, the men have been kept waiting too long. Therefore . . . do you feel faint or unwell?"

"No, no, not in the least!" lied Madeleine. "But I still don't understand how all this concerns me!"

"Then have patience."

"Yes. Yes. I—regret."

The Minister of Police's words contained a rap like that of small finger-bones. His eyes, red-rimmed in the long agreeable face, never ceased to study and weigh his visitor.

Madeleine's age, twenty-six, he knew as he knew so many other facts about her: from the green-bound paper file at his right elbow. More than merely pretty, soft of body without being too heavy or too slender, she looked back at him with the candlelight heightening the warmth of her colouring from pink lips to the dark-lashed blue eyes.

Her heavy, fleecy fair hair had been done up into a cluster of small, shining curls on top of her head; it was unadorned by any headdress of plumes or feathers, such as most women nowadays considered necessary for evening wear. Her face, faintly flushed in the airless room, was a mingling of the sensual and the innocent. Her fingers had ceased to clutch at the arms of the chair.

Instead those fingers, pink-nailed against white, toyed with the silver fringes of a light silk shawl, figured in silver acorns, thrown carelessly across her shoulders. The shawl was mere ornament. Madeleine wore little under her high-waisted gown, of even thinner silk, in that grey colour which French designers called London-smoke.

"Therefore," pursued Joseph Fouché, "this Captain Cut-throat must be found and shot. Anything else would be worse than a crime. It would be a blunder."

Madeleine suddenly laughed.

"I think I have heard those words before."

Up went the red eyebrows.

"Without doubt. I said them myself, about the mur—about the trial and execution of the Duc d'Enghien at Vincennes. And I say them often."

"But, dear M. Fouché! You have so little time!"

"No, my dear," smiled the Minister of Police. "You have so little time."

His oblique glance, sharpening with satire, remained agreeable. But to Madeleine it was as though those long, chilly fingers had fastened round her throat and tightened with a physical pressure.

"I? Arrest a murderer in a military camp? That's ridiculous!"

"Of course. It would be ridiculous—if it were what I wished."

"Then what do you wish?"

"Let us consider your record."

His thin black-clad arm swept to the right. He picked up the green-bound file, set it in front of him with great nicety, and opened it.

"I would not frighten you," he said gently. "Frightened, you would be of no use to me. And I regret that my representative should have been obliged to seek you out in the Palais Royal."

Colour flooded into Madeleine's face. "Probably," she began, "you were surprised——"

"I am never surprised."

"No, no! I mean: surprised to find me living in such a dreadful, squalid . . ."

"Come, we must not scorn the Palais Royal!"

"Must we not? *I* scorn it. It is filthy and odious and I hate it!"

"On the contrary, my dear, it caters for the wealthy; it has all things for all tastes. Dressmakers, jewellers, perfumers, gambling-houses, brothels.——The last word distresses you. I had forgotten you were brought up in England."

"Please don't mock me!"

"Had I any intention of mocking you? Your record, now."

Casually he turned over a page in the file.

"Marie Madeleine Lenormand," he went on. "Born at Paris on 8th July, 1779. Father, French, deceased, was the proprietor of a fashionable finishing school for young English ladies. Mother, English, is still living and is addicted to somewhat dreary charitable works."

"On my word, M. Fouché, I am not disloyal to my own country! I own I have a divided loyalty; I am half English; I can't help that. But I swear I would do nothing against the present Emperor!"

"Tcha," said the Minister of Police.

Madeleine swallowed hard.

"In '93," continued the unruffled Fouché, "the family of Lenormand fled to England to escape what is today known as (tcha, tcha!) the Terror. Your father died. Your mother busied herself charitably and not very profitably with the Fry Society for prison reform, with Dr. Braidwood's London school for the deaf and dumb, and with the Bethlehem Hospital for the insane. You yourself, with a pious and commendable filial devotion, assisted her. In April, 1803, during the Peace of Amiens, you returned alone to France."

"But in what way have I committed a crime? Tell me that!"

"Now remark," insisted Fouché, turning round one finger to point at her, "an exact academic instance of what I mean! You are intelligent, my dear. Very intelligent."

"Thank you."

"Then I would urge you, for your own good, to be frank with me. When you returned to France in April, 1803, why did you not inform the police that you were married?"

"I . . ."

"Come, madame, you cannot control your breathing. When you returned to France more than two years ago, why did you resume your birth-name and fail to report your marriage to an Englishman?"

"Because I was hurt and humiliated, because I wished only to hide myself! That was why you found me in the Palais Royal. It had nothing to do with . . ."

"With what?"

"With any disloyalty to the country where I was born. Believe me!"

Joseph Fouché brushed his hand across the page of the file.

17

"On the 12th June, 1802, at the Church of St. Anne, Soho, you were married to a young man named Alan Hepburn. I applaud your good fortune. M. Hepburn was wealthy, accomplished, the elder son of a noble Scottish family. You were a veritable Cinderella, madame: at Melbourne House, at Devonshire House, at Carlton House, you trod the quadrille in very exalted circles. This marriage, which was one of love and even of violent passion——"

"I beg of you——!"

"——this marrirage, I say, was never dissolved. But at some time in March, 1803, you and your husband officially parted. Why?"

With a spasmodic gesture Madeleine lifted her hands as though to adjust her hair, and pressed her fingers hard against her cheeks.

What had rushed over her was a suffocation of breathlessness, a feeling as though she had been bruised by falling heavily. She did not hate Alan Hepburn: no, not now. Over and over she had assured herself that her feeling, at long last, was one of merciful indifference. She would never have believed that the mere mention of his name should cause a leap of her heart, and a thickening in her throat, and a stab of all the old intolerable pain.

It was unfair; it was even terrifying. But it was true.

For an instant this dust-speckled office, with its frayed carpet and its dingy green panels outlined in blackening gilt, dissolved before a memory of more gracious rooms and a cleaner sky. The fiddles sang under painted ceilings; carriages flowed a-sparkle through the rural greenery of Piccadilly, in smokeless air, past the high stone wall of Devonshire House. And she, uncertain and unsure of herself, amid perfumes and landscape fans and the twittering of gossip, stumbled as best she could through a Whig society more aristocratic than the Tory.

But everything narrowed, with anguish, into some vision of Alan Hepburn. Alan, who preached the doctrine that a man must be eccentric and individual or there was no health in him; Alan, with his charm and his wayward brilliance of mind which (she had often raged and protested) he would never employ to any useful purpose; Alan, who could coax her and laugh her into a state of . . .

"At some time in March, 1803, you and your husband officially parted. Why?"

Madeleine flung the vision away.

"My husband and I separated for private reasons."

"Now God strike me dead," said the atheistic Minister of Police. "I am aware that you must have separated for private reasons. But I would know those reasons. What were they?"

"My husband—chose to desert me."

"Indeed? He deserted you for another woman?"

"I don't know. *I* don't care. Is it of importance?"

"It might be. Had your married life been a happy one?"

"No. Yes. No! I was intolerably jealous; I own it! But he was fully as jealous, fully as suspicious, fully as . . ."

"Yes? Continue."

"I have nothing more to say."

"What I am endeavouring to discover, madame, is the reason for this sudden separation after less than a year of marriage. There was a quarrel, perhaps?"

"No. He left only an order with his banker that I was to be—well pensioned."

"No quarrel? You interest me. No screams or tears or fainting-fits? No note of farewell pinned in tragic grandeur to the bed-curtains? Come, madame! Surely you have been provided with some more convincing explanation than that?"

The extraordinary intensity of Fouché's tone, the dry snake-rustle of his hand on the page of the file, struck a dagger of warning even through her preoccupation. And now, if she had known him better, she would have remarked the most ominous danger-sign of all.

From the tail-pocket of his coat the Minister of Police took out a snuff-box. It was an oval snuff-box of fragile rose-agate, its lid set round with a circlet of diamonds enclosing a bee and the letter 'N,' and its diamonds glittered incongruously in that dingy office. Though Joseph Fouché was a rich man many times over, his tastes remained simple. Clearly the snuff-box had been a present from the Emperor, who hated him with an epileptic rage but found no other man quite so useful.

Gingerly the Minister of Police opened the box and took snuff. His movements were deliberate and even delicate. But his long hands trembled, and his eyes strayed across the desk towards the hand-bell with which he summoned his secretary.

19

"Before I terminate this interview, in a fashion most unpleasant for you . . ."

Madeleine sat rigid.

She had been telling him the complete truth; she could say no more. And yet every one of her nameless fears boiled up in a kind of stifled shriek.

"What is it? What have I done? Do you believe a single word I've been saying?"

"In candour, madame, I do not. Would you deny, for example, that you are still in love with your husband?"

"Well! I . . ."

"Precisely. You flee from him in agony and run away to Paris. It is a coincidence, I suppose, that he arrives here shortly before you arrive yourself?"

"Alan is here? In Paris?"

"You did not know that?"

"No!"

The lid of the snuff-box closed with a snap.

"You were unaware that all this time he has been living in the Faubourg St. Germain, posing as a Frenchman and calling himself the Vicomte de Bergerac? You never assisted him in any of his activities? You were even unaware that for the past seven years he has been the most astute secret-agent in the employ of the British Foreign Office?"

"In the name of God, what are you saying?"

The Minister of Police rose to his feet and towered over her. The thick air of the room stirred sourly, and he reached down with a significant motion towards the handbell on his desk.

"Before I terminate this interview, madame, I give you one more chance. Alan Hepburn was arrested forty-eight hours ago. Unless you are prepared to assist me, he will be shot tomorrow morning."

Chapter III

The Brunette: In the Room of Mirrors

At about the same time, on that same night, a coach with a coat of arms on its panels was driven fast along the Quai des Augustins. And in the coach sat another young woman with some interest in Alan Hepburn.

The clocks had just gone ten. A heavy, sickly moon was rising above the dust-powdered chestnut-trees along the quai. With a lurch and jolt on uneven paving, the coach swung left into the narrow rue des Condamnés, towards the most conspicuous of all entrances to the Ministry of Police.

But the coach, as though from long custom, stopped some distance away. Its travelling-lamps had not been lighted; the lane was as dark as your pocket. The woman, who seemed to be wrapped in a long cloak despite the hot night, disdained any assistance from the coachman. She sprang down with a lithe freedom of movement, and hurried towards an open archway in a grey stone wall on the right.

Faint yellow light, filtering through the archway from a lamp in the courtyard beyond, was cut across by the cocked hat and scarlet coat of a police-guard.

"Eh? Yes? Who's there?"

The woman merely stopped and looked at him. He cursed, growled an apology, saluted, and stood back.

The woman's foot kicked refuse; a cat squalled and scampered. The woman had crossed the courtyard of shuttered windows, and was raising her hand towards the only door in sight, when she stopped to look sharply at a horse tethered to one of the stone hitching-posts outside the door.

It was a light-cavalry horse, with a zebra-skin saddlecloth. That zebra-skin saddle-cloth, the woman knew, was the badge of one of the hussar regiments now stationed in Boulogne . . .

Boulogne!

The woman in the cloak stood motionless, her strong white teeth in her under-lip.

According to rule, no military horse should have been in this courtyard at all. Out of that door, through the archway and into the rue des Condamnés, were borne in great secrecy and closed carriages only prisoners of high political importance, on their way to be shot or imprisoned at Vincennes after "interrogation" in the cells below the Ministry of Police.

But, if Marshal Soult had sent a messenger galloping fifty leagues from Boulogne instead of using the semaphore, if that messenger had slipped by the most secret and urgent way into the presence of Joseph Fouché . . .

It was as though, distantly, the drums of the Grand Army tapped and tapped towards a crescendo. And the woman's thoughts went out to them.

The weather was right. The tides were right. The British fleets had been lured away to Gibraltar and the West Indies, leaving their coast all but defenceless, with only four line-of-battle ships to guard the whole length of the Channel. Admiral Villeneuve, after a sea-victory over Calder off Finisterre, was moving north with thirty-three French and Spanish warships to hold the Straits and cover the passage of the Grand Army.

Now, if ever, was the poised moment for invasion. Now, as the hot night throbbed with drums, was the time to strike.

Drawing a deep breath, the woman again lifted her hand to the knocker on the door.

She was expected. At her brief signal-rapping the door was opened almost immediately. She straightened her shoulders and swept into the hall.

"Good evening, M. Levasseur."

"Madame de Sainte-Elme," murmured her companion, moistening his lips. He closed and locked the door after her.

The hall, not over-large, was floored with squares of dusty black-and-white marble. At the back, facing them, two darkling arches showed staircases beyond. Between the arches stood a marble bust of the Emperor, on a marble pedestal, staring out under the light of three candles in a bronze wall-bracket.

The woman in the cloak took several steps towards the back of the hall. Then she hesitated and turned round.

Ida de Sainte-Elme's shrewdness and self-assurance forever warred with a wholly primitive nature. Her complexion was as golden-brown as that of an Egyptian: the cheek-bones high, the nostrils wide, the lips somewhat broad and hard in edge. Carrying her head a little on one side, under its topknot of glossy black curls, she regarded the world from long and narrow eyes, of a luminous dark brown, with a secret and humourous look at the outer corners.

Now, catching sight of her companion's face, she laughed and let the cloak slip from her shoulders to trail from her right hand. Her tawny skin glistened through a gauzy and transparent gown of Nile-water green, fastened with a gold waist-cord and slit up the sides to allow freedom of movement.

"I obeyed my instructions," she said, "as soon as I conveniently could. I do not wish to risk being seen here more than is necessary——"

"Understood, madame! Understood!"

"And I shall tell the Minister of Police so. Is anything wrong, M. Levasseur?"

"No, madame, no! But I regret that it will be impossible for you to see M. Fouché at the moment. He is . . . occupied."

"Oh? With the messenger from Boulogne?" She laughed again. "Thunder of God, Raoul! Surely it is evident? You must not jump so."

Her companion had not really jumped. All that ailed him was the physical presence of Ida de Sainte-Elme. He was a thin, ugly, dark-faced young man, very humble and soberly dressed, whose position as secretary to the Minister of Police had been the reward of fanatical faithfulness and industry.

She advanced towards him, never taking her eyes from his face.

"Raoul, Raoul, Raoul! Is it necessary to be discreet with me? Have we not been friends?"

"Yes," said the young man, and swallowed and looked away. "We have been friends."

"And shall be again, when I have time."

23

"'Time?' Is that all it means to you? Time!"

"It is all it means to me at the moment, Raoul." Savouring her power over any male creature, Ida delighted to approach him so closely that he flinched. "The future, of course, may be a different matter. What is the news from Boulogne?"

"It—it is bad. Captain Cut-throat . . ."

The expressive face changed again.

"Thunder of God! Captain Cut-throat has not murdered another sentry?"

"No; he has not acted since the night of the 19th. But . . . it is of no importance, I tell you; it is of no importance!"

"Is it of no importance, Raoul? Who is this messenger from Boulogne? And is the news he brings so vital that *I* must be kept waiting?"

Raoul Levasseur made a harassed gesture.

"The messenger is a Lieutenant Schneider, of the Hussars of Bercy. But . . ."

"But what?"

"Madame, I am in hell because of you; I can think of nothing else. In any case, you have not been kept waiting because of the messenger from Boulogne. M. Fouché is questioning someone else."

"Oh? Who is he questioning?"

"The wife of the English spy. The English spy you discovered for us. The English spy who calls himself the Vicomte de Bergerac."

The effect of this announcement was hardly what he expected.

Ida de Saint-Elme backed slowly away, towards the marble bust of the Emperor. She was wearing calf-length buskins of soft white kid-leather, embroidered in gold thread; they made no noise on the black-and-white marble floor. But her body, in the transparent green gown, was polished and silhouetted against the light of the three candles; and now, by some trick of the light, the gown appeared rumpled and disarranged like the moss-rosebuds in her hair.

"Wife?" she repeated in a high, thin voice. "Wife?"

"Yes. Clearly this wife has been aiding him for years. We discovered he had a wife because of a certain book and because the so-called M. de Bergerac, under doses of laudanum, said her name in his sleep. He does not even think we have learned of her existence now. She is a Frenchwoman, brought up in England: a blonde, very beautiful and in some eyes no doubt desirable . . ."

Suddenly Ida flung away the cloak from her right hand, so that it fluttered and fell on the floor.

"I will see the Vicomte de Bergerac," she said.

There was a silence, while the young man stared back at her.

"Sacred name," he said as though praying. "You are in love with the English spy!"

"I am in love with no man! But is the Minister of Police, I ask you, so very squeamish all of a sudden?"

"M-madame?"

"For seven years," said Ida through stiff jaws, "for seven years, here in France itself, a British agent has been upsetting every diplomatic plan and penetrating the disguises of our best agents. For two years he has actually been living among us. And nobody, not a soul, knew who he was or could guess at his identity until I discovered it. This young Vicomte de Bergerac, who entertained so lavishly in the Faubourg St. Germain, who made jokes and threw away money and received the Legion of Honour from the Emperor himself, was nothing but a spy of Pitt and Castlereagh!"

She had backed away until she was standing beside the bust of the Emperor. The chilly sculptured eyes, ruthless even in marble, looked out beside her own.

"You have him now; you have him fast in the cells below. But what happens? He is treated as gently as though he were a friend instead of an enemy. He is not even put to the question," she meant the torture, "though it might tell us everything we want to know.—Yes. I will see the Vicomte de Bergerac."

A belated caution rushed back to Raoul Levasseur and made him flap his arms.

"No, madame! No! I forbid it."

"You forbid it? Why?"

"That is to say: the Minister of Police forbids it. This —this Englishman does not even know it was you who gave him away . . ."

"Nor shall he know, believe me, until I am prepared to tell him."

25

"Madame, listen! The Minister of Police, I may tell you, plays a hidden game of his own . . ."

"Yes!" cried Ida, and clenched her hands. "I thought so!"

"Madame?"

"Always, always, always our good Fouché must play some double-faced game. What is it now? He hates . . ."

Breast heaving, she became abruptly conscious of the marble bust beside her, and glanced round at it.

"He hates . . . no! He does not hate anyone. He is too coldblooded, too detached, too dried to anything except self-interest. But, if he saw the Emperor's star setting and luck turning the other way, he would——"

Though Ida was not overly tall, she was supple and strong of body; and she jabbed out furiously with both hands. The marble bust rocked and tottered on its pedestal. Raoul Levasseur, the idealist, uttered a cry of horror and sprang forward to retrieve it. Then the two of them, both panting from very different emotions, looked at each other past that inscrutable face.

Ida's dusky-red lips folded back over her teeth.

"The Vicomte de Bergerac, I suppose, is still in the Room of Mirrors? Take me to him."

"For the last time, madame, I dare not do it! And, if you have any fondness for me, you will forget what I have just told you about——"

"Take me to him."

From somewhere near at hand there was scrape and grind of metal. Both of them, starting guiltily, glanced round.

Under the archway on their right, as they stood in loving-kindness beneath the Emperor's eye, a marble staircase led up to a waiting-room. Under the archway on their left, another dusty marble stair led down to a heavy door barring the way to the cells.

Beyond this door, now, there was a crash as someone shot back its bar to unlock it from inside. Up the stairs, with enormous self-importance, strutted a fat sergeant of the civil police.

First appeared his cocked hat, then his inflamed red nose set off by a scarlet tail-coat, then the portentous swing of his belly above wine-stained white waistcoat, breeches, and gaiters. Curling his moustache and side-whiskers, he made a dramatic gesture of recognition as he saw Raoul.

"Ah, young man, but this is well met! One requires you, very urgently, in the Minister's Office. My faith, the speaking-tube is whistling itself hoarse. As for me, I go to fetch the lady."

Ida stiffened. "Lady? What lady?"

"Why, naturally, the lady in M. Fouché's office now! She is to be confronted—very suddenly, you comprehend —with the Vicomte de Bergerac."

Raoul Levasseur's hands dropped from the marble pedestal; he gulped, and straightened up. But his sharp rebuke had no effect on this old bottle-nose of the Revolution. At the same moment, as though to add to the secretary's bewilderment, they could all hear the hoof-beats of a horse in the courtyard outside. The hoof-beats cantered up and stopped outside the door.

"Our Vicomte de Bergerac," cried the sergeant, with an explosive smirk and an even greater preening of his whiskers as he beamed on Ida, "has no notion we've nabbed his fellow-spy, too. My faith, Madame de Sainte-Elme! When he's confronted with her, all of a sudden, in the Room of Mirrors: that should be very interesting, eh?"

"Yes. Very interesting, Sergeant Benet."

"You must come and watch it, my pretty. It will amuse you."

"Madame, I forbid it——!"

"Be silent, Raoul!"

A knocking at the outer door, not loud but firm and authoritative, dinned and dinned in Raoul Levasseur's ears. Another courier was expected from Boulogne; he dared not let urgency wait. With the sergeant's hoarse laughter beating about him, he hurried to the door and unlocked it.

Outside, curved sabre bumping at his heels, the dismounted horseman moved stiffly first on one leg and then on the other. His green tunic lined and faced with scarlet, was a blur of dust like his white waistcoat. From busby to red-topped boots he was dust, except for amused eyes and smiling teeth. Raising one gauntlet to slap dust from his busby, as though in compromise for a military salute, he spoke courteously.

"M. Raoul Levasseur?"

"Yes, yes! You are——?"

"Captain Guy Mercier, 2nd Regiment, Mounted Guides. I was instructed to identify myself by . . ."

He broke off, with refreshed interest, at another bellow of laughter from the hall. Raoul Levasseur swung round and muttered despairingly under his breath. Sergeant Benet, slapping his thigh, was now waddling up the stairs to the landing above. Ida de Sainte-Elme's cloak still lay on the floor. But Ida herself had gone.

At that moment, in fact, she was standing at the far end of the underground passage to the cells, looking down imperiously at another red-coated police-officer, who sat behind a table and cursed to himself over an interrupted game of cards.

"Do you hear me?" cried Ida. "By order of the Minister of Police, I am to see the prisoner at once."

"All right, my chicken; keep your stockings on!"

"Then why don't you open the door? Do you doubt my authority from M. Fouché?"

"Doubt it?" snarled her companion flinging down his hand of cards and looking up at her in the light of a fish-oil lamp. "Why should I doubt it? You've put enough of 'em in the cells, God knows."

He spat briefly over his shoulder, and got up. But he did not touch the bunch of keys at his belt. Instead, after picking up a pistol from the table and examining its priming, he stretched out his left hand towards what appeared to be a blank wall.

The famous Room of Mirrors, in which so many had been watched during their last hours, was an adaptation and not an invention of Joseph Fouché. Its four walls and its ceiling, which appeared to have no doors but actually had four, were of skilfully joined looking-glass. Once the principal room of a brothel, it had been thriftily refurbished so that no movement of its occupant, no turn of eyes or twist of facial expression, could go unseen from eight pairs of spy-holes concealed in small and gilded wooden satyr-faces round the mirror-walls.

This room was more than sinister: put to its present use, under ceaselessly watching eyes, its breath of forgotten lusts had an air of ghastliness. As the red-coated jailer pressed a spring and rolled open a narrow head-high panel, it may have been this which made Ida de Sainte-Elme hesitate. But she slipped inside, and the panel closed after her.

There was no furniture here, except a bed now stripped of its canopy, a wooden table, and an armchair. Alan Hepburn—alias Alan Latour, Vicomte de Bergerac—sat beside the table under a brass chandelier of candles hanging from the mirror-ceiling.

Physically, at least, he had been well treated. Alan Hepburn had always kept up the pretence of being a great dandy. He was clean and freshly-shaven; his thick brown hair was brushed in that elaborate style made fashionable by the Prince of Wales. Even his high white collar and white neckcloth of lightly starched muslin, also in the new fashion, were tolerably clean.

He was a thin, wiry, agile man in his late thirties, with a high and faintly-lined forehead. His eyes, cat-green under slanting brows, had a humour and recklessness like his lined mouth.

Since he had been arrested on the way to the opera, he still wore the black satin evening-coat and black satin breeches with gold knee-buckles. So he sat there—one finger marking the page in the book he had been reading, his image endlessly repeated in the mirror-walls—and looked back at his visitor.

And still, as the seconds stretched out, Ida did not speak.

She no longer felt any anger towards him; all her rage had been concentrated on another person. Towards him she felt . . . felt . . .

Alan rose to his feet.

Carefully, as though to keep his hands from trembling, he put down the book on the table. He had been brought up by a French nurse, and learned to speak French before he could speak English; nothing in his accent told of his nationality.

"Hallo, Ida," he said lightly.

"Alan," said his visitor; and then she burst out. "Alan, Alan, Alan!"

She ran to him, across the dirty red carpet; she threw her arms round his neck and pressed herself against him in a fury of tenderness which was at least partly sincere.

"Come now," objected the prisoner, and patted her back. "It isn't as bad as all that, you know."

"Isn't it, Alan? Do you realize how bad it is?"

29

"Well. Let's say that it's damned inconvenient."

"Darling, darling, I rushed here as soon as I heard you were arrested. I only learned of it two hours ago, at a ball at M. de Talleyrand's house; and it's very fortunate he likes me. I pleaded and pleaded with him; otherwise, of course, they'd never have permitted me to see you. Alan, Alan! It breaks my heart to think . . . to think . . ."

Alan Hepburn looked down at her. For the first time his cat-green eyes showed wrinkles of amusement at the outer corners.

"You know, Ida," he said, "this isn't at all necessary."

"What isn't necessary?"

"This flourish of high tragedy. Do you think I don't know, my dear, that it was you who gave me away?"

Silence, while the gilded wooden satyr-faces multiplied round the walls.

The ease with which he could read her thoughts, was the quality which at once infuriated her and attracted her. She could never govern him, never be sure of him, never quench that easy and well-mannered mockery; and rage made her wholly primitive again. There was no anger in his look, none at all. The more philosophically he accepted facts, the more she wanted to scream that it wasn't true.

"*I?* Gave you away? Alan! You can't possibly think that I . . . ?"

"It doesn't matter, I tell you!" Suddenly there was an edge in his voice. "You were an agent of Fouché the Fox; I represented His Britannic Majesty. Why the devil should I blame you for doing your job? I gambled and lost: that's all there is to it."

"But I didn't betray you! I didn't!"

"Just as you please, Circe. Still, if I hadn't left my despatch-box unlocked, on the last night you honoured me with your company in bed . . ."

"I swear to you, on my oath before the Virgin Mary . . . !"

"That you never even looked in that despatch-box?"

"Never!"

He tilted up her chin, and amusement-wrinkles deepened round his eyes.

"In another moment, my dear, you will be taking even stranger oaths before the Virgin Mary. Whiskers to you, Ida. Come off it."

30

Ida wrenched away from hands which made no attempt to restrain her. Her voice shrilled up.

"And if I proved to you, proved beyond any doubt, that I would die and suffer damnation before I would have betrayed you?"

Now she saw him hesitate. Perhaps she did not realize how near he was to breaking-point over a certain problem in his own mind. Alan turned away. He picked up the book from the table. He swung in still another direction, meeting only the turning reflections of his own image and of his companion's pursuing eyes.

Weariness, uncertainty, haunted a lean face which was perhaps a little too fine-drawn and imaginative.

"Ida," he burst out, on an almost pleading note, "let's make an end of pretence, shall we? For years my life has been nothing but pretence. And now I'm in the midst of the worst pretence of all."

"Oh?"

"That is to say——" He glanced at her quickly. "They want me to do something. And I won't do it. I can't! They say they'll give me until tomorrow morning to decide. But my life is forfeit; I know that. Why can't they shoot me and get it over with?"

"You're not afraid, are you? The great Vicomte de Bergerac, with all the prizes in the fencing and riding competition's for civilians? Afraid?"

"Yes," he said flatly. "I'm cursed afraid. I wish I could say I weren't."

"Then you ought to understand, my dear, that there's only one woman who cares for you. Alan, you fool! Do you know who really betrayed you to the police?"

"Yes, naturally! You did!"

"Oh, no," lied Ida, with prepared inspiration. "It was your wife."

Alan Hepburn could control much, but he could not control his response to this. The book, a thick volume with gilt-edged leaves, slipped through his hands and sprawled open on the floor.

"That's imposs—" he began; and then, hoarsely: "How did you know I had a wife?"

Ida had not even suspected it, until Levasseur told her. The success of her purely malicious thrust pleased her as much as it astonished her. Had he some reason to be suspicious of this 'blonde, very beautiful'? If so, how immensely satisfying to sharpen and poison that suspicion!

"And why is it impossible, Alan, that she should have betrayed you?"

"Because——" He started to give one answer, and altered it. "Because, for one reason, Madeleine never knew my identity here in Paris! And Madeleine's in London!"

(He must be telling lies, of course. Break him down! Break him down!)

"And if I proved to you, Alan, that she is talking to the Minister of Police at this very minute?"

The bone-structure of his face showed clearly in the hot, flary light of the candles.

"God Almighty," he said in English, and pressed a hand over his eyes. "Harrowby must have been right."

"Milord Harrowby," cried the astute Ida, instantly fitting together real information with quick flying-guesses, "was the British Foreign Minister in the Addington administration! And your wife is a Frenchwoman! And—of course!" Inspiration opened wide. "I'll bet you were told, weren't you, that your wife has been spying on you for the French?"

"What difference does it make now?"

"Alan, answer me! *Did* Milord Harrowby tell you that?"

"If he hadn't told me, do you think I should have gone away and left her without a word? Harrowby said he was certain; they all said it. Even so, do you think I've never wondered? Or regretted what I did?"

It was as though the mirrors cracked and dissolved before Ida's eyes.

"Gone away and left her?" breathed Ida, with all her calculations upset. "Regretted it? What lies are you telling me now? What do you mean?"

"Just what·I say. Isn't it plain enough?"

"Alan! This—this woman can't mean more to you than I do?"

"She means everything to me. Do you see that book on the floor? It belonged to her. I've kept it by me, like a fool, when it might have led the police to me at any minute. For over two years I've been remembering her, regretting her, picturing her——!"

Ida made a sudden dart to get at the book, but he gripped her shoulder and held her back.

"So that's what you've been thinking!" said Ida, with a little gasp and scream. "And you call her name in your sleep, do you? Well, remember this! No man who has been with me ever forgets it, or forgets me either! In that way, at least, I can make you forget your blonde without half trying!"

"You are mistaken, madame. And, if by any chance Madeleine walked in here now, it wouldn't matter in the least what she had done as a French spy, provided only she hadn't married me just to spy on me!"

"Oh, help me," screamed Ida, now past all endurance. "My God, wait till I get my hands on her! She betrayed you, right enough. Shall I tell you what the Minister of Police means to do, Alan? Well! He means to——"

It would have taken a miracle, apparently, to have diverted Ida's attention just then. And yet something did. She whirled round.

Outside one door of the Room of Mirrors, an invisible door, rose up the voice of the surly and glowering jailer who sat on guard there.

"M. Levasseur!" shouted the voice, dinning back amid the mirrors. "Have you gone crazy? Give me back my pistol, imbecile! Give me . . ."

There was the snap of a door-catch. The invisible panel, pushed by a frantic hand, rolled open. And Raoul Levasseur sprang into the aperture.

Against the prim, snuff-coloured clothes of that conscientious young man, with his hair tied in a neat queue at the back of his neck, stood out the sick anguish of his eyes and mouth. In his hand was the pistol, loaded and primed, which had lain on the jailer's table outside. There was a click as the hammer went back.

"You will betray no more of the Minister's plans, madame," he said.

He lifted the pistol, aimed it at Ida de Sainte-Elme, and fired point-blank.

Chapter IV

Ghost-in-the-Light

Madeleine Hepburn, sitting rigidly in the armchair on the other side of Joseph Fouché's desk, beyond the two burning points of the candles, looked up at the Minister of Police with eyes that scarcely saw him.

"Before I terminate this interview, madame, I give you one more chance. Alan Hepburn was arrested forty-eight hours ago. Unless you are prepared to assist me, he will be shot tomorrow morning."

The words hung there almost visibly, in one moment meaningless and in the next moment weighted with terror.

Joseph Fouché stood high-nosed and high-shouldered behind his desk. A momentary wrath, real or assumed, whittled his emaciated cheeks. In one hand he held the rose-coloured snuff-box with its circlet of diamonds; his other hand stretched down towards the hand-bell whose clang could end everything.

"Wait!" she cried instinctively. "No! Stop!"

"Ah," murmured the Minister of Police.

His hand moved away from the bell, and he sniffed. For an instant longer he studied her out of his red-rimmed eyes, and then continued in his usual emotionless way.

"Now that I find you in a more reasonable frame of mind, madame . . . which I trust you are?"

"Yes! Yes! Yes!"

"Then let me demonstrate to you that further denials would be useless. You are not aware, I suppose, how your husband came to be arrested?"

"No."

"No, I fancied as much. Nevertheless, the name of Ida de Sainte-Elme will naturally be familiar to you?"

To Madeleine the name meant nothing whatever. But, with that bloodless interrogator looking at her fixedly, she

34

nodded and tried to conceal the thick beating of her heart.

"The lady, in short, who has been so much in your husband's company during the past six months?"

"I . . . yes."

"What you are not aware," said Fouché, "is that Madame de Sainte-Elme, who appears to be merely a flamboyant ornament of society, is actually an agent of mine. She is remarkably astute. She might be my best agent if she were not a child of nature, a veritable noble-savage after the style of Jean Jacques Rousseau. Whether or not your husband was pursuing her, she was pursuing him because she suspected him. Examination of certain coded papers, after a happy night of love . . . Did you speak, madame?"

"No, I said nothing. Nothing, nothing, nothing!"

"——examination of these papers, I say, revealed the 'Vicomte de Bergerac's' real name and mission here. Will you acknowledge now, dear leady, that nothing is unknown to us?"

In the old days, when she and Alan had been living in Cavendish Square, the mere mention of this Madame de Sainte-Elme would have put Madeleine into a fury. At the moment, she could think only that Alan was in danger.

Alan an agent of the British Foreign Office? Her Alan?

And yet, the instant Fouché spoke those words, she had known in her heart they were true. Out of the past so many aching contradictions, so many words and looks, so many cryptic scenes were suddenly illuminated like faces in a dark room.

Then Alan may not have deserted her because of another woman, or because . . . ?

But, if that were so, why had the idiot never confided in her? It was a man's world: Madeleine accepted that, as she accepted drunkenness and duels and infidelity. And yet, even if he felt he must go mysterious ways, for duty or for devilment or for whatever reason, why should he never have so much as given her a hint?

Surely he must have known he could trust her? He must have known she would have died rather than breathe a word about this to anyone?

Then why, why, why had he never spoken? The sheer

35

cruelty of what he had done was so inconsistent with his character that . . .

Through these hazy and scurrying thoughts, fast approaching the edge of hysteria, stung a dry and deadly voice.

"Do you honour me with your attention, madame?"

"You—must forgive me, M. Fouché," gulped Madeleine. "The shock of hearing of my husband's arrest . . ."

"Then you no longer trouble to deny that you assisted him in his espionage work?"

Madeleine began to speak, and abruptly stopped.

What if this might be a trap? What if Alan had admitted nothing—or had not even been arrested at all? What, in heaven's name, to do or say now?

"I neither confirm nor deny anything," she retorted, as steadily as she could. "Clearly you want something more from me than confirmation of what you already know,"—good; that shot went home!—"or you would not try to impress me so much with your all-seeing eye. You say Alan is in prison . . ."

"Do you doubt that, madame?" Fouché asked sharply. "Would you care to go and see him?"

Political prisoners, she knew, were held in the fortress at Vincennes. A journey to Vincennes meant a long drive: it meant time, time, time to collect her wits and arrange her defences.

"Yes, I demand to see him!" said Madeleine, clutching at the chance and, at the same time, encountering a new terror. "Alan is . . . he's well, isn't he? You haven't—hurt him?"

"Am I a fool, madame," enquired the Minister of Police, turning down the corners of his mouth, "that I should damage one of the best brains in Europe just before I mean to make use of it?"

"Make use of it?"

"Yes. With your assistance."

"If you have any pity at all, M. Fouché, you will stop this game of cat and mouse! You say Alan will be shot tomorrow morning 'unless' I assist you. But why should you make my terms with me? If Alan is really a spy, you don't spare him and you know it! What can I do for him? What do you offer him?"

36

"I offer him his life," replied Joseph Fouché, "if he can discover the identity of Captain Cut-throat in five days."

During a thunderclap of silence, while nothing on earth seemed to exist except this stifling, dust-speckled room and Fouché's face, Madeleine still sat rigid.

"You would use a British agent," she cried, "to . . . ?"

"To trap a British agent? Obviously. Can you think of a better man than your husband—if he does so willingly? And he will do so willingly, dear lady. You will see to that."

"I?"

"Let me explain very simply," pursued the Minister of Police. "The evening of your husband's arrest coincided with the evening of the Emperor's order from Boulogne. From the first it was evident that the 'Vicomte de Bergerac' was the mysterious British agent who has been plaguing us for so long. As I frequently stated when his identity was still unknown, I wished I could employ the fellow myself.

"I offered him his life he would trap Captain Cutthroat. He replied that he would be shot ten times over before he did any service for 'Boney.'

"Now this intrigued me. Each man has a weakness; it did not take long to discover his. A harmless-looking volume of Shakespeare's comedies in French had on its flyleaf your birth-name and an inscription in his handwriting which it would be mild to call impassioned. Also, if a man of highly-strung temperament be kept awake long hours and then given laudanum, he is apt to speak revealingly afterwards. It took my agents in London only until this evening to identify you as his wife and trace you back to Paris."

Madeleine could keep silent no longer.

"Does Alan know that . . . that . . . ?"

"That you are under arrest as well?" enquired Fouché, with a rap of his bony forefinger on the lid of the snuffbox. "No. Not yet. But you have 'demanded' to meet him; and you shall."

Carefully he replaced the snuff-box in the tail-pocket of his rusty black coat with the pewter buttons. Then he picked up the hand-bell from his desk.

"As soon as I have summoned my secretary," he added, "I shall have you escorted downstairs to his cell."

The bell, vigorously rung, clanked and jangled with a sweep which blew the candle-flames wildly. Madeleine's heart seemed to turn over.

"Alan is not here? In this building?"

"Have I not indicated it?"

"But I don't want to meet him! I—I can't meet him! That is: not just yet!"

"You will meet him, dear lady. While I speak to some other visitors who have been kept waiting too long, my secretary shall take you to the Room of Mirrors. There you will have an interview with M. Hepburn, entirely alone, and you will persuade him to accept this mission."

Madeleine sprang to her feet. Her shawl with the silver acorns fell back on the chair. Her smooth-gleaming shoulders, a white tinged with pink, rose high above the bodice of the smoke-grey silk gown; and she wrung her hands in a helpless attempt to find words.

It was not merely her dread, like a dread of fire, at the prospect of meeting Alan after two years of self-torment.

She had never had a taste for political affairs, and Alan had even encouraged her in this lack of interest. Outwardly he was a Whig. "Buff and Blue!" rang the toast after dinner in Cavendish Square: when the ladies, at music in the drawing-room, could hear their husbands smashing glasses in the dining-room below. "Buff and Blue!" Yet Alan, unlike so many Whigs, had never concealed his hatred of the Emperor's cynical plunderings and diplomatic nose-thumbings.

Men, Madeleine thought, were crazily and inexplicably stubborn about principles. If she now appeared to him out of nowhere, apparently as an emissary of the Emperor himself, when Alan was trapped and in a corner, what mad notions might not come into his head? But the alternative, of death because of a principle, was so absurd and unthinkable that . . .

Fouché could be as patient as a spider.

"If you were the patriotic Frenchwoman you first pretended to be," he said dryly, "you would not hesitate. As it is, since you are a confessed British spy, hesitation will only mean your own death, too. I shall instruct M. Levasseur——"

Abruptly, in the act of putting down the hand-bell, he stopped and glanced over his shoulder.

"By the way," he added, with a sharp new note in his voice, "where is Levasseur? That young man is as punctual as time itself. I have never known him to be a second late in answering a summons. One moment!"

"M. Fouché, wait! Listen to me!"

"One little moment, madame!"

A night-stillness held the dingy green-and-gilt office, with its closely-drawn curtains. Fouché turned round, and made for the central door in the wall behind him. Opening it, he peered out into the anteroom which was brightly lighted but empty.

"Come, I find this even more curious! A rather unpleasant officer of the Hussars of Bercy was waiting for me here. There should also be a lady and another cavalry officer, unless they are both very late. Patience, madame; patience!"

His shoes squeaked in the hollow silence as he returned to the desk. There he snatched up one of the pewter candlesticks, and hurried over to open another door in the wall towards Madeleine's right.

His light, held high, illumined a windowless little box-room beyond. It contained only a dusty oil-painting of the Emperor, shut away there as though in contempt, together with an immense map of Europe and a battery of speaking-tubes. Before turning to one of the speaking-tubes, he dragged the door shut so that Madeleine should not hear.

But, after a few moments of muttered conversation, his voice was raised in wrath and she heard it clearly.

"I am not concerned, Sergeant Benet, with the lateness of the hour," that icy voice said, "nor does it greatly desolate me to interrupt your game of cards. There are two of you on duty at the Mirror-Room. Leave Corporal Chavasse on guard, and come up yourself to fetch the lady. On the way you will find M. Levasseur and send him to me at once. You will also discover what has happened to a certain Lieutenant Schneider, from Boulogne. That is all."

The door flew open with a bang. Fouché appeared in rich satisfaction, holding the candle high.

"I bring good news, madame."

"News?"

"Your husband, though he pretends to sit and read quietly, is showing signs of regretting his quixotic conduct.

39

He is breaking down: not a pretty process. Now is the time to approach him."

"M. Fouché, I . . ."

"As a woman, dear lady, you are a realist. Do you prefer to have him shot?"

"No, no! I will do anything rather than have that! But, if Alan does agree to do as you wish, can you promise to spare his life?"

"In candour, madame, I cannot promise absolutely. Should he fail to find Captain Cut-throat in five days, the Emperor will demand a scapegoat. But I should greatly dislike to lose an excellent new agent, once he is bound to my service——"

"Bound to your service! Dear God!"

"——and I will save him if I can. Very well: then we understand each other. You will persuade M. Hepburn to go to Boulogne on this mission. You yourself, as his confederate of a long time, will of course accompany him."

Madeleine had known certain nightmares in which, though a partial sense of reason told the sleeper that all the actions of her dream were grotesque and meaningless, yet she was forced to walk unprotestingly through them.

This was like one of those dreams in which she could not speak or communicate with anyone. It was like moving among the poor, bewildered creatures at Dr. Braidwood's London school for deaf-mutes: and worse, because with them at least there was an alphabet of the sign-language. 'You yourself, as his confederate of a long time, will of course accompany him.'

"Is it any good telling you," cried Madeleine, "that I'm not a British spy and never have been? How on earth could I, of all people, have been of the slightest use to Alan as a confederate?"

It was the last sentence which roused him. Madeleine, so sensitive to emotional atmospheres, shied back from a new warning of danger flowing from that tall, lean Mephistophelian figure.

"Do you know, madame," the Minister of Police said quietly, "that several times in our talk I have been obliged to wonder about you?"

"To wonder? About what?"

"To wonder," said Fouché, "whether, after all, you might not really be as innocent as you claim to be? Judging

from our conversation, I should have said you were concerned with matters literary and artistic rather than with
intrigue. Though it is clear you are of sensual temperament, I should have thought you too fastidious to indulge
in this work; and M. Hepburn, perhaps, too fastidious to
allow you. How could you ever have been of use to him?
Why, naturally, by using your own kind of professional
talent to extract secrets from other men, as Madame de
Sainte-Elme does! How else?"

Madeleine stared at him. "You think that I . . . ?"

Then Fouché stalked forward, holding the light still
higher.

"Come here," he requested.

"What do you want?"

"Come here, my dear," repeated the Minister of Police,
extending his corpse-like hand. "Come with me."

A while ago Madeleine had thought her terror could
go no further. Now, as those dry and chilly fingers fastened
round her wrist, she realized it had only been increasing
minute by minute.

Walking backwards, he drew her towards the dusty little
box-room which contained only the picture of the Emperor, the battery of speaking-tubes, and the great map
of Europe. Madeleine had a horrible notion that to be
shut in there with him, and the door closed, would be
like entering a grave. She tried to drag away from him, but
her knees refused their motion.

But Fouché did not close the door. Fastening the fingers
of his right hand round her bare arm, he turned her face
towards the map. The light aureoled his red hair and made
skull-pits of his eyes.

"I wish merely," he said, "to repeat some of the lesson
I thought you had learned at the beginning of our talk.
And to make my own deductions about you from that.
No, don't speak!

"Officially, it is true, I have no connection with the
Foreign Office under M. de Talleyrand. But very little they
learn there, or anywhere else in Paris, is unknown to me.
Observe, then, what I indicate to you on this map.

"Here are the British Isles, coloured red. Here is our
own coast-line, sweeping round down the Bay of Biscay
to Spain. Now is the time for the Emperor's stroke,
because the seas are clear. Nelson, with his usual im-

41

petuosity, has allowed himself to be lured away. Collingwood, Cornwallis, Calder are also out of the path. Our own Villeneuve, with a formidable fleet, moves north to hold the Channel.

"Even on land, at the Emperor's back,"—the candleflame swept to the right—"his threats have disposed of all possible enemies. Much as they resent his depredations in Italy, both the Emperor of Austria and the Czar of all the Russias have flatly refused to attack him. He is supreme, omnipotent, the thunderbolt of destiny to strike here. What, then, could possibly prevent invasion?"

Fouché's grip on Madeleine's arm turned her sideways. And, as she caught sight of the Emperor's portrait under its coating of dust, it was as though the living man had come twitching and thrusting to look over her shoulder.

The Emperor was little, delicate-featured, angry of blue eye under the famous cocked hat. In Madeleine's imagination, poisoned by the nightmare, she saw the nervous and recurrent jerk of his shoulder he gave when he was excited. Against his green coat shone only the star of the Legion of Honour and the little silver cross he gave his troops.

"What, then, could possibly prevent invasion?" repeated Fouché, lifting red eyebrows. "I will tell you. A mutiny caused, apparently, by his own generals."

"His own generals?"

"Just that! Some are jealous of his rise to power. Some are genuine republicans who hate the Empire. But for a long time, either loudly or softly, republican principles have been preached by half the able commanders in the Grand Army. Masséna! Augereau! Lannes!——"

Each name, sharp and distinct, rang like a hammer-blow of war.

"——Oudinot! Lecourbe! Macdonald! There also exists a dangerous secret-society called the Olympians, dedicated to establishing a republic and governed by nobody knows whom. The evidence shows its agitation reached a height about a fortnight ago. Then, on the night of 13th August, came Captain Cut-throat."

Madeleine tried to wrench free her arm, but the Minister of Police still held it.

"A sentry of the 3rd Engineers, patrolling the southwest corner of the Field of the Balloons at just past

42

midnight, was caught from the back by an adroit, noiseless assassin of great physical strength.

"This sentry, the first victim, was stabbed through the back of the neck with a heavy and broad-bladed dagger. I have the dagger here in my office now. The victim died without a sound, almost within sight of others. In the blood soaking the back of his tunic was stuck a dirty piece of paper bearing only a few words in a disguised handwriting: 'Yours sincerely, Captain Cut-throat.'

"The second victim, a sentry of the 57th line-regiment guarding an ammunition-store at Le Portel on the night of the 14th August, screamed once before a dagger just like the first was driven through his heart from behind. There was another scrap of paper: 'Yours sincerely, Captain Cut-throat.'

"To be precise: all these scraps of paper, when examined by General Savary's Military Police, were found to be signed with pedantry or from some other cause as 'Captain Cut-the-throat,' instead of the familiar slang-term 'Cut-throat' which would be used by anybody from the highest marshal to the lowest conscript; and, in fact, has been used ever since. For practical purposes, it has not mattered.

"The third victim, a sentry at the quai-side of the inner harbour on August 15th . . . but I spare you all these details, which are familiar to your husband. Each night Captain Cut-throat moved, step by step and murder by murder, from a point far outside the camp to its very centre.

"Violent death is the trade of soldiers. But they meet it shouting in battle, drunk with excitement amid the flags. They do not meet it in the dark, alone, when it takes them without warning. You may imagine the effect on ignorant and superstitious men when a fourth victim died on August 16th: stabbed through the heart from in front, with a straight horizontal blow, by someone whose approach he could not even have heard. Again Captain Cut-throat left his note, but this time he carried away his dagger with him.

"The fifth and sixth nights passed; but there was no alarm, no attack. Then, as the climax of all, came the night of 19th August.

"There is only one space in the camp brightly lighted

after dark. This is, in a sense, its centre: the oblong enclosure round the Emperor's pavilion on the Odre cliff. Round all four sides of this oblong is a head-high fence of stout wooden palings; at intervals, only a short distance apart round the fence, hangs a row of reflector-lamps. These lamps, reflector-side inwards, illuminate everything. Day and night, I might add, the space inside the fence is patrolled by four sentries drawn from the Imperial Guard or the Imperial Marines.

"At shortly before midnight, August 19th, Captain Cut-throat appeared again.

"Grenadier Emile Joyet, of the Marine Guard, was approaching one side of the fence with a loaded musket on his shoulder. Two of the other sentries were actually looking at him, because he was whistling. Grenadier Joyet shouted out and doubled up and fell. The other men could see the whole lighted space for many yards round him, both inside the fence and outside, and not a soul had come near him. But he had been stabbed through the heart. The dagger was gone. And at his feet lay another of Captain Cut-throat's notes."

Joseph Fouché paused.

Still holding the candle high, he released Madeleine's arm.

"Well, madame?" he said.

"Are you telling me the truth?" cried Madeleine. "Or are you only telling me stories of ghosts and goblins to frighten children?"

"It has, at least," said Fouché, "frightened five corps of the Grand Army. Since the night of the second murder, they have talked of nothing else. The Emperor and General Savary, I think unwisely, have refused to make a frank proclamation of the problem. Either the Emperor must launch his invasion at once, which would cure everything by curing inaction, or he must crush Captain Cut-throat before another murder can be committed.—Well, madame?"

Madeleine fought hard against nightmare, both her own and the one he had outlined. She would not, would not, allow herself to be driven to desperation and stupidity. She moved to one side, stumbling, until she encountered the metal mouths of the speaking-tubes and could go no further.

44

"Well, what?" she demanded. "What do you expect me to say?"

"Have you no comment to make on all this? Do you see no indication, at least outwardly, of where we must look for Captain Cut-throat?"

"Of course! This revolutionary secret society called the Olympians: if it really exists . . . !"

"It exists, madame. Believe me!"

"——if it exists, and you don't know who is the head of it, surely they must look for Captain Cut-throat among its high-placed members?"

"Are you quite certain of that?"

"No, I'm not certain of anything! What on earth could I know of ghost-murderers at Boulogne? And, in any event, what has all this to do with me, and whether or not I happen to be a British spy?"

"You are a British spy, madame," replied Fouché, with sudden ferocious tenderness. "I applied a little test, and it has succeeded admirably."

"You . . . what?"

"Be tranquil, my dear: when I thought for an instant you might really be as innocent as you looked, I was half prepared to give you the benefit of the doubt. Now, however, I shall proceed with my scheme exactly as I had intended from the first, after you have been confronted with your husband in the Room of Mirrors. In the Room of Mirrors, at this very time——"

Madeleine had opened her mouth to protest, when she screamed and jumped away from the speaking-tubes.

Had they not been so close to one of those tubes, they might not have heard the noise so distinctly. As it was, piercing up in its metallic thinness, it struck their ears with a sharp vibration of menace and disaster.

A second afterwards, running footsteps pounded through the ante-room and through Fouché's office. An agitated Sergeant Benet appeared at the door of the box-room, his red nose more inflamed and his fat stomach wabbling.

"Citizen Minister," he cried, with the freedom of an old revolutionary, "I can't find Lieutenant Schneider in this wing of the building. The clerks think he went out a few minutes ago to wash at a pump in the courtyard; if so, maybe he's returned by this time and . . ."

Sergeant Benet paused, wheezing, because neither of the others paid any attention to him. The Minister of Police, after putting down the candle on a ledge, still looked at the speaking-tube up which had exploded that eerie noise.

Someone, two floors below, had fired a pistol-shot.

Chapter V

Of a Lady Much Misunderstood

The noise of the shot, fired in that enclosed space, whacked against the mirror walls and rebounded with stunning concussion. A whole genie-bottle of grey smoke, conjured from nowhere, blotted out both Raoul Levasseur and the lanky, blue-chinned jailer in the aperture of the open panel behind.

You would not have thought a single charge of black-powder could have exploded with so much smoke. It spread and swayed; its raw, harsh-burnt odour gouged the nostrils and choked in the throat.

"M. Levasseur!" yelled the jailer, and began to cough. He was still almost invisible in the smoke; he leaped through the aperture, with a few playing-cards in his hand. "Holy Saviour, the boy's gone off his rocker! I'm Chavasse, M. Levasseur! Your friend Chavasse! Hoy!"

Then he ran forward.

The bullet, fired at Ida de Sainte-Elme's heart from a distance of about ten feet, had missed her left side by a matter of inches. Her left arm was lifted, or it would have smashed the arm. Even so, since under the gauzy green gown she wore nothing except a short flower-apron and her kid-leather buskins, powder-grains had burnt the flesh of her side.

But Ida did not even wince. She stood motionless, a rapt look on her face, as Raoul Levasseur took form ghost-like through the mist.

He also stood motionless. But, as Corporal Chavasse called out again, the whites of Levasseur's eyes turned up. An ooze of foam rolled at one corner of his locked lips; he pitched face forward on the red carpet, twitched once or twice like a landed fish, and lay still with his pistol-hand almost touching the fallen volume of Shakespeare's comedies.

Alan Hepburn, heavy and sick at heart, knelt down beside him with Chavasse kneeling on the other side.

"Gently!" said Alan. "Turn him over and loosen his neckband. Easy: that's it!"

"Is he——?"

"No. But he's in a fit, poor devil, and you may have to fetch a physician. You know, Chavasse: he's not a bad sort, this lad."

Chavasse glowered out of a dirty face, hesitated, and spat on the carpet.

"You're not a bad sort yourself, Bergerac," he growled. "It's a pity they've got to put ten bullets into you tomorrow morning." Suddenly he stabbed his finger towards Ida de Sainte-Elme. "But, as for that high-born teaser over there by the bullet-hole . . . !"

Ida, regarding the whole scene from shining and greedy eyes, was glowing and hugging herself with both arms beside the splintered cracks in the mirror.

"Damn my eyes," said Chavasse, "she's enjoying this!"

"And why shouldn't I enjoy it?" enquired Ida, with a graceful little curtsey. "It's exciting, exciting, exciting! One day, mark my words, I'll ride in a cavalry-charge and find out what it's really like! Poor Raoul, though. Poor Raoul! What happened to him?"

"As though you didn't know, my chicken? You've been trying your bawd's tricks on him, haven't you? You're the one who . . ."

"M. Fouché will hold you responsible for all this," said Ida sweetly. "You should have barred the outer door to the cell-corridor, and you know it."

"Now, look," yelled Chavasse, leaping to his feet. "Young Levasseur came racing down here almost as soon as you did. He's got a right to be here, hasn't he? But all he did, as quiet as quiet, was put his eyes to one of the spy-holes and listen while you spouted all you did spout. Then, without any warning——"

Chavasse broke off and swung round. Booted footsteps, with a clink of spurs, strode along the corridor beyond the open panel. Into the aperture stepped, with considerable curiosity, a young officer in the uniform of the Mounted Guides, his busby cradled in his arm.

"Forgive me," said the voice of Captain Mercier, "if I

intrude." He sniffed the powder-reek. "But the Minister of Police's secretary, for some reason, bolted down here without a word and left me standing in the foyer. Then, when I heard what sounded like a shot and I could have sworn the Minister of Police himself ran down the stairs, though I don't see him anywh——"

Here, catching sight of Levasseur's distorted face on the floor, he drew in his lip and stopped. The harassed Chavasse had only time to cry, "Get out, get out!" before more booted footsteps strode along the corridor. Into the Room of Mirrors shouldered another army officer in the uniform of the Hussars of Bercy.

"No, now, this goes too far!" snarled Chavasse, picking up the empty pistol from the carpet. "We shall have all Paris in here, in a minute, because that fool of a Benet left the corridor-door unlocked. You, young man! And you too, in the Hussar breeches! I command you, in the name of the Minister of Police, to leave here now!"

Lieutenant Hans Schneider's upper lip lifted as he stood there negligently.

"You spoke to me, my man?" he asked.

"And I am not 'your man,' high-nose! I am Corporal Chavasse, of the civil police, and in this quarter I have authority!"

"So?" observed Lieutenant Schneider, almost without inflection.

"I am Corporal Chavasse, of the civil police——"

Cat-like or tiger-like, Hans Schneider had cleared away every trace of dust from face and uniform. His dark busby, from which the plume had been removed, made him seem very tall. Against his light-blue tunic, fitting snugly to shoulders and waist, arabesques of silver braid glittered on chest and right sleeve. His light-blue breeches, with a red stripe, ended in polished Hessian boots. Under the fur-trimmed, silver-braided blue dolman, swung from his left shoulder, his left hand supported the long sabre from bumping against the floor.

His pale-blue eyes looked down with contempt at the dirty, ageing Chavasse. A dazzling image in many mirrors, he might have symbolized the youth and arrogance of the Emperor himself.

"Corporal Chavasse, of the civil police," said Lieutenant

Schneider. "Well, Corporal Chavasse, of the civil police," he added in a heavy mimicking tone, "let me show Corporal Chavasse, of the civil police——"

Carelessly, in a leisurely way, he lifted his leather-gauntleted right hand. With the flat of it, backhand, he whacked Chavasse so viciously across the mouth that they saw the broken soles of the corporal's shoes as he sprawled.

"——how an officer of the Emperor deals with insolent civilians," concluded Schneider.

"That's the way to do it!" cried Ida de Sainte-Elme.

"Gently, Lieutenant!" snapped Captain Mercier.

Chavasse's head had struck the wooden side of the bedstead in one corner. The empty pistol flew one way; a few playing-cards flew another. Stunned but not unconscious, Chavasse breathed in whistling gasps and tried to struggle up.

Alan Hepburn, still kneeling beside the unconscious Levasseur with his forefinger on Levasseur's pulse, glanced over towards Chavasse and up to Schneider.

"You take much on yourself, sir," he said.

He spoke mildly, but the emotional temperature of the room shot up several degrees.

Hans Schneider looked down. Marking the other's black satin evening-clothes, the gold knee-buckles, the jewelled watch-fob hanging from the waistcoat pocket, Lieutenant Schneider condescended to notice him. A pleased, wicked smile tightened the corners of Schneider's mouth.

"And if I do?" he enquired.

Levasseur's pulse was more steady and his breathing easier. Putting one arm under the unconscious man's shoulders and the other under the fold of his legs, Alan lifted him as easily as he would have lifted a child, and rose to his feet.

Across the unconscious man, he and Schneider looked into each other's eyes.

"And if I do?" repeated Schneider, lifting blond eyebrows.

"Take care, Bergerac!" croaked out Chavasse, who had stumbled swaying to his feet.

Still Alan did not reply.

He carried Levasseur over to the bed, where he put the man down gently. Levasseur moaned; his eyelids twitched,

50

but he did not recover consciousness. Alan, still watching him, backed away with the table now on his right.

Hans Schneider's voice snapped across the room.

"I think I spoke to you, sir?" he said.

"So you did," said Alan, and turned round with his thumbs hooked in his waistcoat pocket.

"Must I teach you to be civil too?"

"Evidently. Why don't you try it?"

Schneider flicked back the dolman looped to his left shoulder, so that his right hand could dart across to the hilt of his sabre.

And, at the same time, there was a clang and clatter as Captain Guy Mercier, who had been unfastening the straps which held his own sabre to his belt, hurled the sheathed sabre rattling on the table—its hilt within easy reach of Alan's hand.

Alan looked at it, and glanced back at Schneider. The Hussars of Bercy, by a battle-honour won in Egypt, were the only light-cavalry regiment to carry straight sabres. Mercier's sabre was of the usual curved pattern, but it was the same length and the same weight.

And Alan smiled.

An unholy joy shone in his face. From behind his smile, from behind the slightly-hollowed cheeks and the long, green, gleaming eyes under sardonic brows, all the repressions and nerve-strain of years came boiling out.

"Yes, you overbearing swine?" he said softly "Why don't you try it now?"

Hans Schneider made a noise like a man hit in the face. His right hand whipped across to his sabre-hilt. Alan's hand darted at the same time. Then, before either blade could jump more than three inches from its scabbard, both hands were caught and held as though by the lash and coil of a whip.

"That will do now!" said Joseph Fouché from the doorway. "That will suffice, thank you. Finish it, both of you!"

The Minister of Police, in his rusty black coat and pepper-and-salt trousers, snuff-box in his hand, stepped across the threshold. His thin nostrils were pinched. His fingers trembled slightly as he lifted the box, with its diamond letter 'N' glittering against a grubby shirt-front, and took snuff.

"Madame de Sainte-Elme," he continued, "you will please restrain the lust of conflict I see in your face. Captain Mercier, my old pupil, you seem to forget your customary discretion: take back your sabre. Lieutenant Schneider, you have been instructed in a high quarter to receive your orders from me. Let go the sword, young man!"

Fouché's gaze moved across to Corporal Chavasse, still half-dazed and with blood coming from his mouth.

"And a word of warning, Lieutenant Hans Schneider," added the Minister of Police, shutting up the snuff-box and replacing it in his pocket. "Raise your hand against another of my servants; and, army or no army, I will have the shoulder-straps torn from your tunic and yourself reduced to the ranks. Is that understood?"

Schneider's face, under its freckles and red sunburn, was white and rigid. But for some reason, which was not fear in the least, he seemed willing and even glad to let the sabre slip back into its scabbard.

"Minister of Police," he said, "I have more than once spoken my admiration for you and your methods,"—here Fouché looked at him curiously—"or I should not be in Paris now. I was under no compulsion to . . . to carry a despatch. But, when I am no longer under your orders, I have a score to settle with more than one person here."

It was as though Alan Hepburn breathed clean air for the first time. His eyes were fixed curiously on the steel hand-guard of Schneider's sabre.

"If I live until tomorrow, Lieutenant," he declared, "you shall have your wish at the first opportunity. Captain Mercier, I thank you."

And, taking up Mercier's sword and scabbard, he bowed and handed them back.

"Your obedient servant, sir," replied Mercier—in English. "It was a pleasure."

"That will do now, I said!" snarled Fouché.

Nobody spoke. The Minister of Police, like a pursuing death in his creaky shoes, moved slowly over to the bed and stared down at Raoul Levasseur.

"He has had these epileptic attacks before. I do not think this is serious. Still, we had better have him moved upstairs to my living-quarters."

Fouché lifted his hand and snapped the fingers. As

52

though by an effect of magic, another invisible panel in another wall, at right-angles to the first, rolled open to admit two more scarlet-coated agents of the civil police. At his gesture they raised the unconscious man and bore him out of the room. The panel closed.

The Minister of Police moved back, his shoes squeaking. Seeing the volume of Shakespeare sprawled on the floor, he picked it up so that it opened at the title of As You Like It, closed the book, and put it on the table. Grimly he surveyed first Ida, then Mercier, finally Schneider.

"And now," he said, "the three of you will go upstairs and await me in my office. I wish to have a last talk with the prisoner."

"A last talk?" said Ida, her hand flying to her side as though for the first time the powder-burns had hurt her.

"Those were my words, yes. Does it concern you?"

"No; I don't care! But you're not really going to have him——?"

"That, madame, depends entirely on himself."

"And don't you want to know," cried Ida, with a glance at Chavasse, "what happened here?"

"I already know what happened here, sweet lady, after your latest conquest tried to kill you. The noise reached me through a speaking-tube. Within thirty seconds afterwards, I assure you, I was down here listening behind still another door. But that can wait. Go upstairs, all of you! Go!"

Hans Schneider, about to speak, corrected himself and marched out stiffly. Mercier, plainly much impressed and fascinated by Ida, was waiting for her to precede him. Ida was sweeping in her loftiest way towards the open panel, with Mercier following, when Corporal Chavasse found his voice.

"Wait a minute, Citizen Minister!" he snarled, past the dirty blue handkerchief with which he was swabbing at the bloodstains on his mouth. "Wait a minute! That fancy cocotte has more to explain than you think!"

Ida spun round, her green gown billowing, and one hand pressed against the scorched black rent in its fabric.

"And then?" she cried at Fouché. "You would pay attention, I suppose, to a filthy trouserless-one of the Revolution?"

"You must remember," said the Minister of Police, "that I myself was once a filthy trouserless-one of the Revolution—Did you hear my order, madame? Go!"

"Grand God," Ida burst out, "wait until I get my hands on that woman!"

Fouché took a step forward.

"You had better go, Ida," smiled Alan, trying to restrain the beating of a pulse in his temple, "or you will end the night in a place even more uncomfortable than this. Gently, my firebrand!"

Ida, with a last look at Fouché, swept out. Mercier followed her. The panel closed.

Whereupon, in a room where so many emotions had beaten against the walls, only three of them were now shut in amid the staring mirrors. And Fouché, the puppet-master, moved fast in his manipulation of human lives.

"Well?" he asked Chavasse, when he was certain the others had gone. "What exactly happened here, to make Levasseur lose his head?"

"Look, Citizen Minister: it wasn't my fault! I've often said, mind you, that young fellow would go off his rocker if he didn't sometimes forget business affairs and have a woman. But, my word! I never guessed until tonight the cocotte was amusing herself by trying her tricks on *him!*"

"Nor did I," said the Minister of Police. "And, if the lady was merely amusing herself, she is welcome to have an affair with the whole Grand Army. If, however, she has been using him to extract secrets from my desk . . . ?"

"Citizen Minister, Levasseur said so just before he pulled the trigger! He said she'd betray no more plans of yours!"

"Well, well? What else?"

"The rum part of it," said Chavasse, grimacing behind the handkerchief, "is that this tough piece really wants Bergerac there. It's not that she wants him so much, exactly; but her vanity's hurt because Bergerac says another woman is better at the love-business than she is, and she can't endure that."

"Better at . . . you refer to the prisoner's wife, I daresay?"

"That's right, Citizen Minister."

"Yes; I should have known it all the time! But I am patiently waiting, Corporal Chavasse, to hear what happened."

54

"All right, all right! Well, the cocotte came running down the stairs, in a state about something, and demanded to see Bergerac. She said you sent her."

"Yes; I imagined as much. Go on."

Alan Hepburn, with every sense strung alert, was standing by the table and praying for an answer to the question that writhed in his heart and brain.

Was there any possibility, any at all, that Ida had been telling lies about Madeleine? It would not be in the least strange if Madeleine had returned to Paris; Paris had formerly been her home; where else would she go? But the rest of it . . . !

"Well," said Chavasse, with a broad gesture. "Madame de Sainte-Elme rushed in here and played a scene like the best actress at the French Comedy. She said she'd been staggered to hear about Bergerac's arrest. Bergerac, being no fool, gave her the horse-laugh. Then she flew out at him. She swore she hadn't done it. She said Bergerac's wife was a French spy, and was the one who gave him away . . ."

"That his wife was a French spy?"

The boast of Joseph Fouché was that he could never be surprised. Yet Alan, who missed nothing, did not miss the lightning-brief inflection of astonishment on that one word 'wife.' Alan's right hand gripped the edge of the table, in a hope like intense physical pain.

"I don't know what game Bergerac could have been playing," babbled Chavasse. "But, believe it or not, he pitched her a yarn that his wife was a French agent, and only married him to spy on him. He said he'd been told this by somebody name Arrop . . . Arrop . . ."

"Was it by any chance Lord Harrowby? A British Foreign Minister in an interval when Castlereagh was out of power? Was it Lord Harrowby?"

"That's it, Citizen Minister! Aroppi!"

"The prisoner claimed Lord Harrowby had said this?"

"That's what Bergerac told the cocotte, anyway! He swore that's why he'd deserted her!"

Round swung the Minister of Police, an avenging Mephistopheles.

"What does this mean, M. Hepburn?"

"What does," Alan swallowed, "what mean?"

"Did you say all this to Madame de Sainte-Elme?"

"Yes!"

"Why did you say it?"

"Because I believed it myself—until I saw your face a few seconds ago. Now I'm not so sure. Is it true, Father Satan? Is Madeleine a French agent, employed by you or your Foreign Office?"

"Listen to me, M. Hepburn," said the Minister of Police, beginning ominously to reach after his snuff-box. "What you hope to gain by this stratagem I cannot tell. But I know, by an infallible test I applied myself, that your wife is in actual fact a British agent who has been assisting you in your work for years . . ."

"God Almighty!"

"Nor can you hope to gain anything, M. Hepburn, by such a display of histrionics as you are giving now. If you still refuse your assistance, if you prefer to see your wife go first before the firing-party tomorrow morning . . ."

"Madeleine's here, isn't she? She's in this building? She's been here all the time?"

"Yes. She is here."

"But Madeleine—you think she is a British spy?"

"And I warn you, here and now: if you carry this pretence too far, and force me to prove what I say by having her executed in front of your eyes, I am quite prepared to give the order."

"Wait! Listen to me! For God's sake, will you wait?"

"No, my friend, I will not wait. Do you acknowledge this woman as a British spy, or do you not? For the last time: yes or no?"

"If you could have torn yourself away for half a second from the sound of your own voice," shouted Alan, "you would have heard ten minutes ago that you've beaten me; you've won: you've backed me into a corner and scared all the decency and good intentions out of what I like to call my soul! Yes! I'll go to Boulogne. I decided to save my life, and be hanged to the consequences, before you mentioned Madeleine's name at all!"

Dead silence.

Alan Hepburn stood upright, stiffly, supporting his weight with both hands on the table. The sound of his breathing rose, thinly. Then he sat down in the armchair beside the table, and put his head in his hands.

"Ah," murmured the Minister of Police.

The sound of Alan's breathing still went on thinly in the stillness.

"You are sure," enquired Fouché, with a sharp rap on the lid of the snuff-box, "it was not your wife's predicament which caused you so suddenly to change your mind? Was it that?"

"No!"

"I will pretend, at least, that I believe you. But you quite understand the magnitude of the task you undertake? And that it will not necessarily save your life? Listen! A whole Army, crazed and mutinous in the north, is asking but one question. Who is Captain Cut-throat? The risk to yourself, should you fail to find the answer to that question . . ."

Alan Hepburn struck the arm of the chair.

"The risk to myself," he said, "is not worth two sous if you keep your part of the bargain. I can already tell you where to find the murderer."

If there can be degrees of silence, in a room where not one of the three men seemed to breathe at all, this silence had reached its height in the Room of Mirrors.

Joseph Fouché, about to give another rap on the lid of the snuff-box, stood perfectly still. A very curious look flickered in the red-rimmed eyes: flickered, speculated, then cast away doubt and was gone.

"You found your indications of this," he asked sharply, "in the evidence I read to you."

"Yes!"

"And in what indications?"

"Curse me if I tell you that or anything else until I'm good and ready!"

"But are you certain of what you say?"

"No, naturally I can't swear to it! That's why I must do as you ask to be certain." Alan sprang to his feet. "You've put the horrors on me, Minister; you've won. Now make your preparations, summon your post-chaise, set a guard round me to make sure I behave. But, in the meantime, for decency's sake go and leave me in peace!"

"And yet," said Fouché, with his eyes nearly shut, "it is vital that I have at least some inkling of your notion. We agreed yesterday, I think, that Captain Cut-throat was very obviously an Englishman?—Did we not agree?"

"Try to find out!"

"Should I be obliged to force your confidence, dear sir . . . !"

"If you use the iron boot or the water-funnel, Minister, you will only muddle what dull wits I have left. What else can you do? Shoot me? By blue, that's a new way of getting information! If I'm in a corner, so are you and you know it!"

"Yet in the last analysis," mused Fouché, "there is always your wife."

Alan, about to speak, shut his lips and looked away.

"However!" said the Minister of Police, with cheerful urbanity. "It would desolate me to antagonize a new agent who must remain willingly in my service after he has betrayed a fellow-Englishman as being Captain Cutthroat. So I do not compel you—at present."

"Thank you," said Alan. And he swallowed hard and sat down again.

"Let us return, then, to the question of your wife. Since you have agreed to be reasonable, it is apparently not necessary to bring her in here. Nevertheless, you shall have that privilege at once."

"No! It's not necessary now! You said so yourself!"

"On the contrary, I find it even more necessary. You must not be permitted to change your mind; and your wife alone can persuade you against that possibility.—Corporal Chavasse!"

"Yes, Citizen Minister?"

"For some time," pursued Fouché, with his eye on Alan, "Madame Madeleine has been watching and listening to us, under duress, from outside this room. She is in charge of Sergeant Benet, who failed in his search for Lieutenant Schneider and arrived in my office just as that shot was fired. The question of Levasseur's conduct can wait; I am now going upstairs. As soon as I have gone, you will admit the lady to this room."

Again he studied Alan, who sat motionless and did not speak.

"Despite both their protestations to the contrary, these two are undoubtedly longing to see each other. They may be permitted to speak—but not unwatched and not unheard. For the next five days, at least, we must be sure that no secret communication passes between them."

"I tell you," said Alan, whacking his fist on the table,

58

"Madeleine knows nothing whatever about my affairs! She never has known anything! She's your own agent if she's anybody's at all! Don't you understand we're seeing each other for the first time in more than two years?"

"As I was saying, Corporal Chavasse: from your own vantage-point, outside, you will take careful note of everything that is said and done. Be particularly on the alert against any hidden word or whisper. That is all. Pick up your pistol . . . so! . . . and come with me. M. Hepburn, I shall see you presently."

Once more Alan was on his feet. But his companions would not listen. The panel closed after them. He was left alone with the wild vistas of his own image.

He remained by the table, turning slowly round and round, wondering from which wall she would appear, wondering what the first sight of her would be like. One thought in his mind obscured everything else.

He had made the blunder of his life about Madeleine. When it might be too late to mend matters, he was sure of that now.

He and Madeleine had been married for only nine weeks, which were all honeymoon, when they summoned him one night to the Foreign Office and told him what they did tell him. At first he had merely raged and laughed at them: at their admitted lack of proof, at their refusal to arrest Madeleine or even let him question her.

"Damme, old boy, you're in a position to watch the woman! D'ye want to give the whole show away to her?"

But, worst of all, because it infuriated him with the sting of jealousy.

"That look of innocence is the stock-in-trade they all have! D'ye think you're the first man she's coneyed with it?"

And he had stamped away from Whitehall, swearing he would go straight home to Cavendish Square and tell her all this. Then, human nature being what it is, he did not tell her. Madeleine's very beauty of face and figure, the intensity of her dark-blue eyes with the black lashes and strongly luminous whites, became a distillation of poison. Every endearment sounded hypocritical and every embrace grew suspect.

Always in his ear, droned those voices from beyond the lamps of Whitehall:

"Gad, old boy, we never guessed you'd go so far as to marry the wench! Her mother is an English Puritan but a French Bonapartist. Those so-called 'charitable' works of theirs have only concealed . . ."

In the early days Madeleine, white-faced, would cry out and ask him of what his looks accused her: did he think she was having an affair with another man? And he, with his mind on her past, would answer that her experience must be profound. And both of them, tongue-tied, could only look at each other. In later days, when through desperation he might have spoken out, came news of a mission into France which involved a new identity and must not be imperilled for all the marriages in England.

If now, as he believed, he had been grotesquely wrong about her all the time . . .

Alan, waiting in the Room of Mirrors, heard a doorcatch click in the wall directly behind him. Another panel rolled open, and Madeleine's reflected image sprang up in the wall opposite.

She was so exactly like his last memory of her, looking at him mutely on the night he went away, that for an instant he doubted the reality of the mirrored presence. Here, in the reek of gunpowder-smoke, it was all unreal.

Madeleine took an uncertain step forward. The panel rolled shut, and he whipped round to face her. But for seconds, stretching out interminably, they were both as helpless and inarticulate as they had been before.

"Alan," she said in a whisper, and cleared her throat. She was gripping some kind of silvery shawl, and a passion of sincerity consumed her and shone in her eyes.

"Yes, Madeleine?"

"Alan. Listen. There's something I want to tell you."

"No, my darling. There's something I want to tell you! I . . ."

"No! Please! Listen!—Don't do it."

Silence.

"Don't do it!" cried Madeleine, and her whole body trembled and she gripped the shawl harder. "You're going on this mission, aren't you? And you're doing it for my sake?"

Another silence. Alan backed against the table. He could not have expressed the horror he felt to hear this.

"No!" he said. "Whatever you do, don't make me out

60

to be better than I really am! You don't understand! That wasn't the reason at all!"

"Wasn't it, Alan?"

"No! That wasn't the reason! The real reason—I can't tell you!"

Madeleine ran forward, and then stopped when they were a few feet apart.

"Listen!" she said. "They say they'll kill us both, don't they, if you refuse to give up your country and serve them instead? All right, damn them! If you are doing this for my sake, and you hate doing it as much as I think you do, then tell them to go and kill us and get it over with! At least I can prove I didn't marry you to spy on you! Tell them to kill us, Alan! But don't do what they ask you!"

Chapter VI

Of a Lady Much in Waiting

At the same moment, seated behind the desk in his office upstairs, Joseph Fouché had just concluded a statement whose effect on at least one of his three auditors was little more than sensational.

"——and that, as I say," the puppet-master was explaining, "has been my plan from the beginning. That is why I summoned you three here. Very well.

"It is now," he consulted his watch, "half-past eleven. At one o'clock in the morning a special post-chaise departs from here for Boulogne: to be exact, for the village of Pont-de-Briques just outside the camp. This diligence will be drawn by four horses, and will contain four passengers. With a change of horses every four or five leagues, it should achieve a remarkable speed of travelling for this country, and reach Boulogne before dusk tomorrow evening. Certainly it should be there before midnight.

"The four passengers will be M. Hepburn and his wife; you, Madame de Sainte-Elme, and you, Captain Mercier. Following the post-chaise on horseback, at a discreet distance but completely unknown to either of the Hepburns, will be Lieutenant Schneider."

Round that little group, with one accord, ran a pulse of emotion very different in each of them.

Three armchairs, upholstered in dingy yellow damask, had been drawn up to the Minister of Police's desk. But only two of them were occupied, one by Guy Mercier and one by Hans Schneider.

Lieutenant Schneider, his cold countenance alight with pleasure, sat bolt upright on the edge of his chair: his heavy sword-scabbard propped upright on the floor, his freckled left hand gripped hard round the pommel of the sabre.

"I also, of course," demanded Schneider, "shall have a change of horses at every posting-station?"

"Of course. But you will take care that under no circumstances are you seen by M. Hepburn. Understand, Lieutenant?"

"Understood, Minister."

The puppet-master tapped a bony finger on his desk.

"You all apprehend, I hope, the necessity for these precautions?"

Schneider merely fondled the sabre-hilt and smiled to himself. But Mercier, who had contrived to clear much dust from his uniform, was fast losing that air of lightness and tolerance with which he preferred to face the world.

"Their necessity," he admitted, "it does not exactly take an Aristotle to see. Boulogne is the most carefully guarded military camp in the world. At the same time——"

"At the same time," agreed Fouché, with another sharp rap on the desk, "I am sending to this camp a would-be British agent and his woman confederate. This pleases me very much. But there must be no possibility that either of them, at any time or in any way, can send out a message as to what is happening there.

"You, Mercier, will be responsible for the man Hepburn. When I had the pleasure of instructing you in logic and mathematics at Nantes, you were outstanding among my pupils both for intelligence and for good manners. You have changed your vocation, it is true; evidently you found yourself no more suited to the priesthood than I was suited to it . . ."

"A remarkable understatement, sir, as far as both of us are concerned."

Mercier still spoke lightly, and there was a smile on his sun-tanned face. But apprehension was striding closer with each tick of the clock.

"You, I repeat," said Fouché, "will be responsible for the man Hepburn. You will be with him day and night. You will be at his side in the camp and out of it, while Lieutenant Schneider still follows at a distance and covers both of you. I should have preferred to use my own agents for this work, but in a military camp they would be too conspicuous."

"Surely, sir, the presence of Hepburn himself will be conspicuous?"

"On the contrary. He is known as the Vicomte de Bergerac, whose arrest has been kept a secret, and he will continue to use that name. He was decorated by the Emperor, though by proxy and not in person, for winning prizes in the fencing and riding competitions——"

"Is it so, then?" Schneider asked softly.

"——and it will seem only natural for him to be seeking military preferment. As for Lieutenant Schneider here, do you imagine he was sent from Boulogne merely to carry a despatch about a riot at the men's theatre and two duels among senior officers? There was no mutiny in these particular incidents: the riot was caused by a bad singer, and both duels concerned women. No! There is a reason why this officer carries himself with a certain air, and imagines everyone should know his name wherever he goes."

"Well, sir?" prompted Mercier.

"Lieutenant Schneider," said Fouché, "is the best swordsman in the Grand Army."

Ida de Sainte-Elme, standing over by the door of the box-room, gave a gasp but did not speak.

Schneider, with a tight and complacent little smile, turned his head and surveyed Captain Mercier. Mercier returned the look. There was no love in it at all.

"I do not anticipate," said Fouché, "that the man Hepburn will try to escape. However, should he attempt to do so, or in any way get possession of a weapon——"

Schneider smiled again.

"Should he attempt to do so," repeated Fouché, giving Schneider a withering glare, "you will disarm or disable him without killing him. This man is not to die until I say so. Is that clear?"

In none of the looks Schneider had been giving Fouché was there any love either. Now, tense of face, Schneider managed a curt nod and looked away.

"From the moment the coach leaves here tonight," said Fouché, "you and Captain Mercier are responsible for this man both to me and to the Emperor. Remember it!"

Here the Minister of Police's gaze moved across the room and grew agreeable.

"You, Madame de Sainte-Elme," he added, "will of course be responsible for cherishing the woman."

Ida did not move from her position near the door of

the box-room. One of the two candles had been left behind by Fouché on a shelf in the box-room; and it burned beneath the portrait of the Emperor like a taper at the shrine of the war-god. Ida's face was in shadow.

"Do I make this clear, madame?" enquired the Minister of Police. "For the next five days you will be closer to Madeleine Hepburn than a sister. You will live with her, eat with her, sleep with her; you will even do your best to win her confidence. Is it agreed?"

Then Ida spoke.

"But of course, it is agreed!" she replied, in a ringing voice which was clear and vibrant and sweet. "Perhaps after all, she is a dear creature who ought to be cherished. I shall treat her, believe me, as she has never been treated before!"

Fouché whacked the desk again.

"If you meditate any of your tricks, madame . . . !"

"Tricks?" exclaimed the incredulous Ida, and threw out her arms in a gesture of innocence. "Am I foolish enough to meditate any such thing? After all, dear Minister, you pay me very generously; should I risk your displeasure for a whim? I shall cherish her and comfort her, and be as kind to her as a sister."

Such a load of emotional gunpowder, a detached observer might have reflected, could seldom have been packed into one coach as that which would presently rock and plunge on its race to the north.

But, if Fouché must have known this, he gave little sign of it.

"Make sure that you do, dear lady. Already, tonight, you have lost me one faithful servant in young Levasseur——"

"Poor Raoul? But he is not dead!"

"He is dead as far as I am concerned. He leaves my service immediately. In the meantime——"

"In the meantime," continued Ida, approaching the desk in a way which had its own strong effect on Captain Mercier, "this experiment of yours should be exciting and exciting and exciting! Where shall we live, dear Minister? At the Château of Pont-de-Briques, together with the Emperor's household?"

"No. This so-called château is a small box of a place,

not even big enough for His Majesty's own followers. But near it are several guest-houses, opulently and most vulgarly furnished for distinguished visitors . . ."

"Ah!"

"——because there is nothing the Emperor uses so well as a dramatic gesture or a theatrical display; that is half the secret of his power. You are going to one such guest-house, called the Park of Thirty Statues, until recently occupied by an American envoy named M. Hopewell. But you will encounter those from the château——"

"And the coach, you say, leaves here in an hour and a half? My clothes, dear Minister! What of my clothes!"

If either Mercier or Schneider expected the Minister of Police to treat this as a frivolous request, neither of them could have been well acquainted with Joseph Fouché.

"That is understood." He merely nodded. "Your own coach, I suppose, is outside now? Good! Then you will just have time to go home and prepare. Madame Madeleine shall have the same opportunity as yourself . . ."

"Dear Minister, I should be desolated if she hadn't! Has she, by the way, consented to your experiment?"

"Yes. She consented almost from the first, and her husband has agreed as well. We should have no more trouble with either of them."

Ida approached closer to the desk, watching him.

"In this matter of clothes," pursued Fouché, "I want you both to look your best, for reasons it will hardly be necessary to explain. I must warn you there will not be space to transport more than one large portmanteau each. However! Since my wife assures me that even the day-costume of a modern lady, including shoes, weighs only eight ounces . . ."

Mercier, jarred out of a philosophical calm not as strong as he imagined, was so startled that he left off tugging at his glossy black moustache and sprang to his feet.

"Your wife?" Mercier exclaimed, and instantly grew contrite. "Please to pardon me, old teacher! But I never thought you were interested . . . hem! That is to say——"

"Now God strike me dead!" said the atheistic Minister of Police, and also rose to his feet. "I am an excellent family man with a devoted wife and six children, all of whom play in this very building. Must you assume I have

66

no heart or feelings, merely because I will not display them in public? My children alone . . ."

"Sacred name, what an example they have!" breathed Ida, whose eyes were shining with concentration. "Conceive of it, all of you! Six little Fouchés growing up at the Ministry of Police, learning to betray their parents and each other!"

"Betray, madame?" repeated Fouché, stung for the first time. "Is this the devil rebuking sin? You use rather a strong word, I think?"

"No stronger, dear Minister, than the situation calls for. And I ask you, before these two others!"

Ida flung forward. She pressed herself against the desk, leaning her weight on the top with both hands, and looking at him with the light of the solitary candle illuminating her inspired face.

"What, precisely, is behind all this?" she cried out. "And what double-faced game are you playing now?"

Up went the red eyebrows. "I fail to understand you, madame."

"Attend to me, dear Minister! Does the Emperor know that your agent to Boulogne, your alleged Vicomte de Bergerac, is really a condemned Englishman?"

"No, he does not. His Majesty is much too impatient. When he discovers a spy, he wastes good material and has the fellow shot immediately."

"Ah, I thought so!"

"Meaning, madame?"

"The Emperor, you tell us," said Ida, "calls for a secret-agent to find Captain Cut-throat and gives you only seven days to accomplish it. Yet you waste two of these days persuading a rebellious man who may fail after all! I'll not even mention your apparent insanity when you deliberately open the gates of Boulogne to a British spy.

"No, I'll not mention that! But would you dare risk your own position by entrusting this mission to a solitary agent, an unwilling agent, a man who might hand us all over to the English? Would you dare risk that, Minister, unless . . ."

"Unless what?"

"Unless behind it you had some twisted plot of your own?"

This time it was Lieutenant Schneider who sprang to his feet, but nobody noticed him.

"I don't know what it is!" persisted Ida, groping for inspiration with her hands at her temples. "I can't quite fathom it——!"

"If you could, dear lady, you would be as successful as Joseph Fouché. But there is no such plot. Even if there were, and in the unlikely event you could fathom it . . . !"

"Oh, I know how to be silent! I have certain plans of my own, and I won't pry into your conduct if you don't pry into mine. Sacred name, Minister, how I could make you writhe (and how I would) if I could only discover your scheme! In sending Alan against such impossible odds, it would almost seem——"

Suddenly Ida became transfigured.

"You don't really want him to succeed, do you?" she burst out. "You think he can't possibly find Captain Cutthroat! Answer me one question, sweet Minister! What chance does he have to save his life?"

In the thick silence, pressing down like an extinguisher-cap, they could distinctly hear the ticking of Fouché's watch.

"In candour, madame, very little indeed."

"So!"

"But that, I do really assure you," said the Minister of Police, twinkling at her urbanely and showing his bad teeth, "is merely because of the heavy odds you mention. I have done my part. I have chosen the best agent. And under no circumstances can he communicate with the English."

"What is behind this? What is in your mind?"

"No vestige of deceit, at least. I have my human feelings, dear lady. I rather like this young man. It is remotely possible that he may suffer no harm after all. Meanwhile, be tranquil: with Madame Madeleine to persuade him, he will serve me very willingly. What else can he do?"

The eerie noise which jabbed at them then, thin and shrill and strangely inhuman, was in fact no more than one of the speaking-tubes whistling through its perforated mouthpiece as someone frantically blew into it from the other end.

It whistled, gasped, and whistled again with increasing urgency. Ida and Mercier had jumped at the first sound;

Fouché and Schneider remained unperturbed. But all four looked towards the box-room, where the candle burned steadily below the portrait of the all-conquering Emperor.

"I would wager you," sweetly declared Ida, "that you are hearing the speaking-tube from the Room of Mirrors. You had better answer it, dear Minister. Perhaps the prisoner has notions you have not even fathomed yourself."

Chapter VII

"The Semaphore-Lamps Burn Late Tonight"

If Madeleine Hepburn had not spoken those words in the Room of Mirrors, and spoken them just when she did, Alan realized afterwards that he would not—and could not—have believed her, and all his later conduct would have been different.

In the snap-judgment of shock, just before she entered, he had decided that his past suspicions of her had been unfounded. But this, he knew in his heart, was partly the wish to think it so. All the naggings of distrust, whispering away at the mind for years, are not cast out quite so easily. A revulsion would have come soon after he saw her.

If Madeleine, then, had pleaded with him to be sensible and obey Fouché . . .

But she had done nothing of the sort.

"All right, damn them! If you are doing this for my sake, and you hate doing it as much as I think you do, then tell them to go on and kill us and get it over with! At least I can prove . . ."

Still the seconds went by, and he did not speak. When he looked down at her, after all that long separation, the only revulsion he felt was one of greater tenderness.

And yet, ironically, these very words of hers only created for him a new quandary and a worse difficulty.

He did not touch her, much as he wished to do so. A brief time longer he studied her: the blue eyes, wide-spaced, the short, straight nose, the smooth-gleaming shoulders rising high from the bodice of a grey silk gown.

Then he turned his back on her, and walked to the other side of the Room of Mirrors.

"Alan! What is it?"

At the other side of the room Alan faced her, leaning casually against the wall near one of the gilded wooden satyr-faces. Hitherto Madeleine had spoken in English,

70

because they had always spoken English in the past. But Alan addressed her in French.

"Madeleine," he said, "how is your mother?"

It was as though he had hit her in the face.

When she had been waiting outside, in the narrow corridor which ran round all four sides of the room, it had struck her to the heart to see how much older he looked—and how different from the Alan she had known in the drawling, baaing Whig circle. With one of Sergeant Benet's hands pressing her face against a grotesque spyhole, and the other hand ready to clamp over her mouth if she should cry out, she had watched Alan seem to falter and weaken when her own name was mentioned. And Madeleine had made her decision.

She was not a girl given to rhetoric or empty gestures. Passionately she had meant every word she said about dying with him, and had thought he would understand.

But now . . .

"Then the culprit, it seems," said Madeleine, pressing a hand against her breast, "is not to be given a hearing after all."

Despite herself, and to her horror, tears stung into her eyes.

"The French are quite convinced I'm a British spy," she said. "And you, all this time, have been thinking I was in the pay of the French! I, of all people! It would be comical if it weren't so horribly ironic!"

Alan did not move.

"Since we can't speak of anything else without being overheard," he said, "let us at least speak of the old days in London. Madeleine, how is your mother?"

There was no very strong emphasis on those last words, not even a raising of the voice. But, Madeleine, catching his eye, stopped abruptly in the very act of speaking.

What stopped her was not even a tone, a warning, an inflection; it was that eerie emotion-transference which can be fully known only to those who, however bitterly they misunderstand each other's motives because they are in love, can sense each shading of the other's mood.

Listen to what I mean rather than what I say! it called to her across the room! *Listen! Listen! Listen!*

Madeleine, with a shock at her heart, flung the tears out of her eyes.

71

"My—my mother is well," she answered, instantly following his lead. "I—I haven't seen her since I ran away and hid here in Paris, but I have had news in spite of the war."

"Does she still pursue all her charitable works, my dear?"

"Y-yes! Why?"

"Does she still protest that the madmen at Bedlam should receive soothing treatment instead of being starved and flogged?"

"Yes, more than ever!"

"And still instruct pupils, as you used to do, in Dr. Braidwood's school at Hackney?"

"Yes, though that c-can't go on for long. Dr. Braidwood is growing very old."

"That's a pity," said Alan. "It's a great, great pity!"

And then, metaphorically speaking, the hair rose on Madeleine's head.

Alan's left hand was hooked in his waistcoat pocket. Raising his right hand carelessly, fingers upward and thumb across the palm, he folded the fingers downwards and then made a careless gesture sideways with forefinger out and three fingers folded under.

Beneath the steady gaze of Sergeant Benet and Corporal Chavasse, whose eyes Madeleine could see glistening behind two of the gilded satyr-faces, Alan had just formed the letters B, E, and G in Dr. Braidwood's manual alphabet for the deaf-and-dumb.

(Steady! Steady! Steady!)

"But my heart is too heavy," Alan went on, in a voice that seemed to ring with uncanny loudness, "to go on discussing happier times than these. Credit me, Madeleine: I understand your generosity and I appreciate its motive. All the same, my dear . . ."

B.E.G.M.E.G.——

(What was this? Take care! For God's sake, Alan, take care!)

And yet, if done slowly and with gestures, that deaf-and-dumb alphabet was completely undetectable to the probing eyes outside: even if they had known such an alphabet existed at all. Though for centuries efforts had been made to instruct deaf-mutes, it was only in the past forty years that the Abbé de l'Epée and Dr. Thomas

72

Braidwood had evolved a practical sign language, first for two hands and then for one.

"All the same, my dear," continued Alan, striding to another side of the room, taking out his watch and consulting it, "we should only be idiotic and futile to obstruct the Minister of Police any longer. I was given until to-morrow morning to make up my mind, and I—I put off the decision almost too long."

B.E.G.M.E.B.O.U. . . .

For an instant Madeleine herself imagined that she had been dreaming all this; that the words were gibberish or that he was not even signalling at all. Then the mute syllables flashed out in English.

BEG ME GO BOULOGNE.

"We must think of ourselves, my dear," persisted Alan, replacing the watch in his pocket and continuing to pace. "We must consider the safe and prudent course for both of us. I have no choice in the matter now; and neither, believe me, have you."

"I have always obeyed you, Alan, and I always will. Perhaps it was a stupid—and silly notion, not practical, out of a novel by Mrs. Radcliffe! But, if I said it, I think you know"—it was her eyes which made the word a question —"why?"

(Take care, take care! A pair of the eyes shifted round then!)

"Yes," snapped Alan, picking up the volume of Shake-speare from the table, "I have already told you I apprehend your excellent intention. But I am far from being a hero, my dearest, and the safe and prudent course is wisest in the end!"

Bang went the book, down on the table, while the hot room seemed to grow hotter, and Alan paced, and the mute language flowed on.

"It should be evident, by this time——"

BEG ME GO BOULOGNE. ALL PART OF MY PLAN.

She did not clearly hear the words he was uttering aloud, like a man whipped and hunted to the end of his courage. When he paused she made a plea of her own, urging him to be sensible and obey Fouché with diligence. And, all this time, Madeleine's thoughts ran riot.

Well, then, Alan had meant to obey Fouché from the

very first! If he feared anything he had feared only that his pretence of reluctance might have been kept up until it was too late, and he would be shot instead. But, if he wanted to go, it could only be because he was using this mission as a pretext to hide . . .

As though Alan were reading her thoughts, the deaf-and-dumb alphabet flashed back.

ONLY WAY ENTER CAMP. MUST LEARN BONEY'S PLANS.

The implications of this, and all the new dangers it opened, boiled up in Madeleine so that she could hardly hide her own feelings.

Turning away from him, more than ever conscious of the staring eyes from the wall, Madeleine threw her shawl on the table and pressed her hands together. Alan was speaking aloud again, for effect; again she scarcely heard him.

But surely . . .

Surely Alan had not deliberately allowed himself to be suspected and arrested, in the mere hope that he would be chosen to find Captain Cut-throat? No! Incredible beyond all reason! Even if he were willing to take so mad a risk—and, one night at Brookes's Club, he had wagered sixty thousand pounds on the turn of one card—even then he could not possibly have known or suspected in advance the design of Joseph Fouché.

If he had contrived to get himself arrested at the in-stigation of his latest mistress, Ida de Sainte-Elme, in the ordinary way it would only have meant suicide. A blank wall at dawn; a firing-party; then a stroke-of-mercy pistol-bullet through the ear.

Briefly Madeleine entertained the wild notion that Alan and Fouché, for some obscure cause, were secretly working in league together. But this, for a dozen reasons, she dismissed as even more incredible; and rightly so. Alan and the Minister of Police were engaged in a fast-moving contest of wits whose end had not even come in sight.

There must be some very good reason, which she dared not ask at length, why Alan knew or at least strongly suspected that he would be asked to find a murderer. But what reason could it be? What reason?

Then Alan's voice struck through her thoughts.

"Did you hear what I said, Madeleine?"

74

Conscious of an alteration in his tone, she looked at him quickly. He regarded her with the old twinkle in his eye and the old amiable expression, quickly veiled. She felt he had never been so much master of the game as when he seemed beaten and in a corner. But this only prompted new terrors, because of his eternal and hair-raising jugglery with risks.

"Alan," she cried—take care, now!—"how did you come to be arrested?"

"It would seem, my dear, that I carelessly left a despatch-box unlocked one night when I should have been on my guard. Afterwards I was not sure whether or not it had been tampered with. So I went away . . ."

"You went away?"

Here, very slightly, he hesitated: why?

"Yes. I left Paris and went to take thought of matters, alone, at a shooting-box in the Forest of Marly. When I returned, nearly ten days later, I was instantly arrested and haled off to Fouché's office. But never mind that! Did you hear what I said?"

Now she understood the alteration in his tone. He was not talking for effect on the listeners outside. His face had darkened and there was fierce sincerity in every word.

"You need have no fear, I tell you! You were impressed into this accursed business through my fault and mine alone . . ."

"I don't care, Alan! I prefer it so!"

"But I care. So be easy: I will make some bargain with the Father of Lies upstairs, and he'll set you free as soon as it can be managed."

"You can't, Alan! And you mustn't!"

"Why not?"

"In the first place, he would never believe you! In the second place . . ."

What Madeleine wanted to say was that in some fashion she meant to help him. The memory of her offer to die beside him, however well-intentioned, now covered her with a hot and pouring humiliation which she determined to live down.

"In the second place," she retorted, "at least we can be together. They are sending me to Boulogne with you. Did you know that?"

Plainly, as she saw by his expression, he had not known it. He drew back a little, poised: his eyes roving and his mind sorting thoughts.

"Then that's it," he said softly. "That explains much I ought to have interpreted before this! That's why Ida was here tonight."

"Ida?" repeated Madeleine—and stiffened a little in spite of herself.

"Ida de Sainte-Elme! The dark-haired woman who was here with Fouché and those two officers. If you were anywhere outside the room, you must have seen her?"

"Yes. I saw her."

Alan, deep in mazy thought, had drawn back still more. His eyes were fixed on the crown of candles hanging from the ceiling, the candles flaring low in broad winding-sheets of grease and dripping hot wax on the table-top beneath. And Alan nodded.

"The semaphore-lamps burn late tonight," he said.

"What?"

"Already a message has gone out on the first stage of its journey to M. Bourrienne, the Emperor's secretary." Then Alan's face grew sardonic. "Tut, no! I had forgotten: Bourrienne was dismissed from his post for taking bribes from Fouché to spy on the Emperor. That was fair enough, though; because M. Desmarest, the Prefect of Police, had been bribed by the Emperor to spy on Fouché."

"Alan, is anybody at all to be trusted in France now?"

"Nobody! Please to remember that. However: a message has already gone out to General Duroc, the Emperor's secretary, at Pont-de-Briques. A coach leaves here at one o'clock in the morning. According to what Fouché told me today, my only companion in that coach was to have been Captain Mercier: an old and trusted pupil, who incidentally speaks perfect English. A captain in the Guides, with dark hair and moustache: you must have seen him as well?"

"Yes! The one who offered you the sabre when . . ."

Alan had resumed his pacing, and was speaking more rapidly.

"Well, clearly, the Father of Lies has had a different design all the time. That other officer, from the Hussars of Bercy, doesn't count; Corporal Chavasse said earlier he had come here to carry a despatch. But, if Fouché insists on sending you to Pont-de-Briques, it can only mean Ida de Sainte-Elme is going as well."

He faced her fully; he struck the table; a full-blown bitterness flared out.

"And I very much fear," he said, "that you and I will not be together after all."

Madeleine moistened dry lips.

"Do you mean to imply," she cried, "that you will be with her instead? Your latest mistress? The veritable noble-savage out of the pages of Jean Jacques Rousseau?"

They looked at each other. Spectres of old days, of white-faced suspicions and misunderstandings, crowded round and troubled the air even now.

"Listen to me!" said Alan. "I merely mean that she is to watch you as Mercier is to watch me. But, whatever happens or seems to happen in the future, will you promise me to be as civil to this woman as though she were your closest friend? Can you promise that?"

"Do you take me for altogether stupid, Alan? I know what you're doing! You—you may even make love with her while I'm there, if there is any possible good reason for it!"

"There is the very best reason in the world. For I tell you this, without any exaggeration at all: that the future of several countries for the next fifty years may depend on what can be discovered at Boulogne in the next few days."

Another splash of burning wax, unheeded, fell from the chandelier on Madeleine's shawl across the table.

"And—and this Captain Cut-throat? You intend to find him, too?"

In her excitement Madeleine did not notice the slipping-out of that dangerous word "too." Fortunately, it seemed, neither of the wall-listeners noticed it either.

"That is what I am pledged to do," retorted Alan, giving her a glance which shocked her back to alertness; "and, what is more, to find Captain Cut-throat before there can be another murder."

"But that's impossible!"

"Is it, my dear?"

"For some reason," said Madeleine, "your so-called Father of Lies told me the whole story tonight and seemed to think I ought to understand it. According to what he

77

said, a sentry named Grenadier Somebody was patrolling in a brightly-lighted space with two witnesses actually looking at him. Nobody came anywhere near him to stab him with a dagger; and yet he was stabbed and a message dropped at his feet! Can that possible be true?"

"As I read the evidence, it is quite true."

"But how could it possibly be?—And, anyway, can you ever dream of finding one person lost in a whole army? It might be anyone! Isn't the choice far too wide?"

"The choice," he answered, "is not nearly so wide as you think. Nor is the assassin's method at all mysterious. Would you care to hear, for instance, how he committed his latest murder?"

In the pause Alan deliberately allowed, both of them became intensely aware of those two other presences, Sergeant Benet and Corporal Chevasse, listening and listening as though with stopped breath.

There was a gulping, strangling noise of breath released. Then one of the gilded satyr-faces flashed into witlessness as a pair of eyes disappeared from behind it. Somebody stumbled in the corridor outside. They heard the frantic whistle of a speaking-tube, summoning the Minister of Police to come and listen to a prisoner all suddenly grown garrulous.

Alan, as urbane as Fouché himself, removed his gaze from the mirrored reflection of that satyr-face. Taking the watch out of his waistcoat pocket, he opened its lid, glanced at it, shut it up, and replaced it.

"The way in which that sentry was really killed in a lighted space——" he began.

A speaking-tube whistled again. The time was just ten minutes to twelve on the night of Monday, the 22nd of August.

Chapter VIII

Gunpowder in a Coach

Tuesday, August 23rd. A quarter to nine in the evening, with a lurid yellowish sky fading to ghostly twilight over the heights of the Forest of Harbelot far ahead.

Crack! went the whip of the leading postilion, plied ever more freely as the coach, built high off the ground with large back wheels and smaller front wheels, rolled at a faster pace along the Emperor's new military road.

Drawn by four horses with two postilions up, it had clattered through Amiens at mid-morning; through Abbeville and Etaples; and now, in the twilight, it was on a straight run of a league and a half to its destination at Pont-de-Briques outside Boulogne.

A cleaner, fresher wind from the sea stirred through groves of spruce and fir and pine. The air was pine-scented and aromatic; it cooled hot foreheads inside the coach as one of the four passengers—he wore dusty day-clothes of blue coat and buff waistcoat above white doeskin breeches and black top-boots—made the first remark in some time.

"Well!" began Alan Hepburn. "If you would care . . ."

Alan, sitting with his back to the horses and with a leather-covered box across his knees, paused to glance first at Captain Mercier seated beside him at his right hand. Then he looked across at Madeleine Hepburn and Ida de Sainte-Elme, who sat facing forward.

"Come!" he added, with weary and ironic affability. "Are we all asleep, then? Can we show no trace of good spirits, any of us!"

It would have been surprising if any of them could; it was not unexpected when Ida de Sainte-Elme screamed out at him, and brought the whole group again to a tension of nerves.

Nearly nineteen hours' continuous bone-jolting over bad and dusty roads, with brief halts only for changes of horses or for what scanty meals could be obtained, are not conducive to good spirits at the best of times. Unlike the posting-system in England, French posting-stations were operated by the government and were very seldom situated at inns, so as to have food or drink awaiting the traveller at any hour.

And, when these travellers had left Paris at two o'clock in the morning instead of one, rumbling out under the Porte St. Denis with the glow of their own carriage-lamps reflected through the windows on claret-coloured upholstery, more than one condition of nerves was already manifest.

Guy Mercier, with a deprecating grimace, had propped a sabre upright in the corner beside his busby, and put down a loaded pistol on the cushion at his right hand.

"Very well: I regret this!" he had said, glancing at Alan beside him. "But there you have it; the Minister of Police gave me no choice."

"Is it any good telling you, Captain," said Alan, "that I have no intention of trying to escape? For example! Would you accept my word of parole?"

"I should accept it, happily. The Minister of Police is a different matter. It is not that I object to keeping awake all night . . ."

"Keeping awake tonight? After you have just ridden post-horses more than fifty leagues from Boulogne?"

"There are far worse things on campaign. No, it is not that; but the idea of failing in this trust——!"

Mercier's gaze strayed towards Ida: who, occupied with her own simmering and seething thoughts, for once in her life was not trying to enslave every man in sight. She paid no attention whatever to Mercier; and Mercier, it was evident, had been enslaved long ago.

"The idea of failing——!" he repeated. "Do you understand, M. Hepburn, that I have never before been given a serious responsibility in my life?"

"You offered the hilt of that sword to a contemptible prisoner, Captain; and we are at least friendly enemies. You don't think we can both hope to keep awake every minute from now on?"

"So far as I am concerned, only until we arrive at Pont-de-Briques. After that, the matter arranges itself with laudanum."

"Laudanum?" Alan repeated sharply; and the whole atmosphere quivered with a slight but perceptible change.

"Given in large doses, it induces sleep. For better or worse, M. Hepburn, you are carrying a pass, signed by General Savary, which allows you to go anywhere inside the Boulogne Camp during the day. Very well! But every night, by instructions from Papa Fouché . . ."

Here Mercier reached down beside him and tapped the flat leather pouch, called a sabretache, which swung low from the left hip of every cavalry-officer.

"Every night," he repeated, tapping the pouch, "I am to give you sufficient laudanum to keep you asleep for seven or eight hours at least. There must be no chance of your wandering about the camp in the dark hours."

"But that's not necessary, I tell you!"

"Then why do you object to it?"

"Captain Mercier, there are more reasons than you can ever guess."

"Listen!" interrupted Madeleine, who had raised her head. "Don't you hear hoof-beats following this coach now? Isn't there some horseman after us?"

"La, there can be nobody following us!" instantly declared Ida, and laughed and was merry and affectionately patted Madeleine's hand. "Even if there were, could we hear it under all the noise of this diligence?"

There was some truth in what she said. The coach, flying out through the suburbs of Paris, crashed and swayed on creaky springs. Since Ida had insisted on bringing two portmanteaux of clothes as well as a wooden hat-box, these objects bumped about on the roof together with the other luggage and Mercier's saddle, sliding from side to side like loose cargo in a ship's hold.

But Captain Mercier's attention would not be distracted.

"And there is a further consideration, my friend," he said. "When we reach this guest-house near Pont-de-Briques, you will still be posing as the Vicomte de Bergerac. Can you guess how much your life would be worth if the Emperor should discover who you really are?"

"Frankly," confessed Alan, "I have once or twice wondered if the discovery might not perhaps annoy him."

"Annoy him? For your own sake, M. Hepburn, I counsel you to walk warily and avoid rashness! You would not live a quarter of an hour—and neither, I regret to say,

81

would your wife—should the Emperor learn the true identity of either one of you."

Madeleine Hepburn, from the corner of her eye, glanced quickly round at Ida de Sainte-Elme. Ida, with a quiet and satisfied smile, looked fixedly ahead.

"But don't misunderstand me, Madame Hepburn," urged Mercier, instantly contrite. "I have no wish to alarm a lady. And I meant only to warn your husband against his own plain recklessness. After all, it is certain that neither Madame de Sainte-Elme or I would ever give you away."

"And why is that so certain?" cried Ida.

"If for no other consideration, dear lady, because we dare not. We have put our own lives in hazard by accepting these orders from Papa Fouché; he knows it; we must protect our two hostages in order to protect ourselves."

Ida, opening her mouth to speak, kept it open for an instant in a kind of seething dismay. Then, wrapped like Madeleine in a dark cambric dust-cloak, she sat back and clasped one hand round the gold-embroidered reticule hanging from her left arm.

"In the meantime," reflected Mercier, "we shall only reach a state of nervous crisis if we keep on imagining traps for the future. This is an unpleasant duty and an unpleasant journey for all of us; but we must at least try to make it as agreeable as we can. Surely, for instance, we can speak of more cheerful subjects?"

Then out of the gloom, honey-sweet and charged with yearning, rose the voice of Ida de Sainte-Elme.

"Yes, yes, yes! That is true and it must be done!—Captain Mercier!"

"Madame?" said Mercier, jumping a little in spite of himself.

Ida, who was seated opposite Mercier, leaned forward with her knees almost touching his, and her intent face upturned. Alan, seated opposite Madeleine, exchanged a quick glance with her. But, ever since meeting Ida, Madeleine had been as eager and wide-eyed and innocent-seeming as a girl of eighteen.

"This wretched affair," pursued Ida, "will drive us all to distraction and leave us not a second's peace of mind! But only you, Captain Mercier, have had the good sense and the good heart to recognize that!"

"Come, madame makes too much of a trifle!" protested Mercier, and laughed rather self-consciously. "When I recall that a few days ago, out of sheer imagination, I was picturing just such a scene as this . . . !"

"But I don't quite understand, Captain Mercier. You imagined," and affectionately Ida touched Madeleine, who beamed back at her, "you imagined us two?"

"Not you two ladies in particular, naturally. Still! When I thought of just such a situation as this, and in my innocence believed I should enjoy taking part in it . . . !"

"Oh, really? And don't you enjoy it at all, dear Captain?"

"With you here, madame, enjoyment is inevitable."

You're damned well right it is, thought Alan Hepburn; and through that devious labyrinth of treachery, he wondered, was this female squirming and writhing at the present moment?

"That woman," Madeleine was afterwards to exclaim, "is so horribly obvious in what she does that at first you are furious and think she must seem only comical. And then, all of a sudden——!"

By every law of poetic justice, reflected Alan, Ida de Sainte-Elme should have been the wife of Joseph Fouché. For all his withered looks, the Minister of Police was only forty-two years old. Whereas Fouché's real wife was a dusty, ugly little woman known to everybody as Bonne Jeanne, who——

Meanwhile, since they had galloped past the last dark house-windows to throw back reflected gleams of their own coach-lamps, faces faded away against claret-coloured upholstery and the inside of the coach grew dark. The floor jolted and rocked. The rolled-up blinds rattled. But the inside reflector-lamp remained unlighted. Feeling Madeleine's gaze steadily on him in the dark, Alan reached out and gripped her hands while desperately he revolved more problems than one.

And still Ida's conversation with Mercier, sinking to intimate whispers, flowed on and on.

Ida asked about his past life. She offered him a sip of brandy from the miniature flask in her handbag. She was by turns coy and full-throatedly alluring. If this sort of talk continued all through the night . . .

It did continue for most of the night. But by the next

day, when the coach had passed its halfway mark at Amiens where there was a jubilant sign-board reading "To England," incessant jolting and noise and discomfort had brought them all to a pitch of nerves, at which anything might have happened.

The lurid afterglow was fading to a ghostly twilight. They were within sight of the Forest of Harbelot. And Alan made up his mind as to the only course he could take.

"Well!" he began. "If you would care . . ."

Madeleine, wrapped in her cloak and with a kerchief over her hair, saw with apprehension that he was pale. Slapping dust from his blue coat and buff waistcoat, he shifted on his knees the flattish wooden box—it was bound in the green-and-gold leather of the Imperial colours— which he had carried all the way from Paris.

"Come!" he added, with weary and ironic affability. "Are we all asleep, then? Can we show no trace of good spirits, any of us?"

And Ida exploded.

"Good spirits, eh?" she screamed at him. "Will you look at my hair? And my clothes? And with no drop of water to wash in? There are times, Alan when the prospect of having them kill you——"

"As a matter of fact," snapped Alan, "it was the subject of killing I wished to discuss. If you would care to hear, at long last, what I have discovered about Captain Cutthroat and how the assassin committed his last murder . . . ?"

Crack! went the whip of the leading postilion. Madeleine, who had been speculatively studying Ida as though Madeleine too had made up her mind about something, twitched her head round. Alan felt rather than saw Captain Mercier grow tense at his right side. Ida de Sainte-Elme forgot even the disarray of the journey.

"Do you mean what you say?" she demanded.

"Yes! Every word of it!"

"As for me," amusedly said Mercier, who was the most hollow-eyed of the four, "I shall believe all this when I actually hear it. It seems to me that in the Room of Mirrors, about a century ago, you made just the same offer. Did you not?"

"Yes! Granted!"

84

"And afterwards, when the guards had whistled us all downstairs in a hurry, you calmly refused to say another word. I shall not soon forget Papa Fouché's face at the time. Frankly, now: weren't you deliberately trying to infuriate him and no more?"

"Frankly, yes! I was! Damn it all, could I resist the temptation to give him a dig when it was too late for him to make reprisals?"

"Once again, M. Hepburn," said Mercier, seeing Ida's angry eye, "I must warn you against this line of conduct. You may joke with us; you may even joke with Joseph Fouché; but you joke with the Emperor at your own risk!"

"And who is joking with the Emperor? Am I? Listen to me! If you maintain my foolery has rebounded straight back on my own head, very well. I won't gainsay it. But this decision to keep me quiet with laudanum has altered every move I make. Do you agree, all of you, that it is vital to stop Captain Cut-throat?"

"Yes: naturally we agree! Well?"

"Well!" said Alan, tapping the box. "This murderer strikes at night, and only at night. With the whole camp in a turmoil, with a campaign looming close, he may strike again at any minute. When that happens, my friend, they will call for the man who was supposed to prevent it. How will you explain to the Emperor the fact that I am lying stupefied in a drugged sleep?"

Crack went the postilion's whip.

Mercier, so bemused with Ida that he seemed to have lost the power to think, consulted her face for inspiration and found none. Alan was peering round at him. A bounce of the coach threw Madeleine and Ida against each other; they smiled mechanically and hastily scrambled apart.

"It is a difficulty," admitted Mercier, "which should have occurred to me. But it's no affair of mine! I am acting under orders, on the Minister of Police's responsibility——!"

"And do you think Fouché will accept any responsibility whatever, once all four of us have landed in the same bath? Knowing his past history as you do, can you possibly think that?"

"But what is Fouché trying to do?" cried Madeleine. "Surely he must have thought of this difficulty himself?"

"Of course he did, Madeleine. He thinks of everything.

This is simply part of the web he has spun round you and me——"

("I knew it!" breathed Ida.)

"——because the old twister is sure I can't find a way out of it. Can I persuade you, Captain, that you will hardly aid your investigator if you drug him before he even begins to investigate?"

"My friend, you are very persuasive. Even if I were inclined to credit your sincerity . . ."

"For God's sake, Captain, believe me! I was never more sincere in my life!"

"Yet I still tell you," retorted Mercier, "that I cannot do this. If you like, I will forego the drug for one night more; at least I can keep on my feet to watch over you. Otherwise I am a soldier under orders; I must obey them!"

"Thunder of God!" said Ida de Sainte-Elme. "That I should be placed in a position like this! If I go straight to the Emperor with the entire story——"

"And have Alan immediately shot for espionage?" cried Madeleine. "Try that, Madame de Sainte-Elme, and you may find certain things used against yourself!"

"Meaning what, Madame Hepburn?" demanded Ida, beginning to shiver.

"Stop this!" said Alan.

There was a silence. Alan drew a deep breath and settled back.

"No," he admitted. "I had not expected you, Mercier, to say anything else. So I must make a final effort to persuade your good sense, flat against your orders. I must tell you everything I know about these murders, including the trick by which the murderer killed one victim without being seen. You say you have never had a serious responsibility. But do you accept the responsibility for knowing the truth about these crimes?"

"If only from curiosity," smiled Mercier, "I accept *that* responsibility."

Alan nodded. He opened the box across his knees, took something out of it, and laid it across the lid of the box.

"This," he said, "is the dagger with which the first murder was committed. Sapper Robert Duchêne, 3rd Engineers, was stabbed through the back of the neck at the south-west corner of the Field of the Balloons."

It was as though all the stormy perplexities of the Boulogne Camp—hitherto only a confusion of drums and shouting—came near and closed round them at last.

The dagger, carefully cleaned of bloodstains, glistened in the last light from the sky. Its handle was of black polished wood with a plain steel crosspiece. Its blade was flat and straight, some six inches long by an inch and a half broad; it did not even taper until it reached the point, and one edge of the long blade was razor-sharp. Lying against the green-and-gold box-lid, it rattled and quivered with their motion.

"Now where the devil," exclaimed the protruding-eyed Mercier, "did you get that dagger? How did you come by it at all?"

"Papa Fouché gave it to me," Alan said simply.

"Fouché?"

"Yes. You have heard one thing, I imagine? In the first three murders, the weapon was left behind in the body of the victim?"

"Of course I have! Everybody has!"

"Very well. As soon as our Father of Lies was told to investigate, he sent a semaphore message for the three daggers and the five scraps of paper signed by Captain Cut-throat. Let's see what he found."

Alan picked up the dagger and handed it to Mercier.

"Take a close look at the blade," he suggested.

"But there's nothing here!" protested Mercier, after holding it against the light from the window and tilting it back and forth. "The maker's name has been filed off."

"Yes. Now look at it through a strong crystal-lens," said Alan, giving him a lens from the box, "as Fouché naturally and immediately did.—Good! You see something, don't you? The maker's name has been filed off, but not so completely filed off that it can't be distinguished under scrutiny; and the name is Andrews of Sheffield. All three of those daggers came from England."

"England, eh?" repeated Ida de Sainte-Elme, and drew her lips back in a brilliant smile. "More and more interesting! England!"

"Finally," said Alan, producing his third and last exhibit, "here is one of the notes left by Captain Cut-throat. Do you find anything odd about this?"

The spots of blood on the paper were only brown and dim in the gloom as Mercier held it up to the window.

"Admittedly," said Mercier, "admittedly we have heard a good deal about these notes from the murderer; but——"

"But," Alan interrupted, "nobody has actually seen them except General Savary's Military Police, who are not famous for their brilliant intellects and are damned lucky if they can read and write at all. Pay no attention to the handwriting; that tells us nothing. Look at the signature itself."

"Just a moment!" Mercier almost shouted, after a long pause. "Give me time to think! This message is signed . . ."

"Yes. It is signed, curiously, as *Captain Cut-the-throat.* But that is a misnomer: no throats were cut in the literal sense. Any Frenchman would simply have written *Captain Cut-throat.* To Fouché's logical mind it meant only one thing. Some foreigner, trying too hard to write correct French, had overreached himself and used a word which nobody in the Grand Army would ever use. Captain Cut-throat, then, must be an Englishman spreading terror in the pay of Pitt or Castlereagh."

"And it's true, isn't it?" cried Ida.

Alan did not seem to hear. Dropping the exhibits back in the box, he closed it with a snap.

"Didn't you guess anything of this!" he said. "Fouché asked me, in plain words, if the murderer must not obviously be an Englishman. No, stop; you weren't there at the time. But you, Madeleine, heard some interesting things from the old boy himself."

To Madeleine it was as though the presence of Fouché peered in at the coach-window like a devil-in-the-box, raising its red eyebrows and pinning her into a corner as the Minister of Police had done the night before.

"Yes!" Madeleine said in an anguish of bitterness. "He told me the whole story of the murders as though he expected me to understand it. Naturally he did! Since he thought I was a British spy, and that a Frenchwoman ought to have seen the point about the mistake in grammar, of course he expected me to understand!"

"Did he say that nobody in the Grand Army would ever have written 'Captain Cut-the-throat?' "

"Yes! He said it and he even stressed it, and pointedly asked if it didn't mean something to me." Madeleine, in a quiet rage at having to admit this before Ida, could have killed herself for not seeing the explanation before; but the fright and confusion of last night had been too great. "Then, of course," she added, "when I said Captain Cutthroat must be a highly-placed member of a French secret-society called the Olympians, he thought I knew better but was deliberately misleading him . . ."

"In short," interrupted Ida de Sainte-Elme, with a sudden snap, "that you were the sweet-voiced and innocent-looking liar you actually are?"

Madeleine flung her head round.

"Take care, my lady!" she said. "The Minister of Police is one thing. But if you think I am afraid of you or your stupid bluster——!"

'Gently,' thought Alan, 'for God's sake let there be no open row between these two women!' The coach swayed and banged, ever closer towards trouble.

"Now one moment!" urged Mercier, waving his hands. "How long has Fouché known or believed the murderer must be an Englishman?"

"Since the evening of the 21st, at least. That was when the notes and the daggers came into his hands. Yesterday morning he sent a long despatch by special courier to Savary and the Emperor. It must have arrived at Boulogne well before the time we were leaving Paris."

"But—sacred name! Savary and the Emperor are not still keeping the whole affair a secret? To our troops this knowledge will mean everything. The news that Captain Cut-throat is not one of their own comrades, but a hidden English spy they can find and tear in pieces, will lift their morale to the skies again! Surely the Emperor must immediately publish it?"

"I have no doubt he already has," returned Alan dryly, "and that we shall run full-tilt into its effects very soon. That's why I must take immediate steps to disprove it."

"To disprove it? Are you mad?"

"No."

"But why disprove it?"

"Because I don't believe a word of it," said Alan. "I maintain, just as Madeleine says, that Captain Cut-throat is the head of a revolutionary secret-society called the Olympians: whose symbol, by the way, is a blood-stained dagger. I further maintain that 'Captain Cut-throat' hired a certain person to do the killings for him. And I am prepared to give the name of the hired killer at this very minute."

In the excitement of those hurtling words, both he and Mercier were partly standing up. Now they staggered with a jolt and nearly fell.

"*Ohé, there!*" screamed out a youthful voice from a little way outside. "*Ho-là! Stand fast! Pull up!*"

In a snorting of horses and a swaying of wheels, the coach bumped and slowed down with an abruptness which flung them all together. As the youthful voice cried out something else, they came to a dead stop in the twilight.

Chapter IX

The Three Daggers

Guy Mercier, infected by the general atmosphere, instantly snatched up the loaded pistol which lay on the cushion at the right hand.

Briefly they all felt the loneliness and emptiness of the countryside at nightfall. Mercier, in his dust-spattered green coat with the single gold epaulet, was leaning out of the off-window. Alan had suddenly twisted to his own left: head up, intently listening.

"What is it?" Mercier called out of the window. "What's wrong?"

"Wrong Captain?" yelled back the youthful voice, and approached closer.

"Yes! Why are we stopping?"

Since all the work of managing the vehicle was done by the two postilions riding the off-horses, there was no coachman or guard on the box. Into sight strutted the leading postilion, a cocky and diminutive youth of sixteen, in the usual blue coat and white breeches. Already, since they picked him up at the last posting-station only a short distance back, he had informed them grandly that his name was Michel and that one day he would be a greater cavalry-commander than Michel Ney.

"What's wrong, Captain?" jeered Michel, giving him a reluctant military salute. "Got to light the lamps, haven't I?" He produced a tinder-box and waved it. " 'Tisn't quite dark yet, maybe, but we're on the edge of the Forest of Harbelot and it'll be very dark in there."

"And that's what all the fuss was about, then? Couldn't you have——"

That was when Alan Hepburn, moving very quickly, slipped open the opposite door of the coach and sprang down outside.

Instantly there was a click as Mercier drew back the hammer of the pistol and whirled round to cover him.

"No," said Mercier flatly. "Don't try it! Come back in here!"

Alan, who had not moved after his jump, was standing beside the door with the coach-door as high as his waist, and staring straight ahead up the road. He replied only when Mercier had repeated the order.

"After all I have just told you," said Alan, turning round an exasperated face, "do you still think I am trying to escape? If I had wanted to do you any harm, couldn't I have killed you with that dagger a hundred times during the night?—No, all of you: listen for a minute!"

He lifted his hand and held it there, intently. In the ensuing silence a light wind whispered at a conference of leaves, and a moist night-fragrance breathed up from soil and trees.

"There is a horseman following us," Madeleine said quietly. "He's been following us all night and all day. The sound stopped just now, but I'm sure of it."

"That may be true," said Alan, still on an edge of nervous impatience. "But I was thinking . . ."

"Of what?"

"Of someone ahead of us. The road through the forest throws the noise back like a tunnel; it sounds like another coach or carriage with a cavalry escort. Now who would be going to Boulogne, with a cavalry escort, at this particular time?" Alan stared round. "Where's the expert in these matters? Michel! Hoy! Michel!"

"Sir?"

"Is that what it is, Michel? Another coach with a cavalry escort?"

Since Michel had been trying to show off in front of the women by leaping dramatically on each front axle to kindle the wicks of the brass-bound coach-lamps, and resented his performance going unnoticed, he made quite a show of answering Alan's question.

"Not so bad for you, town-toff!" he screeched, after running into the forest to listen and running back again. "It's a light carriage, but not many cavalry: four or six heavy 'uns, maybe, going at a quick trot."

"Can you overtake and pass them, do you think?"

"When they're only going at a quick trot? Ho!"

"Can you overtake and pass them, I mean, without giving any offence or having them block the road?"

"Ho!"

Alan nodded, and a coin spun from his hand. Soft yellow

light, shining out from a square lamp on either side of the coach, flashed on a new-minted gold napoleon as Michel caught it. Paralyzed at such generosity, he clutched the coin in one hand and the tinder-box in the other.

"Sir!" croaked Michel, and added a fervent string of obscenities to show his gratitude. "Would you like . . . I don't know! Ohé! Would you like me, perhaps, to light the reflector-lamp in this old salad-basket?"

"A reflector-lamp is it?" asked Alan, craning round and peering up inside the coach. "Yes, so it is! That's most appropriate. A good idea, Michel: light it! In you go, then; mind the ladies' skirts, and don't tread all over their feet. Good; that's it. Now——"

"By the so-and-so of Saint So-and-so," swore Michel, jumping down beside Alan in a puff and swirl of white dust, "I'll never forget you for this, toff, even when I'm a marshal. It's almost as good as winning the Emperor's reward for Captain Cut-throat."

If before he had failed to attract their attention, now at one stroke he held it spellbound.

"The Emperor's reward for Captain Cut-throat?" repeated Mercier, appearing suddenly at the open door on Alan's side. "What's that?"

Michel stared at him.

"What are you singing there, Captain? You're in the Invasion Army, aren't you? It was published last night."

"Yes; but we've just come from Paris. What do you mean by the Emperor's reward for Captain Cut-throat?"

Michel looked at all of them: but especially at Madeleine leaning forward, and at the suspicious dark-eyed face of Ida de Sainte-Elme beyond. Then, drawing himself up, he made the most of the opportunity.

"By order of the Emperor!" shrilled Michel, at attention. "To any man or boy in the five corps of the Invasion Army, below the rank of a field-officer, bringing to military-police headquarters, alive, the person of the criminal known as Captain Cut-throat, now proved to be an Englishman disguised among you——"

Michel's breath soared up and ran out into pantomime for a dozen syllables more; then it caught power in the soaring finale.

"——the sum of one hundred gold napoleons, to be paid immediately, and as much wine or brandy as can be drunk in one night. Signed by me, Savary, Chief of Brigade and Commander of Military Police. And my faith, ladies," added Michel on his own, "the whole camp's gone detective-crazy. My cousin Louis-Cyr, in the Horse Grenadiers, says they're tearing the place to pieces!"

Nobody spoke.

"And you toff," yelled the grateful Michel, with his eyes on Alan's clothes, "I hope you're not a stranger at the camp, and I hope to so-and-so they know you. I wouldn't like to be the so-and-so they even suspect of being Captain Cut-throat."

"No, that's all right," said Alan. But a small bead of sweat ran down his temple. "I carry credentials, fortunately——"

"But I tell you, toff——"

"Look here, Michel!" said Alan, with a snap and snarl almost unknown to his nature. "That other carriage is drawing farther and farther ahead of us. You'll lose it altogether if you don't make haste. Whip up your horses and pass them, but don't provoke a quarrel with anybody. Off you go, now!"

Michel kissed his hand to Madeleine and ran. Without a word Alan swung himself up into the coach; but not before he had intercepted a very curious look, abruptly grown speculative, in the long and languishing eyes of Ida de Sainte-Elme.

The whip cracked and cracked with a new fury of energy: the coach, bouncing, gathered speed as the horses smashed into a gallop through the Forest of Harbelot. But Alan, slamming the door and sinking back with the box across his knees, still felt Ida's sharply suspicious gaze fixed on him.

"Peace be on your house!" he said. "Let's forget the Emperor's reward, shall we? That gentleman's invariable device, in difficulties, is to distract people's attention and give them something to talk about. After all, couldn't we have expected this?"

"Yet perhaps," said Ida, "it is not alone his device. Perhaps others use it too. What do you think, Alan?"

"Nobody's attention," cried Madeleine, after a quick glance at Ida, "has been in the least distracted by any talk about a reward. Has yours, Captain Mercier?"

"No!"

94

"Alan was arguing," Madeleine went on rapidly, as though by will-power driving and forcing Ida's mind away from something, "that Captain Cut-throat must be the leader of this revolutionary secret-society. I don't understand it; but I must understand it! Go on, Alan!"

"Let's think for a moment," said Alan, looking from Ida to Mercier, "about the secret-society called the Olympians, whose symbol is a blood-stained dagger. Of necessity it uses firework methods; and its leader, Captain Cut-throat, employs a hired killer for a series of ghost-murders to spread panic and mutiny. But will he ever once allow the world to suspect that his hired killer is a friend, a comrade-in-arms, a member of the Grand Army who sits down at table with them?

"You can bet your life he won't! That's why I don't believe for an instant in this so-called Englishman; and neither, under the surface, does old Papa Fouché himself. Would any real English agent leave behind him three daggers, all of them conspicuously made in England and all with the maker's name not quite filed off? Would any real agent of Castlereagh, who must speak French as well as he speaks his own language, make such a blunder as writing 'Captain Cut-the-throat'? These things were easily detected because they were meant to be seen at once. Captain Cut-throat, of necessity, was creating a mythical person to take the blame.—Just tell me, Mercier: isn't this reasonable?"

"It is reasonable as a theory, yes! And no doubt it is very interesting! But as for actual evidence . . ."

"The betraying evidence," said Alan, "can be found in the last two murders. Will you hear it?"

"Of course!"

"On the night of August 16th, then, Private Felix Saulomon of the 7th Light Infantry was killed not far from the house of Marshal Soult himself. Saulomon was stabbed through the heart from front, with a straight horizontal blow, and the weapon was taken away by the murderer. Or had you heard the fourth victim was killed like that?"

"I had heard it!" replied Madeleine: truthfully, but throwing the lead straight back to him.

"Very well," said Alan, opening the box and again taking out the dagger. "Now, Mercier, let's suppose you are the

95

actual assassin who strikes the blows. Imagine you are walking up to your victim. And show me how you would hold this dagger so as to stab any man through the heart in a perfectly straight line. Show me!"

The reflector-lamp, swinging back and forth on the rear wall of the coach, flickered as it swung. Inside the lamp, which was flat and rather small, a candle-flame burned against a round, concave shield of tin polished as bright as a mirror. The lamp threw a wild, wicked light on the sharp blade of the dagger, and on Guy Mercier as he began to twist his arm into contorted positions.

"But there's something wrong here!" Mercier began. "You can't——!"

"No," said Alan. "However you hold it, at least with enough strength for a heart-wound, the line of the blow will never be straight. You can't do it from in front; you can't even do it from the back. Imagine a sentry carrying a large musket on his right shoulder, and try."

"But it was done somehow!"

"Of course it was. Now look at the blade of the dagger. Does it remind you of anything?"

"In what way?"

"Stop thinking of it as a dagger. Think of the blade and the blade alone.—And in Satan's name don't look at me as though I were off my head! I tell you that as soon as you think clearly of the last murder, inside the fence round the Emperor's pavilion, you will see the whole crude trick in a flash!"

And now, he knew, he had caught Ida's full attention at last.

Desperately he was fighting for that, fighting to hold her attention, fighting to turn her mercurial hatred away from Madeleine and her mercurial suspicions away from himself. And always, with every sense alert, he was listening for the wheels of that other carriage they were pursuing through the echoing forest.

The noise of horse-hoofs drummed and reverberated back; the luggage, the wooden hat-box, and Mercier's saddle clattered on the roof.

"I ask all of you," said Alan, "as Papa Fouché would ask you, to picture what happened towards midnight, August 19th, at the Emperor's pavilion on the cliff above the Channel. The pavilion itself is dark and deserted. It is

96

a windy night; overcast, with the moon obscured, and the four sentries pacing inside the fence."

"You sound," muttered Ida, "as though you might have been there yourself."

"I was not there, Ida. But Captain Cut-throat's killer was there. Shall I go on?"

"Yes!"

"Admittedly," said Alan, "it is a lonely and desolate place for those four sentries of the Marine Guard. They are inside an oblong fence of wooden palings built head-high, each man patrolling one side. At short intervals, all the way round inside the fence, hang reflector-lamps to make the place bright. This light, and their own company, is good enough reassurance.

"Grenadier Emile Joyet, it may be, does not feel quite so assured. He is whistling to keep up his courage; and two of the others are looking at him, because whistling is forbidden on sentry-go. Still, what actually has he to fear? The gate in the fence is locked. This ghost-murderer, with a dagger, cannot climb the fence without being seen and shot; this ghost-murderer cannot even thrust an arm through the narrow spaces between the upright wooden palings. Safety!

"Such night fears, are childish, unworthy of the Grand Army. As Grenadier Joyet paces towards one end of his beat, nearer and nearer to the north-eastern angle of the fence, he is walking nearer and nearer to his death. But he does not know it. He knows he can see every lighted inch inside the fence, and he thinks he can see sufficiently far outside . . ."

Ida could not restrain herself.

"He thinks he can see outside the fence? But, as I understood it, there was no doubt! The witnesses swore they could see outside! Weren't they telling the truth?"

"No!" said Alan, "although they all believed they were telling the truth!"

"Why?"

"Because that is the whole meaning of reflector-lamps turned inwards: look at the one behind you. They do not blind witnesses; but they deceive the eyes. A figure dressed in dark clothes, standing just outside the fence, would have been totally invisible against a black sky. Now, do you see it?"

"But the murderer," exclaimed Mercier, "still had to get inside the fence in order to strike down his victim!"

"Not in the least," said Alan. "And we can understand at last why Private Saulomon and Grenadier Joyet were both killed with a straight and level thrust. We can understand why in each case the dagger seemed to have been 'carried away' from the scene of the crime. Because, in those two instances, no dagger was used at all.

"The hired killer, with a certain type of weapon in his hand, made one deadly and unerring thrust between two wooden palings of the fence; and he let his scrap of paper flutter through before the eyes of men who could not see it. Now look again at the dagger in your own hand; notice its flatness, its one sharp edge, and its broad blade that does not taper; and tell me finally—what does it remind you of?"

Mercier sat up and swore.

"The blade of a straight sabre!" he said.

Alan rapped his knuckles on the lid of the box.

"Not only a straight sabre," he said, "but a light-cavalry sabre of a pattern carried by just one small group of men in the whole of the French Army. Well, who is this hired killer who loves violence for its own sake? He is a man of great physical strength; when he did use a dagger, he had to risk a fight with the sentry. He is exceptionally skilled in the use of the sabre. He is a man of immense courage or else arrogant self-confidence——"

"Are you describing," demanded Ida, "a man exactly like yourself?"

"I am describing," retorted Alan, "a man even more like Lieutenant Hans Schneider, of the Hussars of Bercy. It was by no chance or accident, believe me, that Schneider of all people appeared at the Ministry of Police last night. And next, with your permission, I will try to offer you absolute proof. But do you accept, all of you, that Grenadier Joyet was probably killed in the way I say he was?"

"My friend," said Mercier, spreading out his hands, "I can't help accepting it. The same principle, that the colour black cannot be seen against black, was demonstrated during a conjuring show at Talleyrand's house two years ago. But . . . !"

"But what?"

"The assassin, you tell me, lunged through the fence

with a sabre. Good! But sabres are of polished steel. What if some witness had seen a flash of light on the blade? Surely Captain Cut-throat would have told his tame assassin to darken the sword or paint it black?"

"He did," snapped Alan. "That is how we know the murderer is Lieutenant Schneider."

"What?"

"Do you really imagine," asked Alan, with a sort of kindly and sardonic fury, "that the secret-agents of Lord Castlereagh have no information whatever about the Grand Army or its more notorious characters? Last night, in the Room of Mirrors, Hans Schneider was in all his glory. His uniform shone like the hope of heaven. He walloped Chavasse in the face as he would have walloped any other man on earth. He didn't fear me or a dozen like me. But he wouldn't draw his sabre: did you notice that? He wouldn't draw his sabre, that is, until I goaded him so far he had no choice. Even then, when he had lifted it only a few inches, he was damned glad of an interruption to let it drop back again. *That sabre-blade was painted black.*"

Alan Hepburn paused.

The sweat was running down his forehead and into his eyes; the faces of his companions swam before him; all the noises of their flying passage crashed and dinned in his ears.

"Ida," he said, swallowing a lump in his throat, "I cry Q.E.D. and I leave it there. Think of that man's face and his temper; picture him, wherever he is now . . ."

Mercier sprang up, holding the edge of the coach-door, and seemed to be staring hard at the reflector-lamp on the back wall of the coach.

"Wherever he is now!" repeated Ida in a high, strange voice.

Perhaps Ida was thinking, perhaps Mercier was thinking, of a solitary horseman riding hard through the night in pursuit of the coach; a straight sabre at his side, a tight-set smile round his jaws. But who could tell what they were thinking? Who, in this game of rapid move and counter-move, could tell what anybody was thinking?

Alan turned to Mercier.

"The sword was painted black," he said, "because Schneider is ready for more killings at Captain Cut-throat's order. Now you are warned, and you may act as you like. But it is certainly one of the reasons, at least, why I don't care to be dosed with laudanum at night. If Schneider is permitted to prowl loose, wherever he likes . . ."

"Hepburn!"

"Well?"

Mercier, holding the dagger in his left hand as though it burnt him, and clasping the coach-door with his right, was still trying to stand up on the rocking floor.

"I can't believe you're deceiving me in this," said Mercier, staring hard at Alan. "If there is any truth left in human nature, I don't believe you're deceiving me. Therefore," and he moistened his dust-caked lips under the dark moustache, and glanced towards the back of the coach, "there is something I ought to tell you."

"No!" said Ida sharply. "No! You're not to tell him! I forbid it!"

"But, madame——!"

"He *is* deceiving us! I know his ways! I forbid this!"

Mercier's anguish, as Ida turned up at him her full fleshy appeal, was as vivid in the coach as Ida's own personality

"And yet, madame," he told her, "I do not believe this is deceit and I am certain that in your heart you don't believe it either. But if it is true," and he stared ahead, "who the devil is the real Captain Cut-throat? Who hired Schneider? Who is planning all this mummery to wreck the Army?"

"I don't know!" Alan admitted bitterly. "I never said I did know."

"But I understand, from certain remarks made by Fouché himself . . ."

"Never once did I claim to know the identity of Captain Cut-throat himself. For reasons of my own I took a long gamble and said I knew where to find the assassin: because the first place to look for him, clearly, was in the Hussars of Bercy. Then, when Schneider appeared afterwards . . ."

"You had reason to suspect Schneider in particular?"

"No, of course not! Not until that black sabre-blade jumped three inches out of its scabbard and every fact fitted together at once. Up to that time I had simply been on edge and spoiling for a fight. Afterwards, in the light

100

of revelation, I kept looking at the sword so much I was afraid you noticed me."

"And the real Captain Cut-throat . . . ?"

"The real Captain Cut-throat," said Alan, "may be anybody. It may be someone of high official position, It may be someone relatively humble. It may even conceivably be a woman——"

"A woman?"

"It would not be the first time, in France, that the motivating force behind a secret-society has come from a woman. I don't know; and it doesn't matter! What we have, or what you have if anything happens to me, is a clear lead to the secret god through Schneider. We have only to keep the closest watch on Schneider . . ."

"Madame de Sainte-Elme," Mercier said formally, "I am going to tell him."

"Answer me one question, darling Guy," cried Ida, with her shoulders back and her head up in silhouette against the swinging lamp. "Do you obey the orders you are given, or do you take orders from the prisoner in your care?"

"Madame, that has ceased to be the question!"

All this time Madeleine Hepburn had said not a word. Yet anyone would have suspected that Madeleine, with her intense intuitive powers, already divined something which may have been hidden from the far more clever Alan. Madeleine sat tense, but trying hard to smile, while she looked sideways: first at Ida's face, then at the gold-embroidered reticule in Ida's hand.

"And when," Ida was demanding of Mercier, "will it cease to be the question so long as a British spy is loose at Boulogne? Why, for instance, is Alan so interested in that other carriage?"

"What other carriage?"

"The other carriage," snapped Ida, "that Alan bribed the postilion to overtake. Why is he so concerned with someone going to Boulogne, if he is thinking only of Captain Cut-throat? Look!" she added, starting up and brushing past Madeleine to point out of the right-hand window. "We are overtaking the other carriage now!"

Chapter X

Hoof-beats in the Forest

"Except that it can't be the Emperor himself on the road," Mercier gestured, "I beg your indulgence, madame! Is it of any importance at all?"

"Alan thinks it is," Ida retorted. "And do put away that dagger, if you please, before you cut my own throat with it."

Alan, snatching the dagger from Mercier's hand, dropped it into the box, closed the box, and pushed it under the red-upholstered seat. Then he leaned out of the window beside him, with Mercier leaning on his shoulder and looking out, too.

"The Imperial livery, eh?" cried Ida. "Stand aside, can't you? Stand . . ."

Inside the Forest of Harbelot it was cool, even chilly, with a damp air which for some time had stirred inside the musty coach. Ahead of them, travelling fast, was a light closed-carriage with shining green-and-gold panels; a coachman in green-and-gold livery cracked his own whip over its two horses. Four troopers of the Breastplaters, an escort from the Emperor's heavy cavalry, rode two in front of the carriage and two behind it.

They were big men with formidable moustaches, these Breastplaters, riding big horses. From the crests of their brass helmets, shaped in the Roman style, streamed out long scarlet plumes. Their brass chest-and-back armour glimmered in the glow of the carriage-lamps. Long and heavy sabres jingled against blue saddle-cloths.

By tradition they were the most dreaded of the cavalry: silent and moody of temper, ready for a quarrel on any pretext. And yet, as the coach thundered up to overtake the carriage, one of the troopers glanced back over his shoulder —and slightly smiled.

Alan, leaning out of the window and craning round

towards the left, saw sixteen-year-old Michel and his fellow-postilion. Both these youths, rigid with ecstasy or a good imitation of it, were standing straight up in their stirrups, heads back and hands stiffened at salute.

"Live the Emperor!" screamed Michel.

"Live the Emperor!" shouted his companion, all but drowning him out; and the cries rang and echoed in the spectral forest.

The Breastplater's smile broadened under his lowering moustache. Indulgently half-returning the salute, he nodded and made a gesture with his gloved hand for the coach to pass.

"Michel," observed Mercier dryly, "is earning his gold napoleon by tribute to another——" And Mercier stopped dead.

It was not the Emperor in the closed carriage. It was someone who should have been in Paris at that time, unless . . .

For an instant, as the horse-hoofs hammered in unison and the windows of the two vehicles drew level, a face peered out of the other window. It was a withered, sharp-nosed, aristocratic face, its smile a diplomatic leer between the wings of grey hair. And Charles Maurice Talleyrand de Périgord, Foreign Minister of the French Empire, raised his hand in mock-pious blessing as the coach rocketed past.

During a little space afterwards, while Alan and Mercier sank back into their seats, Alan's face had grown completely expressionless. But Madeleine knew he was even more desperate than before.

"Not important, eh?" crowed Ida, shivering so much that the kerchief slipped off her dark hair. "Not important! Oh, no!"

"You were saying, my dear Hepburn?" blurted Mercier. "You were saying about Captain Cut-throat——?"

"Put me peace to your talk of Captain Cut-throat, both of you!" said Ida. "Talleyrand is here! Can't you guess what that means, without any trouble?"

"I opine, madame . . ."

"Why should Talleyrand, a cripple and a man who hates travel, be hastening to the Emperor's side at this hour? Don't you realize what they plan for tonight, of all nights?"

Mercier, like a man flinging from his mind thoughts

which he must not entertain, made another remark about Captain Cut-throat. But Ida gave him no refuge.

"Captain Cut-throat has lost his gamble. Forget Schneider! It does not matter now if Schneider kills fifty men. The Emperor has given the word, and in a few hours the drums will beat to arms all along the coast. This is the night of the invasion!"

The night of the invasion.

Long awaited, long expected, looming closer and closer with the thunder of its final shock . . .

"And I shall not be there," said Mercier, pressing a hand against his forehead. "I can't help the first thought which occurs to me: I shall miss it all, damn me, when the barges set out. Never mind! My duty, my only duty, is to guard this prisoner of ours."

"Then guard him well, I counsel you, and give him an extra dose of laudanum for good measure. Tonight, of all nights, he will try to send a message to the British!"

"Madame, how the devil can he possibly send a message to the British?"

"I don't know. But he'll try. He'll risk every bayonet on the Iron Coast to try! Or, if you think using laudanum is unworthy of a gentleman like yourself . . ."

The creepy part of all this, a detached observer might have said, was that Ida's mind did not really seem concerned with what she was saying.

Her dust-cloak had fallen back; before leaving Paris, she had put on a scarlet-and-black travelling-dress which, while not transparent like her evening gown, was fully as exotic and flamboyant. The fingers of her right hand were fastened round Madeleine's left wrist; and yet Madeleine, though tense and white-faced, smiled and made no effort to wrench her wrist away.

"If you think using laudanum is unworthy of a gentleman," jeered Ida, rather implying that it *was* unworthy, "at least don't tell him what you proposed to tell him a minute ago. With that safeguard following behind us (do you understand me, Guy?), he will be as helpless as though he were tied with ropes." Here Ida broke off. "Alan! Are you up to your accursed tricks already? What have you got there?"

Alan, though still on edge, had regained all his usual

suavity and his most amiable expression. From the inside pocket of his blue coat he was taking out a folded oblong of heavy paper, and carefully spreading it out on his knees.

"This is a map of the Boulogne Camp and its environs," he said. "You needn't look so surprised, any of you; this was also given to me by Papa Fouché himself."

"Guy!" screamed Ida. "Make him put away that map! Make him . . ."

"Why should I put it away?" enquired Alan, looking up. "I don't and can't deny I'm interested in what is happening tonight. Which of us isn't interested? But, as Mercier says, what can I possible do at so late a date as this?"

"I tell you——!"

"Mercier," said Alan, "if our good Ida insists on your following the strict letter of your orders, she can't have it both ways. In any case, I was only trying to discover . . ."

Abruptly, as though his alert ear had caught some other noise, he craned his neck out of the window to peer at the road behind them. He was sitting back again in a flash; but, to Madeleine, his eyes seemed to have changed their colour from green to black.

"No, it's nothing!" he said; forestalling the quick questions. "We must be sure Talleyrand is not delayed, that's all; and he's still there. Nothing is likely to happen, is it, until he's at the Emperor's side?"

"By the splendour of God!" breathed Mercier. "If I had guessed last night what I have learned since, I would rather ride at a square on a spent horse than accept any responsibility for you. No wonder Fouché wants you in his service! If you don't mean to communicate with the British, what do you want with that map now?"

"I'll show you. At the present time we are travelling north and still going uphill. But at any moment we'll be going downhill, and shortly emerge from the forest . . ."

"Well?"

"Emerge from the forest," Alan tapped the map, "into a valley with a village called Condette on our left hand facing forward. Look here! On our right hand, beyond and above several kilometres of open fields, will lie the Forest of Boulogne."

"Yes, I know all that! What about it?"

"In the Forest of Boulogne, hidden in a very large open

105

clearing, is the Field of the Balloons. Those are the balloons the Emperor means to use for his invasion. Well! Isn't it evident——"

Interrupting him with a curt gesture, Mercier turned round and darted out his hand. "That's enough," he said. "Give me that map!"

Alan snatched it sideways. "But I was only trying to——"

"Hepburn, don't force me to be melodramatic and threaten you with the pistol again. I can afford to take no chances. Give me the map!"

"As you please," replied Alan after a hard-breathing pause. Carefully he folded up the map and handed it over. "Perhaps, after you've heard what I have to say, you'll let me have it back again."

"I very much doubt that. But what *did* you want to say?"

"Estimates as to the number of the Emperor's force," said Alan, "vary from a thousand balloons, each with a car carrying ten men—which is far-fetched—to a hundred balloons, each carrying the same number of men—which is more probable. In either event! Given a favourable wind, such as there is tonight . . ."

"How do you happen to know all this?"

"Know it?" demanded the exasperated Alan. "For three years the Emperor's balloons have been the subject of engravings in the window of every print-shop in London. Everybody knows it! Still! Once we're on our way downhill and out of this wood . . ."

"Don't you feel the motion of the coach?" said Madeleine, sitting up. "We're on our way downhill now."

"Very well! Once downhill and out of this wood, we should be able to see the Forest of Boulogne, as plain as print on the other side of the open fields. If there are lights inside the forest, if the balloons are fully inflated—and we can't help seeing them above the trees—it's a fairly sure sign the Emperor means business at last."

"So!" muttered Mercier.

"That's what I meant, and all I meant. If you'll give me back the map . . ."

"Not a chance, my friend; and sit still! We don't want trouble now! What I can't understand is the criminal negligence of Papa Fouché, who is usually so careful, in presenting you with a map at the outset."

106

"Can't you?" said Ida. "I can."

She flared out in a glory of inspiration which caught them all with its heat and fervour. Her high cheek-bones, her long and full-lipped mouth, shared with those narrow eyes a vividness of personality which had in it almost a touch of the insane.

"I knew from the beginning," said Ida, "Fouché was playing some double-faced game! This is the only thing that will explain it all. He hates the Emperor; he's never lost his revolutionary principles; he sees advantage to himself if the Empire cracks. He called Schneider to Paris, and all but went into a fit when Schneider tried to draw that sword." Convulsively Ida gripped Mercier's knee. "Thunder of God, it can't be anything else! The Minister of Police is Captain Cut-throat!"

Michel, the postilion, had no longer any reason to use his whip.

The coach was rushing downhill in a clatter and clank of the swing-bar. At any time, no doubt, the other postilion must crawl back hastily to the box and apply the brake. Ida, in the certainty of her inspiration, turned her eyes towards Alan—and stopped dead at his richly sardonic look.

"What's the matter with you?" she cried. "This is true, isn't it?"

"No," Alan replied with great distinctness. "Did you fall into that trap, too?"

"What?"

"I nearly fell into it myself," said Alan. "It might have been designed to trip an investigator. Fouché would mock the Emperor; he might even defy the Emperor . . ."

"Well, then?"

"But he's not Captain Cut-throat, because he is too cautious ever to plot treason unless someone else begins it first. Remember the history of all his turncoat policy, and you must agree I'm right."

"Then who is Captain Cut-throat?"

"A minute ago," retorted Alan, "you were saying it didn't matter. Speaking personally, to me it doesn't matter at all. But it must matter to you as a Frenchwoman (doesn't it?) that someone at Boulogne—someone using methods that are crude and showy but effective—will continue to give orders for people to be stabbed in the back, perhaps orders to kill the Emperor himself at the hour of the invasion?"

Here, breaking off, Alan lifted his head sharply.

"Steady, as she goes, Michel!" he called to the empty air. "You'll tumble us all out in the ditch if you drive like that!—So we can agree, I think, that following Schneider is just as important as it ever was. Mercier!"

"Yes?"

"When we come out into the valley, we shall be very close to Pont-de-Briques itself. Exactly where is this guest-house called the Park of Thirty Statues?"

"That's very close, too. We can't be far away from it now."

"And I suppose, if this is the night of the invasion, they'll insist on holding both you and me indoors? Who keeps the guest-house?"

"A woman—(steady, Michel!)—a woman called the Duchess."

"What duchess?"

"She isn't a duchess, actually; that's a nickname; and she is quite a character. No; she won't hold you indoors; and neither will the servants nor the two sentries of the Guard who are always there. But I will very much keep you indoors whatever happens."

"Mercier, listen to me!"

"My friend, I beg you not to argue! You will leave that house only if I am dead!"

"But, man, is there no getting away from your decision alone? For instance, could I appeal to the Emperor himself?"

"At a time like this? Impossible! If, as you say, the signal will be given tonight—"

Mercier stopped, catching his breath. All of them, with one impulse, craned towards the right-hand window facing forwards.

Though the coach still rocked and plunged, they were warned by the different sound as they swept out from under the trees into the open air and gradually slowed to a steadier pace.

It was dark, in the brooding hush of a sultry night, but with that greyish light in which blacker shapes can just be distinguished close at hand. North-eastwards, on high-rising ground fully two miles away, a long dark blur marked the tree-tops of Boulogne Forest.

Alan had badly misjudged his distances. They were too far away, and it was too dark, to make out with any clearness the details he said he had hoped to see. But there could be no mistaking those acres of firefly glimmers moving low against tall trees, or above trees the vague shimmer of colour where acres of gaudily-painted monster-shapes swayed ready. The balloons for the invasion, however many of them had been commissioned, were fully inflated and tugged hard at their guy-ropes.

Mercier's voice clove through the pause.

"Madame Hepburn!" he said: not loudly, but in so odd a tone that Madeleine's heart jumped. "Madame Hepburn! Please change places with me, and sit beside your husband. Do not argue or hesitate, I beg of you! Do as I ask!"

Whereupon Madeleine, who had never turned her gaze from Alan, received an even worse shock. Alan, though all attention, was not looking at those monster-shapes at all.

Craned far round, he was looking back over his shoulder in the direction of Boulogne itself. Through the Forest of Boulogne dimly showed another kind of light: a light as though along a road, faint and reddish from lanterns or torches, but a long line distinctly moving southward.

And Alan's fists clenched.

"Madame Hepburn!"

"I—I beg your pardon!" said Madeleine. Instinctively speaking in a whisper, because Mercier himself now spoke in a whisper, she stumbled past him and sank into the seat beside Alan.

She had forgotten her coach-bruised body and the aching cramp of her knees and back. Now Mercier had seen the moving lights; or perhaps he had observed them from the first; and Madeleine's thoughts spun in circles.

Invasion, yes! Portentous events taking shape in the night, without a betraying drum-beat or a sound from afar. But what, exactly, did this particular move mean?

"I think, friend Hepburn," Mercier said abruptly, "you have seen enough."

Raising his hand to the blind over the centre window above the coach-door, he drew down the blind sharply.

109

Then he drew down the other two right-hand blinds, covering the open panels beside the seats on that side.

"Madame de Sainte-Elme," he added, "will you be good enough to draw all three blinds on your side?"

"But we'll stifle in here!" said Ida, making fierce fanning motions. "There's no air in this coach as it is. We'll stifle!"

"Then we stifle," said Mercier. "At least, for the short time until we reach the Park of Statues. Do as I tell you!"

"And what is the meaning," demanded Ida, "of that moving line of light? What *is* it? Why are you two both looking so strange?"

"Our friend has already guessed," said Mercier, "what is happening tonight. There is no need to tell him exactly how it will happen, too. Will you pull down the blinds, madame, or must I do it myself?"

Down came the blinds on the other side, while Ida cursed like an ostler, and they were sealed into darkness except for the yellow flame of the reflector-lamp swinging again the rear wall.

Nobody spoke. Mercier, with the pistol in his hand and the map thrust between two gold buttons of his partly-undone waistcoat, stared across at Alan, while the coach raced forward towards its last stop. The time, by Alan's watch as he hastened to look at it, was five minutes to ten o'clock.

At five minutes to eleven o'clock, over coffee and brandy at the end of a dinner, something happened which gave the events of that night their final and most deadly turn. And at twenty minutes past eleven precisely, in an upstairs bedroom of the house called the Park of Thirty Statues, the long pent-up conflict between Ida and Madeleine burst out at last.

Chapter XI

The Other Dear Charmer

Ding! rapped the little marble clock, on the first stroke of eleven. *Ding! Ding! Ding!* . . .

Madeleine, dressing with feverish haste in the bedroom, scarcely glanced at the clock on the white marble mantelpiece.

Whatever happened at Boulogne tonight, it could not happen for a few hours yet. But that was not her immediate concern. Now that she had joined in the game and dared to try a trick of her own, Madeleine prayed and prayed it would be successful.

It must be successful, or . . .

Everywhere lay the same uncanny and oppressive silence. Alan and Captain Mercier were still downstairs over their wine. Even aside from the Duchess herself, there were in the house at least two maids and two liveried manservants, to say nothing of a presumed cook and kitchen-staff. And yet, except for the sound of Ida de Sainte-Elme splashing bath-water in the little room adjoining the bedroom, and the thin but resonant throat-notes of the clock, it was as quiet as a desert.

Ding! Ding! Ding! Ding! . . .

A puff of wind stirred the curtains, heavy dark-blue velvet bordered in gold, on full-length windows in this ornate jewel-box of a bedroom, with its gilt-and-white furniture and its glazed wallpaper in vertical stripes of blue and white. Over the bed, in its alcove, hung a bronze medallion-head of the Emperor. Everywhere was the presence of the sharp-eyed Emperor, even though you never saw him.

It had been the same ever since they arrived at the Park of Statues: when Mercier, as they turned in at the entrance-gates, permitted the coach-blinds to be raised. At Pont-de-Briques they saw nobody on the road except a courier of the Mounted Guides, bent low and galloping hard with a despatch, yet the air quivered to an omnipresent sense of waiting.

At the gate of the park they saw the two grenadiers of the Imperial Guard, burly men distinguished by the bearskin hats they wore on formal occasions to replace their usual brass-decorated helmets, each man standing before a sentry-box under a lighted gate-lamp on either side of the entrance. These sentries were as immovable as the statues beyond them, except when they recognized Mercier and brought their muskets to salute as the coach passed.

Up a gravel drive lined with statues out of classical mythology, the coach finally swung round in the grass courtyard of a two-storeyed stone house, its roof of slate and its long window-frames painted white, which was built round three sides of a square.

In the courtyard a fountain splashed and glimmered in light from the open doorway. And the Duchess was waiting to greet them.

"The Vicomte de Bergerac?" she had intoned. "Madame Ida de Sainte-Elme? Captain Guy Mercier? And,—" here Madeleine had started,—"Mademoiselle Madeleine Lenormand?"

The Duchess was somewhat overpowering. At times she reminded Madeleine of London and of Mrs. Siddons playing Lady Macbeth at Covent Garden Theatre. At other times she overflowed with geniality and with confidences of an embarrassingly intimate kind, which she imparted to women and men alike. Overriding all protests about bathing and changing first, she had insisted that they sit down at once to dinner.

And afterwards . . .

Afterwards, while Madeleine exulted with secret joy, the trouble was on its way.

When Ida and Madeleine went upstairs in silence, it was Madeleine who raced ahead and secured first use of the copper-and-mahogany bathtub: the only one she had ever seen in her life into which hot water flowed through pipes instead of having to be carried there in buckets.

Still saying not a word, the stormy-faced Ida walked in and watched her, assessing her carefully in the water. Madeleine, though defiant and not at all unwilling to be

112

assessed, nevertheless made haste through the process because at any cost she must be dressed long before Ida.

If her plan succeeded! If it succeeded, as it certainly must!

Ding! Ding! Ding! rapped the clock on the last stroke of eleven. It whirred in its throat and was still.

Madeleine, listening so tensely for some word from Ida in the adjoining room, had forgotten to make haste at all. Standing motionless in the blue-and-white bedroom, she still wore nothing except the silk stockings, fastened with buckled garters, and the flat heelless evening-shoes of satin—hers were coloured blue—which the year's fashion dictated.

She must hurry and hurry hurry!

The remainder of her dressing was not a complicated process: she had only to draw over her head a low-cut evening-gown of blue bordered in white, and dust a little rice-powder on her face and arms and shoulders. But dressing her hair before a full-length mirror took much longer. This room, like the whole house, had a comfortable scent of old curtains and new furniture-polish, which Madeleine breathed deeply while her pulses hammered and the seconds ticked past . . .

There were three hollow and ghostly knocks at the door to the corridor, making Madeleine all but jump out of her gown. The door opened. The Duchess herself, large and impressive and much decorated with dubious jewels, moved in amid trailing draperies like Lady Macbeth for the sleepwalking scene.

"If you are provided with everything you desire, my dear," said the Duchess, pointing one finger ceilingward, "I shall take my most formal leave and retire to my couch. What a day! Ah, my God, what a day! If the Emperor himself were to call at the Park of Statues to-night . . ."

"The Emperor?" exclaimed Madeleine, turning round from the mirror. "Is the Emperor likely to visit here?"

"Only a figure of speech, ducky," the Duchess assured her. "Today, behold, he is not at the pavilion: no! He is at the château of Pont-de-Briques; and his presence anywhere near disturbs me like a galvanic battery. I swear this!"

Madeleine glanced nervously at one of the windows.

"All day, they say," pursued the Duchess, "he walks up and down the balcony, dictating to General Duroc. And the cocked hats of the marshals crowd round him and crowd closer! What with all the excitement in camp today over chasing Captain Cut-throat, and now this silence—silence, silence, silence!—I am frightened and I wish myself back in Marseilles."

Drawing a deep breath, and making a broad gesture as though trying hard to dismiss this, she studied Madeleine for some moments.

"Ducky!" she said in a somewhat different voice.

"Yes, madame?"

"About your lover, my dear . . ."

"My lover!"

"Come, my dear!" cried the Duchess. "It leaps to the eyes that for this occasion you are the little friend of the Vicomte de Bergerac, eh? And I, being a woman of good heart: it desolates me, my dear, that I am unable to put you in the same room. But we are servants of the Emperor; always, always, always it is necessary to have dignity; and how I wish, in this world of ill-breeding, that others would remember as much!"

Out flared her grievance.

"Figure to yourself!" said the Duchess. "Only the day before yesterday there comes to see me Marshal Ney himself, who is also of good heart and an old friend of mine, but a rough diamond whose manners I can only deplore. And what must this vulgar type do, I ask you, but laugh coarsely and slap me on the behind? 'Well, Madame the Duchess,' cries he, 'and how are all your little daughters of joy today.' "

Here an expression of outrage spread over the Duchess's face, and she drew herself up as majestically as Lady Macbeth bidding the guests depart from the banquet after her husband has seen Banquo's ghost.

"I ask you," she repeated.

"But, madame . . . !"

" 'Marshal Ney,' said I, 'I would inform you that I was once the owner of the most esteemed tolerance-house in all Marseilles,'—and so I was, too!—'with my girls everywhere known as the most agreeable and the most ladylike; and I would further inform you that such low and vulgar talk as yours, you son of a bitch, ill becomes a Marshal

114

of France and the Commander, 5th Corps, of the Grand Army!'

"Oh, I gave it to him, I can tell you!

"And you asked me a moment ago, ducky," swept on the Duchess, "whether the Emperor might call here, and why it is necessary to maintain a seeming and fitting dignity? I reply to you: His Majesty did call here. It was upon the occasion of a visit paid to us two days ago by the American envoy and his wife, a Meester and Meesus Opevell, of the city of Philadelphia, who . . ."

Here the Duchess, who could not fail to notice her companion's expression, pulled up short with a shake of her bosom and a rattle of her jewels.

"And pray what ails you, ducky?" she demanded. "Is there something wrong?"

There was.

On any other occasion Madeleine, who it must be confessed was not at all a high-minded girl, would immensely have relished the Duchess's confidences. But the shock of hearing a certain name, amid all her other perplexities, drove the blood from her heart and brought more difficulties to thicken and stab.

"Did you say Hopewell?" she cried. "A Mr. and Mrs. Gideon Hopewell? Formerly attached to the American Ministry in London?"

The Duchess considered this.

"Of the first name I am not sure. And London? Bah! Madame Hopewell is a lady of the most charming, who in private asks me many questions about my profession and is altogether genteel. But her husband . . ."

"A rather portly middle-aged man? Gideon Hopewell?"

"Ah! He is in truth distinguished-looking, like my first-class clients in the old days. But stern? Oo la la! I tell you! When the Emperor was here . . ."

"But you say they've gone, haven't they? They're not here now?"

"Am I not telling you, ducky? Sweet Jesus! They have been gone only for one night, so that M. Opevell may inspect some new guns that fire shells for a league and a half. They return at any moment, perhaps tonight. That is why, even aside from my instructions from M. Fouché, I could not allow myself to admit you to the same room as the Vicomte de Bergerac!"

115

Madeleine, her back to the mirror and her hands pressed under her eyes, stood motionless. When all Whig doors in London were open to Gideon Hopewell and his wife, because the buff and blue of the Whig colours had been adopted from the buff and blue of General Washington's army at the time of the Rebellion, both Madeleine and Alan had met the Hopewells everywhere.

If Lucy Hopewell at least could be told now, and told beforehand, they might well keep silent. But if unexpectedly, here at Pont-de-Briques village, they encountered 'the Vicomte de Bergerac' and 'Mademoiselle Madeleine Lenormand'—|

And then, following quickly on the Duchess's news, everything seemed to happen at once.

A heavier gust of wind swayed and belled out the curtains at the long windows. Distantly but vividly, a wink and flicker of lightning dazzled at the corner of Madeleine's eye; and thunder smote low in pursuit. The breeze swirled through the room, fluttering at discarded clothes and making a dozen candle-flames flicker even inside their glass shades.

A storm tonight? A storm at a time like this?

Madeleine's mind went back to that angry-looking sky at twilight; then, instinctively, she glanced across at the bronze medallion-head of the Emperor above the bed in the alcove.

But this was impossible! Wouldn't the Emperor have weather-forecasters to warn him, long and long beforehand, that he must not trust his two thousand barges to the uncertainty of the Narrow Seas in a gale? Or was it simply that he struck hard and cared not a groat for the weather?

Madeleine had no time to think of this, or of the Hopewells; or, in fact, of anything except Ida de Sainte-Elme. For the partly open door to the bathroom opened fully, and Ida sauntered out, and the emotional temperature of the room soared to its top.

Tonight Ida wore another gauzy and transparent gown trailing the floor, this time of a jonquil-yellow colour. Underneath it she had discarded her buskins for gold-hued slippers and for an even narrower flower-girdle of scarlet roses. Her glossy black hair was done up into its topknot curls and bound with a gold fillet. Bedecked, bedizened,

116

and resplendent in her self-confidence, she exuded the very odour of feminine triumph.

Scarcely troubling to glance at Madeleine, she picked up a heavy gold-backed hand-mirror from the dressing table. She regarded herself this way and that, moving her mouth. She smiled slightly. Then she lowered the mirror and looked at the Duchess with detached contempt.

"Get out," she said curtly.

"What's that, ducky?"

"I said get out," repeated Ida, with her voice and eyebrows going up. "Surely you are not altogether hard of hearing too?"

"Now, now, ducky, there's no call to go and talk like that! I'm sure we all want to be friendly, don't we? I was only trying to be friendly, just as this young lady's been very friendly to me since . . ."

Ida lowered the mirror still further, and looked at the Duchess again.

"I have had enough insolence," she said through her teeth, "from underlings who cannot seem to learn their place in life.—Get out!" screamed Ida. "Get out, you filthy old bawd, and don't let me see your face in this house again!"

Madeleine held her breath.

Remembering that Lady-Macbeth stateliness, remembering the Duchess's past profession and how she had dealt with the redoubtable Marshal Ney, Madeleine expected a mighty wrath to burst in reply. And yet, before Ida's self-assurance and glory, the Duchess's big face suddenly sagged and retreated and crumpled up. With horrifying grotesqueness, as though a tower had fallen, she blundered back against the door and attempted to bob a curtsey.

"I am sorry, my lady," she said. "I meant no harm, my lady. It was only my way."

"Then see to it that you keep out of my sight!" said Ida. "Like the Emperor himself, I will not endure insolence. The Minister of Police may allow any Jacques Bonhomme to speak as he likes; but I do not. Now go!"

"It was only, my lady, that——"

"Did you hear me tell you to go?" enquired Ida, advancing towards the door with the mirror in her hand. "One more word from you, I warn you, and I will have

117

you dismissed from even such a position as you hold now."

With even more an effect of grotesqueness, two tears gathered in the Duchess's eyes. Fumbling to open the door, she bobbed another curtsey, backed her way out, and closed the door hastily.

They heard her tripping and stumbling in her skirts as she ran hard down the painted corridor outside. And Madeleine sensed the terrifying insecurity behind all the Duchess's ranting talk, like the insecurity in France itself as the threat of the Emperor hovered like a hawk over Europe; and, on this trivial incident of all things, Madeleine's rage boiled over.

"Had you any reason on earth," she cried out, "to speak to the woman like that?"

"The old harlot appealed to your taste, no doubt?" demanded Ida.

"Yes, she did! Why shouldn't she do as she does? And haven't you got a most astonishing nerve, Ida de Sainte-Elme, to call any woman what you actually are yourself?"

Ida, who had been staring at the closed door with the mirror uplifted as though to strike a blow, whirled round.

Nostrils dilated, eyes widening, Ida looked at her companion; and Madeleine, with only a heightening and intensifying of the same emotions, looked back.

"I think, Madame Hepburn," said Ida in a high voice, "it is time we settle certain matters between ourselves."

"Yes! I think it is too!"

Ida flew back to the door and twisted the key in the lock. Snatching the key out of the lock, she set her back against the door.

"Lock it!" said Madeleine. "Yes: lock it, by all means! Do you imagine it will do you any good?"

"Yes, I am sure it will," said Ida, with ferocious sweetness. "Tell me, Madame Hepburn: how do you feel?"

"Very, very well indeed!" said Madeleine. "I can seldom remember feeling better in my life.—How do you feel?"

"Meaning what?"

"You don't want Alan!" said Madeleine. "You never did want him. Corporal Chavasse was right in every word he said!"

"Corporal Chavasse? And pray who is he?"

"You know very well who he is. I heard him tell the Minister of Police the real truth about you. Your vanity was just scratched raw when Alan said he would rather have me than have you, and you swore to get level with me if it was the last thing you ever did. You underestimated me, didn't you? I prayed and prayed you would underestimate me. Do you think I don't know," said Madeleine, "do you think I don't know you stole the laudanum out of Captain Mercier's sabretache last night?"

Ida, though staring at her hard and strangely, did not move from the door.

"And who," demanded Ida, "told you about the laudanum?"

"Nobody told me. Nobody needed to tell me. Anyone would have seen it as soon as you grew so crudely amorous with Captain Mercier."

"You dare say to me . . . !"

"Dare Madame? I'll challenge you at wits and at any of your other pleasures, too!—The laudanum was in that sabretache at his left side as you faced him. It was dark in the coach, and jolting so much he'd never have noticed if you opened the pouch. You didn't dare steal the whole laudanum bottle, in case he missed it. But the brandy was gone from that little flask in your reticule, so you poured all the laudanum you needed into the flask. Didn't you?"

"And why should I have done that, Mademoiselle Boarding-School?"

"You don't know?" said Madeleine. "You don't know?"

"If you imagine . . ."

"I don't imagine! If you drugged my coffee after dinner, and then drugged Captain Mercier's coffee too, you could have all the time you wanted alone with Alan, and get your best possible revenge by humiliating me!"

Madeleine, in a paroxysm of rage and with her blonde beauty flushed to loveliness, took a step forward.

"Oh, you'd never have risked Alan getting out of this house!" she cried. "You're too fanatically loyal to the Emperor; you worship war just as he does. You'd never have risked drugging Captain Mercier, and letting Alan get out to discover the invasion plans, unless you knew it was perfectly safe. But there's another officer following us, isn't there? And he's been following us all the way from Paris? And he'll do his best to kill Alan and rouse the whole camp, won't he, if Alan tries to leave the house?

So you knew it was safe. And that's what you did, isn't it?"

Ida threw back her head and laughed.

"Yes, of course I did!" she said with exultant triumph. "And tomorrow you'll understand, Mademoiselle Boarding-School, how easy it is to make any man forget you. I've been waiting, and listening patiently to your raving, so that I could see the symptoms come on. Don't you feel the giddiness in your head and legs? You drank the coffee, you know!"

"Oh, no, I didn't!" said Madeleine. "You drank it yourself, and I hope you liked the laudanum-brandy taste of it. Don't you feel the giddiness now?"

Ida straightened up violently. The back of the heavy hand-mirror banged against the panel of the door.

"What . . . clumsy . . . lie . . ."

"You drank it yourself, I tell you," said Madeleine, stamping her foot on the floor, "because I changed the cups when you were so occupied with Alan. And, what's more, you can tell it's true! You thought it was only the heat of the bath-water making you giddy, but you know now it's not that at all! Don't you?"

Ida sprang forward, whirling up the heavy hand-mirror. But she had to catch herself, with panic in her eyes, to keep her balance. Spreading both arms wide, arching her back, she fell against the door and trembled there like a figure crucified.

The mirror dropped from one of her hands. The key dropped from the other. Again lightning dazzled beyond the swirling window-curtains; the candle-flames flickered inside their glass vases; and thunder shocked distantly with the onrush of the approaching storm.

Chapter XII

Thunder Over Europe

The storm approached with stealth, with movements like those of one who stirs in unquiet sleep. There was a scent of rain in the air before any rain had fallen. That same distant rumble of thunder, heard by Madeleine in the perfumed bedroom, was also heard by Alan Hepburn downstairs.

In the large, lofty dining-room at the front of the northern wing, there was a scene just as wild but to Alan completely mysterious.

The furniture of the dining-room, of heavy and polished black wood inlaid with designs of yellowish metal, stood out in sombre vividness against a crimson carpet and against high window-curtains of dull scarlet and gold. Captain Guy Mercier sprawled face downwards across the refectory table, sitting there as though dead drunk. His right hand lay near an overturned brandy-glass, and the right side of his face rested against a crushed bunch of grapes. It was twenty seconds since his sabre had bumped and stayed motionless against the floor.

Alan, with a brandy-glass in his own hand, was standing up on the other side of the table, and looking at his companion in stark incredulity.

"Mercier!" he called sharply, putting down his glass after still more seconds had elapsed. "Mercier! What the devil's the matter with you? Mercier!"

There was no reply.

Alan glanced at the decanters on the table beneath unsteady candle-flames. They were depleted, but not so much as all that: even considering Mercier's sleepless night after a gruelling fifty-league gallop on post-horses.

"No!" he said aloud. "If I weren't sure it couldn't be possible, I should think from the look of you . . ."

Alan hurried round to the other side of the table. He lifted the left eyelid of the unconscious man. Though the eyeball rolled up, he saw that the pupil had shrunk to the size of a pin-head.

"Wow!" he said in English.

Bending down quickly, he unfastened the catch of Mercier's leather sabretache, took out a brown glass bottle of dark-brown liquid, and held it up to the light. Enough laudanum was gone from the bottle to do more than render a man insensible. Carelessly used, it would have poisoned him as well.

The curtains here had been not quite drawn. The whole dining-room went deathly white with lightning; another rumble of thunder, striking closer yet, set vibrating the gold dinner-service and the frame of a portrait over the sideboard. Alan hastily thrust the bottle back into the sabretache, removed from that pouch the map Mercier had taken from him, put the map in his pocket, and then stood up straight, listening.

There was not a sound in the house. Not a sound!

The Duchess had said she was going to bed some time ago; the servants, she had proclaimed, were already abed with the exception of a liveried manservant named Victor, who had been very talkative during dinner and who, the Duchess announced, would attend to anything the gentlemen might require.

"Ah, my lord viscount," he could still hear Victor's voice during dinner, "now that the authorities have seen fit to act in this matter of Captain Cut-throat; depend on it, my lord viscount, they will deal with the English ship! More Burgundy, my lord viscount?"

"Just a little if you please."

"The English frigate, my lord viscount, which every day sails in during the morning or the evening, and insults our good men to frenzy by thumbing its nose at the shore-batteries, and sails out again without firing a shot. If M. Decres cannot spare ships of the line, at least there are enough Imperial gunboats! Depend on it, my lord viscount . . ."

Alan threw the memory away.

(Hurry, you fool! Hurry!)

Diving underneath the table, where Mercier had tactfully concealed the pistol which was never very far away

122

from him, Alan made it harmless by blowing the loose powder out of the firing-pin, and then replaced it.

Next he hastily unbuckled and removed Mercier's sword-belt. But, about to buckle the belt round his own waist, he first went to one of the front windows, pushing it open.

A swoop of wind rushed past him, carrying with it the noise of frothing leaves from the park and all the magic of the French countryside at night. Diagonally ahead, past the grass courtyard where someone had thriftily turned off the fountain, and past the double line of classical statues leading to the front gate, a dim oil-lamp still burned atop each gate-post. The two sentries of the Imperial Guard paced back and forth between the gates, past each other, as regularly as a double-pendulum: aloof, incurious, unwarned.

Alan could hardly credit what had happened. What a piece of good fortune, he thought, had been delivered into his hands! Whoever drugged Mercier, wittingly or unwittingly, had done more for him than all of His Britannic Majesty's secret-agents put together.

Hurrying back from the window, he was again about to buckle on the sword-belt when he hesitated. No! If the inquisitive Victor were still about . . .

Alan turned towards the sideboard, and his gaze automatically lifted to the big portrait above it.

Of course it was a portrait of the Emperor. Here at the Park of Statues, or anywhere within reach of the little autocrat's hand, no visitor could expect another portrait. And Alan Hepburn—a man essentially humble of soul beneath all his vitality and all his pose as Corinthian and dandy-lion—Alan Hepburn knew that every moment of his own worthless life had been leading up to this night, to the 23rd of August 1805. All the thoughts and feelings which rose up in him, as he saw the portrait, could have taken shape in one fierce and silent heart-cry:

Boney had been stopped.

A heavy crash of thunder, exploding close over the house, rattled the whole picture-frame and split into tumbling echoes down the sky. The glare of lightning which preceded it, the jump of the candle-flames immediately following, brought out all the shadings of the portrait above gold plate on the sideboard.

It showed the Emperor on his white horse Marengo,

which was rearing up on its hind legs while the Emperor stood in the stirrups, his eyes blazing wide, and pointed up a finger dramatically at painted lightning in the sky.

And yet Boney had been stopped.

No, Alan corrected himself bitterly: no, it would be foolish even to think that much. Undoubtedly Boney's greatest victories were yet to come; his star was still in the ascendant; perhaps he could never lose. But Alan, remembering the crawling line of light he himself had seen in the Forest of Boulogne on the road to St. Omer and Lille, would have staked everything on one belief.

Boney could never invade England now; and, what was more, he must have learned by this time it was impossible.

The actual length of time in which Alan stood looking up at that portrait, measured by the clock, was only the few seconds while the reverberations of the thunder-peal died away. But in those few seconds he examined thoughts at which he had not even dared to look too closely as yet, including the real reason why he was here in Boulogne. And all these images still resolved themselves into a picture of Boney—on a white horse.

'Here's to you!' Alan thought, raising an imaginary glass. 'And to the future! And to what, with any luck, I can prove tonight in Boulogne Forest!'

The Emperor had made only one blunder: he was rather contemptuous of sea-tactics, and thought it a simple matter to use them. For a long time he really believed that his enemies the goddams, whose sole strength was their apprenticeship in sea-tactics for five hundred years, had been hoaxed and gulled into scattering their ships over far places and leaving their island all but defenceless. On August 8th, elated by Admiral Villeneuve's apparent victory over Calder, the Emperor had triumphantly ordered Villeneuve to sail north, join Admirals Ganteaume and Allemand, and hold the Channel for the crossing of the Grand Army.

But the practical-minded Villeneuve, then at Vigo Bay with the Spanish Admiral Gravina and their large but shaky and ill-trained fleet, knew better than the Emperor what he could do and could not do. "Our condition," he wrote, "is frightful." He obeyed orders and set out, though he quickly learned what had happened.

Straight in his path was gathering the whole British

Channel Fleet: twenty-seven sail of the line, including ten three-deckers, and now joined by Nelson with twelve ships more. At any moment Villeneuve feared to raise their topsails and sight the dreaded Cross of St. George.

Villeneuve altered his course and took refuge in the port of Ferrol; against such a fleet he could do nothing else; his despatch informing the Emperor of his decision reached Boulogne as early as the 14th of August.

And most of these despatches were being intercepted, before they were sent on again, by the British espionage-system in France.

The Emperor, outwardly professing to believe success still possible, screamed in his own despatches that the enemy were in confusion, that they had only four effective ships in the Channel. But his acuteness must have divined what British agents more than suspected: if Villeneuve ventured out of port again, Villeneuve would only retreat still further to avoid Nelson. The Grand Design was smashed, the invasion in ruins.

True, it was a check only to the Emperor's sea-tactics. He would not wait idle at Boulogne, considering what had happened since. Everywhere the earth was humming, the semaphore-arms clacking like an articulate gallows, with news of an outbreak in Europe at his back.

To Alan, and Alan's colleagues in Paris, this fresh news ten days ago was as surprising as it was surprising to William Pitt in the map-room at Whitehall. So far the Emperor of Austria and the Czar of Russia, apprehensive of the Emperor, refused to stir against him. In a decision made almost overnight, they had changed their minds: Austria and Russia, leagued together in secret treaty, were now pledged to strike westward into France.

Unfortunately, this news could not fail to be known to Boney. If he discovered he could not invade Britain, it must have been just what his heart most desired. To swing round his mighty forces, to outwit Austrian and Russian commanders in the kind of campaign of which he was supreme master, to march with the Grand Army first behind the advancing Austrians in a thrust at Vienna; then, perhaps, to cut between two armies and defeat the other enemy at his leisure . . .

If the Emperor meant to take this course . . .

It was highly probable he did mean to take it. But there

125

remained just a possibility, remote and unlikely yet not to be disregarded, that he might still fling the dice for his invasion of England.

And so Alan, standing before the dark sideboard with the gold plate, and looking up at the portrait as the echoes of the thunder died away across the valley, silently addressed the portrait with more than usual vehemence.

'That, O Father of your People,' he was saying, 'is what has landed me in this scrape. Somebody had to get inside the fortress of Boulogne. Somebody had to discover what your real design was. Somebody has still to verify what I am dead certain is true; and tomorrow, with luck, to get the news out of this camp to London when they say it can't be done.'

Whereupon Alan, more moved than he knew, was astounded to hear himself speaking aloud.

"By God!" he muttered, and half lifted the sabre. "If the cursed slow-moving Austrians can be warned in time that Boney in person is counter-marching against them! If I can verify the facts, send that message safely, and still get out of this scrape alive with Madeleine and a new life . . . !"

But that was the trouble.

He himself was probably finished; he knew that, and he ought to be honest enough to face it. His chances of getting out alive were almost as remote as those of Boney dining at Buckingham House next week. Against him, from the beginning, Joseph Fouché had been playing a game which was unlikely to fail. Now that Alan really was in a corner and no mistake, any move he made would be countered by a more adroit move from the wily Minister of Police.

In Paris, when he had deliberately got himself arrested for a very good reason, he thought he could face it: that is, if his none-too-dependable courage did not collapse under fire. But that was before he had known about Madeleine.

Madeleine . . .

He could still save her, or believed he could. But to lose her now, when all his jealousy in the past had been insane self-delusion and nonsense——!

More thunder shocked out across the chimney-tops of the Park of Statues, and again set rattling the gold plate and the glassware on the dinner-table. As it did so, Alan heard a heavy thump behind him, and turned round.

The inert figure of Captain Guy Mercier, who had stood his friend at a difficult time, had slipped sideways out of the chair and sprawled on the crimson carpet beside the table. Involuntarily Alan looked across the table, towards the large double-doors of the dining-room.

Madeleine herself, as though conjured there by his imagination, was just closing one of the double-doors. Wrenched out of despair in this particular way, he could only stand and stare at her.

"What is it?" she asked instantly, and in English.

"I was thinking, Madeleine, that it's damned funny."

"What is funny? What is? What are you thinking?"

"I was considering," he said, "the map of Europe and all the kingdoms on it. I was weighing men and guns and the blood that will be spilled for nothing. But mostly I was thinking that I love you."

"Don't ever stop, then," said Madeleine. "Don't ever, ever stop!"

And she ran round the table towards him.

What these two said or did, during the next few minutes of frantic and broken endearments, should not matter to a story which concerns men and guns and the map of Europe. They spoke in English, perhaps incautiously; but they did not speak much, and, while they were speaking, the skies opened and the rain tore down and roared round the house.

Still, whether their state of mind was of much consequence set against the towering portrait of the Emperor, it mattered very much to them. It was only after some time that Alan, conscious of minutes ticking past and of a mission in the Forest of Boulogne, began to babble of this to her; and Madeleine, he realized, was babbling to him some incoherent words about Ida.

"Listen, my dear!" he said. "There's something——" Again he tried to think, and failed. "I have no notion of what is happening here, or why Mercier should have been drinking his own laudanum . . ."

"I can tell you," said Madeleine.

Between defiance and a kind of bursting pride, Madeleine poured out the story. The realization of what it meant shocked him fully awake.

127

"Then *both* of them are insensible? Both guards are out of it?"

"Both of them are insensible, yes! But there's something you don't know! There's another——"

"What happened to Ida, finally?"

"She had dropped the key on the floor," answered Madeleine, quick-breathing and flushed and disheveled in a blue gown. "Then she—she tried to find it. But it was a brass key against a blue-and-gold carpet, and she couldn't see it. Finally she tried to reach the bell-rope in the alcove, and collapsed beside the bed."

"What happened then?"

"I—I managed to lift her up and put her in bed as though she were naturally asleep. Afterwards I locked the door on the outside. Here!"

Moving back from him, Madeleine held out the key in the palm of her hand.

"Just before Ida collapsed," Madeleine went on, "she said . . ."

"Said what?"

"She said," Madeleine hesitated, and then spoke in a rush, " 'You damned traitor and spy, I'll tell the Emperor himself about you; that's what I meant to do at first.' I never thought of it before, Alan, but she was right; that's just what I am; and I don't care in the least.—Alan!"

"Yes?"

"There was something I wanted to ask you in the Room of Mirrors, and on my life I couldn't! But I can ask you now! If you would let me help you in all this . . ."

"No!"

"Darling, what's the matter? What have I said? Why shouldn't I help you?"

"Because it's a cursed ugly and dirty game; you don't know how ugly and dirty it can be; and I won't have you concerned in it!"

"But I am concerned in it, whether we like it or not! Won't you sometimes, sometimes let me think I'm essential to you and a part of your life, which is what I could never think in the past?"

(*My God, so that's it!*)

The rain roared round the house; draughts trembled in the red-curtained dining-room, whisking the candle-flames above the strewn debris on the table. For a moment Alan could not reply. He had never felt so proud of her or so happy as at the time when he must lose her within twenty-four hours.

"Madeleine," he said. "If you really mean what you say . . ."

"I do! You must know I do!"

"Then keep that key you have." His voice grew sharp and intense. "Now don't lose your head; don't ask questions; but remember everything I tell you. We don't know how much laudanum Ida swallowed. Still, if it keeps her insensible until late forenoon tomorrow, my whole mission here may be accomplished by that time."

"Your——?"

"Yes! Everything I am to do was planned beforehand by our people in London, and here is what I want you to remember best. Each evening now—don't ask me how or why—a small boat from England will touch at the coast here just an hour after sunset. It will touch near the village of Condette, where there are sand-dunes, just beside an inn, 'At the Sign of the Sleeping Cat.' You can easily walk to it from where we are now."

Madeleine began to speak, but he cut her short.

"Repeat that after me, my dear. A village named Condette! The Sign of the Sleeping Cat! An hour after sunset! Repeat it!"

Madeleine did so, with her eyes never leaving his face.

"Very well! The inn is kept by smugglers," he went on, "who don't care a curse about the war provided only it goes on and furnishes them with business. With good fortune, both you and I will be able to leave in that boat tomorrow night. But if anything should happen, and I am unable to be there . . ."

The intuition of her eyes was almost terrifying; he flinched from it.

"I merely mean," he said patiently, "that I may be delayed. In that case, the boat will return for me on the following night. Whatever happens, you must promise to be in that boat when it leaves tomorrow.—Now don't argue, Madeleine! Will you promise that?"

"I . . ."

"Do you mean to help me, or do you mean to hinder me? This is your opportunity, if you say you want to help! Do you promise: yes or no?"

"I . . . All right, all right! Yes!"

"Good; that is settled. There is not time to explain much more, because I must leave the Park of Statues for a little while tonight . . ."

Then Madeleine burst out.

"I know that!" she cried. "But it's just what you mustn't do! You mustn't leave this house, or you will meet the worst trouble of all! I know you want to discover the invasion-plans . . ."

"Hell's death and God's damnation, will you be silent and listen to me?"

He was white to the lips; she shrank back from him.

"It is a thousand to one against there ever being an invasion of England at all. S-h-h! Quiet, now! That is what I must prove to my own satisfaction, and its implications will contain everything Whitehall wants to know. Tonight (do you remember?) we saw a mile of dim lights moving along the road through the Forest of Boulogne. In which direction were they going: north or south?"

"South of course! Why?"

"Away from the camp. Boney, without any of his usual band-music, is secretly moving out a very large body of troops or equipment of some kind. Mercier saw that; and he was so paralyzed with astonishment he tried to throw me off the scent by suggesting it was part of the invasion of England. Of course it wasn't. Those lights were moving too quickly for infantry but too slowly for cavalry. What must they have meant?"

"Darling, I can't solve a military problem! What were they, then?"

"Guns," said Alan. "Only artillery need lights at all, when mishaps block the whole column on bad roads."

He looked at the sword-scabbard in his hand as though he had never seen it before. Intent, gnawing at his under-lip, he took a turn towards the table and back again.

"If Boney is moving out his artillery days and days ahead of his main body of troops—hang it, he can't even have completed his campaign-plan yet; that's why he was dictating on the balcony at the château today!—then this moving of guns is no feint or manoeuvre. Guns mean a full-scale attack."

"And everything else?"

"Everything else," said Alan, "is a feint to hoodwink

the world he still means to invade England. By the Lord! When I heard Mercier's saddle bumping on the roof of the coach all the way from Paris, I never thought it was going to help me so much."

"Mercier's saddle?"

"Yes! He ordered them to have a horse ready in the stables, in case he needed it. The column of troops, whatever it was, will have passed through the forest long ago. But one look at that road, if it's rutted with the tracks of light and heavy guns, will tell me whether I'm right. It will prove——"

He stopped abruptly, because of the look on Madeleine's face.

"And this is the information," she asked, "you must take back to London in such haste?"

"Yes!"

"Alan, don't lie to me."

"Word of honour, those gun-tracks can tell us——!"

"I don't mean about the guns! I mean about the boat that's supposed to touch the coast here tomorrow night. Do anything else, but don't lie to me! You say you may be 'delayed,' and you may not be in time to go with that boat. But, if this information is so vital, mustn't you be there at all costs to take back the news?"

"I can tell you what the news is, and you can——"

"Maybe, maybe! But that wasn't what you had in mind when you told me about the boat. For pity's sake, Alan, tell me the truth!"

And in this respect, at least, he was telling her bitter truth.

"I am bound to warn you, my dear, the boat may not be able to reach here at all. Our people at Whitehall were doubtful; they say the whole coast-line, even down as far as this, is patrolled by Boney's pramcs and gunboats. That was why we had to devise a means of sending a message even if I never left France or——"

Again he stopped, trying in vain mentally to drag back the words. He had gone too far, blurted out too much; and he saw her eyes as he said it.

"Then you are going to send a message out of the camp!" said Madeleine, with a tense and quivering calmness. "The very thing Captain Mercier said you couldn't do! How?"

131

"My dear, there is no time——"

"How, Alan? I don't ask you out of curiosity, you know. I ask you because I can face anything, anything, if only I know the extent of the danger and what it is you have to risk. How, Alan? Tell me!"

"As you like! It's not at all difficult," he answered, with fear growing inside him as he spoke, "but I can only hope I don't lose my nerve at the crucial moment, or it will mean failing all the people who depend on me. The method, you see, is——"

Neither of them had heard the double-doors of the dining-room open on the far side of the long table. It had opened, and closed again softly, before a faint movement at the corner of Alan's eye warned him.

The inquisitive footman Victor was standing there and looking at them. Tall and impressive in his green-and-gold livery, except for a look of slyness which darted and was gone from the dark eyes on either side of his large, Casanova-like nose, Victor remained as immaculate as he was impressive, save that flecks of white hair-powder had dribbled down on his collar.

Bowing with a somewhat ironical respect, Victor spoke easily and fluently.

"My lord viscount desires something, perhaps?"

But this time, mockingly, he spoke in English.

Chapter XIII

Midnight at the Park of Statues

This was the moment at which Alan, at all times for it to come upon him, felt his courage begin to waver and falter. He might have lost the game then, losing it before a servant who (perhaps) suspected nothing at all, if one glance at Madeleine had not give him heart.

For Madeleine, very proud and exultantly happy in her new role as his confederate, had not faltered for an instant. God help her, he thought with a pang, if she imagined she would enjoy this dance for very long. And yet, as he realized instantly afterwards, what an actress the superb little devil could be when she thought she had reason for trying! If they could have been spared more time together—as somehow, somehow, they must be—they could have made a team to meet even Joseph Fouché on equal terms!

Madeleine, chin slightly raised and with a languid smile, did not make the blunder of changing the conversation to French. She continued in English as though it were the most natural course in the world.

"Indeed my lord viscount did ring!" said Madeleine, with a little shiver and an outward twitch of her fingers. "Poor Captain Mercier, I fear, has become most revoltingly and disgustingly intoxicated, as men *will* do . . ."

"Ah, well, Miss Lenormand!" cried Victor, at his most expansive. "That happens to all the gentlemen, and especially to those who visit us here at the Park of Statues. You would wish me to carry the gallant captain up to his bed, perhaps?"

"Yes, Victor; if it would not be too troublesome to you?"

"It would be my pride and privilege, Miss Lenormand!"

"You speak English very well, Victor."

"I was about to compliment Miss Lenormand, if I may

133

be permitted to do so, on her own accomplishment in that respect."

"And why not?" demanded Madeleine, a little haughtily and regally. "The Vicomte de Bergerac and I have been practicing very hard for the benefit of Mr. and Mrs. Hopewell."

Mr. and Mrs. Hopewell?

Alan, turning round to meet Madeleine's significant smile, had no opportunity to think of what her reference to the Hopewells might mean.

It came to him with instant certainty that Victor was acting. Victor's eyes, swiveling on either side of his Casanova nose, moved shrewdly in watchfulness; Victor's big figure, in livery and hair-powder, was as tense as a panther's as he slid round the table toward Mercier. If Victor had not heard everything, under the crashing tumult of the storm, he had at least heard enough to . . .

"I do not think," Madeleine was saying loudly to Alan, "you have ever met Mr. and Mrs. Gideon Hopewell, of Philadelphia. They were formerly attached to the American Ministry in London. They have been here at the Park of Statues for two days, and are expected back tonight——"

Alan, his scalp tingling at the imminence of rushing danger, knew he could not afford to delay much longer. He must hurry on to the Forest of Boulogne, taking his directions in pitch darkness by the lights at the Field of the Balloons. In the event that Victor gave any trouble . . .

Victor, sidling round the table like a big dancing-master, bowed and knelt by Mercier's recumbent figure.

"If Miss Lenormand and the Vicomte de Bergerac will allow me," he said, "I shall just——"

Then, as more thunder tore through the screen of the rain, the whole scene changed. Victor's right hand went under the table, and caught up Mercier's pistol from the crimson carpet. Up to his feet leaped Victor, the pistol-muzzle levelled at Alan.

"Stand still, Mr. Hepburn!" he said, continuing in English. "The Minister of Police, of all people, would not neglect his precautions at this house. Stand still, Mr. Hepburn!"

And, as he said it, there was a hiss and slither as Alan whipped the curved sabre out of its scabbard.

Bright steel glittered level with the pistol-muzzle, point presented to it like another pistol. Immediately the nimble Victor, his legs shuttling so that the brass buckles twinkled on his big shoes, backed away very fast round the dining-room table, the pistol still levelled.

Alan followed him.

"Stand still, Mr. Hepburn!" repeated Victor, his left hand groping behind him towards the heavy bell-rope at the side of the double-doors. "I am the Minister of Police's representative in this house. Shall I prove it? A special courier on horseback, from Fouché himself, arrived here at the Park of Statues on Monday night at ten o'clock precisely on his way to Pont-de-Briques château. Ask any-one here! He carried a message for the Emperor and General Savary, telling them that Captain Cut-throat was an unknown Englishman—in fact yourself, Mr. Hepburn, because you yourself are Captain Cut-throat . . . !"

Alan, saying not a word, still followed him with the sabre ready.

Victor's voice went higher and shriller.

"But that was not contained in the message, about you being Captain Cut-throat, so how else could I know it? Stand still, Mr. Hepburn! I am instructed not to kill you, but if I am compelled to fire and wound you . . . !"

"Fire," said Alan. "I blew the powder out of the lock not twenty minutes ago. It's not bounce, what I say; if you don't believe me, pull the trigger!"

Victor pulled the trigger.

The resultant noise, only a sharp click, was blotted out by thunder. Alan's right arm swept out and up as he lunged forward, the sabre-blade flashing high.

Victor dodged by instinct, but it was not necessary. The sabre-blade whistled above his head. It severed the heavy bell-rope high out of Victor's reach so that the rest of the rope thumped down half-coiled on the carpet behind his back.

Then Alan darted back, sabre at guard-position and scabbard in his left hand.

"You stand still," he said softly. "Madeleine!"

"Yes?"

"Can you tie his hands with that bell-rope? The walls of this house are stone, and there's a cupboard here in the dining-room. No, stop! That's no good! There's not enough rope to tie him completely, and we haven't anything at all to use as a gag."

"Oh, yes, we have!" said Madeleine.

She ran to the table, snatched up a very sharp fruit-knife from amid the litter, and ran to Alan's side. Catching up the hem of her gown, which had cost a good hundred gold louis at Madame de Centlivre's in the Palais Royal, she slashed deeply into the hem and began to rip the silk in sideways swathes to make both ropes and a gag.

What we all do or say or think, under the wildness of heightened feelings, will not follow an established rule; we blurt out our innermost thoughts, and remember it afterwards only with astonishment. What flashed into Alan Hepburn's mind, and what he said instinctively without even stopping to think was what he would never otherwise have dreamed of saying in public.

"Damme, madam," he yelled, "are you clad in nothing whatever under that gown, without so much as a shift to your name? Must you disport yourself before every man's eye in a condition even more naked than Ida de Sainte-Elme herself?"

"Alan, we are not in England now! It is the custom in Paris; it would be the custom in London if it weren't for the climate! I am only——"

And Victor, who had lost none of his alertness and little of his courage, sprang straight for Alan's throat.

Out flashed the sword-blade with such eye-wink speed that Victor hardly saw it before the razor-edge slashed a patch from the side of his wig without even touching the hair underneath; without more than crushing and crumpling the curls of the wig grotesquely over his right ear. And Victor, halted in mid-flight with sweat-drops starting out on his forehead, stood still with the breath stuck in his throat.

"Don't do that again," warned the civilian epée-and-sabre champion of France, "or I'll cut to hurt you.—Madeleine, pray accept my apologies and oblige me by appearing publicly in as naked a condition as you please. Meanwhile, madam, for God's sake cut up your skirt and tie him!"

It was the sheer humiliation of his position which made Victor desperate then.

136

"Was it by accident, do you think," he cried, "that Mr. and Mrs. Hopewell have been here at the Park of Statues? Do you think the Minister of Police did not know you were well acquainted with them in London? You are Captain Cut-throat, Mr. Hepburn!"

"Down on the carpet, Victor," snapped Alan, but with a quick sidelong look at Madeleine. "Down on the carpet, with your hands behind your back.—Madeleine! The ropes and gag!"

"You killed all those sentries yourself," screamed Victor, "and you cannot prove you were not at Boulogne during the week it happened. Very soon you will be convicted as Captain Cut-throat, and handed over to the Grand Army for judgment. That will be pleasant, eh?"

Alan whipped the sword-blade high.

"Down on the carpet, do you hear me?—Ah, that's better! Madeleine! The ropes and gag!"

'You are Captain Cut-throat, Mr. Hepburn!'

To Madeleine, with those words ringing in her head, came the prospect of a worse nightmare than she had known forty-eight hours ago in the office of Joseph Fouché. Her body went limp, and the knife wabbled in her hand.

"Madeleine! The ropes and gag! *Madeleine!*"

Holding her nerves tightly, pale as a ghost, she hastened to obey.

"No, wait!" Alan said feverishly. "There is a better way than that. Gag him; tie his arms and hands behind him; but leave his legs free."

"W-why?"

"He can walk upstairs ahead of us. I'll carry Mercier, and we'll lock both of them in the room Mercier and I were to occupy. So far as the Park of Statues is concerned, this business with Victor has finished us. But then, once I can make certain of the wheel-ruts in the forest road, we needn't trouble further about what happens here. We can always go to ground at the smugglers' inn. Quickly, now; and then upstairs!"

Again measured in time, by the clock, it was little more than five minutes before these two hurried conspirators were alone together as the clocks struck midnight.

They stood in the upstairs corridor, which was illuminated only by an occasional flash of lightning through a round window at the front. The walls of the corridor had been painted in scenes from classical mythology, and rioted with the adventures of the god Zeus amid his throng of human nymphs; the adventures of Zeus among mortals appealed to the Emperor's taste when he directed everything.

But lightning flickered less frequently on the colours of the walls; and, for the most part, the corridor was left in chilly darkness echoing to the noise of the rain.

Alan, who had put on a loose waterproof mantle of the cavalry pattern, together with the sabre under it and spurs to his boots, loomed up before his companion in dim outline. It may have been only the darkness which made Madeleine think him transformed for a moment or two into an eerie, remote stranger.

Madeleine fought this off; she told herself not to be a fool, and she tried hard to drive away morbid fancies.

"I understand you must go out there!" she said. "But how long will it take? How long must you be gone?"

"With anything like luck, not much more than an hour. In the meantime, though, you must lie low and hold on here. Can you do that?"

"Yes, of course I can! But—actually, what I wanted to ask you——!"

"Get yourself ready to leave as soon as I return. You can't take your luggage; but put on a travelling-dress and a cloak, and a bonnet if you brought one. We haven't the slightest idea where or how this night will end."

"Alan! About what Victor was saying . . ."

"Don't speak of that! Don't even think of it!"

"It's completely absurd, isn't it? You're not really Captain Cut-throat?"

"No, no, of course not! Could you ever seriously think I might be?"

"No! It's—no, it's ridiculous. But in the Room of Mirrors you told me you spent that week all alone, at a shooting-box in the Forest of Marly; wherever you really were, I knew that wasn't true. And tonight, when Ida seemed to have some kind of suspicion of you, you acted so strangely I couldn't tell what it meant, except that I tried to divert her. It's comical, that's all: you can't be Captain Cut-throat!"

"Then be resolute in your belief. It's their pleasant game

to drive me into just that corner, and my game to keep out of it if I can."

"Then all the time they've been intending to accuse you—?"

"While I'm gone," he swept this aside, "lock yourself in the bedroom; blow out the lights if you feel up to it, but at least don't attract attention whatever you do. I have only to send my message to England tomorrow . . ."

"But can you possibly manage to do that, Alan? Isn't the camp too well guarded? In Paris we read in the Monitor about a dozen spies being shot for trying to send messages, and none of them could ever do it!"

"No," he said flatly. "None of them could ever do it."

"Well, then?"

"That's why we have to adopt this kind of method. But Boney's plans are the most vital news of all the war; and it is worth any method we use." Alan's voice, gnawed with anxiety, grew harder yet. "I'm certain Fouché himself doesn't suspect it. I only hope Victor hasn't come to suspect it somehow. If he has——! But it may only have been an accident when he mentioned that ship."

"Ship? What ship? No!" Madeleine said fiercely. "You can't leave me in a state of uncertainty like this! And you promised! Tell me! And then——"

"Then you will know everything, except what is going to happen when this powder-keg explodes? Very well!"

Alan drew a deep breath.

"Every day for some time past," he said, "the forty-four-gun frigate Medusa has been appearing off Boulogne and sailing straight at the harbour-mouth. That was to get the French accustomed to her. Medusa's only apparent purpose is to insult the shore-batteries."

"Her only 'apparent' purpose?"

"Yes! The French see nothing strange in it; it's the sort of gesture they would dearly love to make themselves. But our own staid lords of the Admiralty would never permit such useless heroics without a good purpose. As a rule you can sight that ship either between five and six in the afternoon or between ten o'clock and noon in the morning. Medusa has been ordered never to fire a shot; and her captain is so disgusted that he won't even break out his colours . . ."

"Never to fire a shot? But what——"

Alan's voice grew louder.

"She can't fire a shot," he said, "because the smoke of her own broadside might interfere with her view at a crucial moment. Anyone with a telescope, standing on the cliff near the Emperor's pavilion, can see the wrinkles in the face of *Medusa's* captain. Conversely, anyone aboard *Medusa* can see the hands—the hands—of someone standing on the cliff near the pavilion."

Into Madeleine's mind flashed the image of a device so simple, yet so hideously fanged with danger . . .

"Yes!" said Alan. "I am wearing a conspicuous civilian costume, and I am to be on that cliff tomorrow. Using Dr. Braidwood's alphabet, the alphabet you first taught me, I can send to an interpreter aboard *Medusa* the news of what Boney means to do. That's all there is to it!"

Yes; she understood. And Madeleine now believed she was not frightened at all. She was only wildly enraged, perhaps a little inconsistently considering her own conduct, at the risks people would plan and run in even the smallest hope of toppling an autocrat from his pedestal or of spoiling one scheme of the all-conquering Boney.

"And if they catch you?" she cried. "Do you understand what you're doing? The whole of the Boulogne Camp will be looking straight at you! You're a stranger; it's a different thing from deceiving guards at the Room of Mirrors. If you make one false move, and they see it . . ."

"They mustn't see it, that's all!"

"But——!"

"A far greater danger is that *Medusa* may not arrive in the morning, or even in the afternoon if there should be a dead calm. With three persons, Ida and Mercier and now Victor, who are bound to be discovered by forenoon at the latest——" Alan paused. He spoke in a strange, uncertain, repressed voice she had never heard from him. "You see, Madeleine," he said, "that is why I am a dismal failure at this work, and why I have a confession to make to you."

"A failure?"

"Yes! You see . . ."

"Alan! What is it! Tell me!"

"When I volunteered to do this," he said, "I promised to let nothing stand in its way. I swore to be guilty of no false pity or bloody snivelling sentiment. And that was right; that was only just! Thousands of lives may be saved, and a European disaster averted, if only Austria and Russia can be warned in time that Boney is marching against them, and may mean to cut between them and crush them separately."

Alan smote his hand on the pommel of the sabre.

"I tell you," he said, "when I thought Victor suspected the ship I should have rammed this sword through him and had done with it then! Even before that time, I should have put Mercier out of the way for good. As soon as I saw those lights in the forest, I knew I was bound to leave the house tonight; Mercier alive will always be a danger until this mission is completed; I should have taken him unawares and stabbed him dead with Captain Cut-throat's dagger.

"And I couldn't do it, Madeleine.

"God help my weak guts, I couldn't do it! I can't kill any man except in a fair fight; and even then I'm not at all sure of myself. It's easy to fight mock-duels with blunted sabres or buttoned foils; but how do I know how I should behave in a real sabre-duel with razor-edges and murder on both sides? I may fail you, Madeleine, when I mustn't fail you; but there it is; and I've got to warn you of that no matter how weak it is or how much it lowers me in your eyes."

There was silence.

"And you think," Madeleine said out of a full and over-flowing heart, "you think it would be likely to lower you in my eyes?"

"I think you ought to know the truth, anyway. For some reason you've always exaggerated my courage; and I've suspected for some time it wasn't worth a button. There's the plain truth; now I am going out to that forest; and all I can promise, my dear, is that I won't let you down if I can help it."

"Yes, go!" said Madeleine, with the tears stinging into her eyes. "Please go!" He tried to take her hand, but she pushed him away. "Go on, my darling, before I make a complete fool of myself. But don't forget to come back, or it won't be worth living at all."

The rain smashed and drove on the slate roof of the house, swirling and gurgling across the eaves. Then he moved, a darker shadow in a dark corridor. She heard the quick rattle of his spurs descend the marble staircase, and presently die away.

And she was alone.

Groping towards the head of the staircase, she felt the cold metal of the balustrade; she grasped it hard, biting at her lips furiously determined not to give way. Yes! That was better.

Seconds passed while she stood there, and closed her mind to all but the immediate concerns. A last dying flicker of lightning, kindling up through the round window at the front of the corridor, illuminated the wall-panel beside the staircase. It was a painting representing the mythological character of the alluring Leda; its subtle flesh-tints, no less than the dark hair and dark eyes, gave Madeleine a sudden sharp reminder of Ida de Sainte-Elme.

The woman could not possibly wake up, it was true. She was safe enough, locked into the bedroom under the blowing draughts and the sinking candle-flames.

But to Madeleine it brought back all the ache and upset of her encounter with Ida at the approach of the storm. She remembered Ida's collapse, and afterwards how she herself had locked the bedroom door from outside; and how, almost noiselessly in her flat-soled slippers of soft leather, she had flown downstairs to warn Alan of something he had not suspected: to warn him . . .

Madeleine, standing in the dark at the head of the stairs, went cold all over.

She had warned Alan of everything, hadn't she?

Chapter XIV

The Field of the Balloons

Down the broad gravel driveway, between the line of statues on either side, the dapple-grey mare flew at the gallop towards the entrance-gates.

She was a beauty, that horse. Alan found her ready-saddled with Mercier's saddle and green saddle-cloth. He imagined she was Mercier's own horse. From the first whisper and pat, in a deserted stable, they understood each other. She put back her ears; she responded to a touch or even a thought, without need of the spur. He immediately christened her Fancy Girl, after a favourite horse at home.

And so, despite the sheets of rain whirling into both their eyes, he put Fancy Girl at the gallop down the gravel drive, where he would have first to pass the two sentries at the gate.

He was wearing Mercier's busby, fronted with the metal letter "N" which marked it as the badge of the Mounted Guides. His flapping cavalry-mantle covered his clothes. But there was a light on top of each stone gate-post; and every one of Boney's cavalrymen wore side-whiskers, or a moustace, or both.

However, if he kept his head lowered and a corner of the mantle up as he whisked past . . .

Down the gravel drive flew Fancy Girl, with the white statues from classical mythology unreeling on either side.

'Damn this busby,' thought Alan. And then, 'First hazard!'

At the thudding onrush of his approach, the two sentries of the Imperial Guard stopped their pacing and drew back to each side.

Sodden with rain loomed their high bearskin caps; which, with the mingling of shaggy hair and bearskin, made their broad sun-burnt faces seem to be all eyes and

143

moustache. They had drawn on the long overcoats they usually kept stored in their hairy parade-knapsacks. Up came their muskets to salute as he swept past.

Alan, remembering in time to return the salute palm-inward in French style, ducked his head before he swung Fancy Girl to the left. And the accursed busby all but toppled off.

It was not so bad as he had imagined wearing such top-heavy headgear. It fitted down over his neck and almost to his eyes, like a helmet; but, for all the brass links of the chin strap, it must not be wagged or waved without practice.

Past dashed Fancy Girl, out into the hard good-surfaced main road. Alan had a glimpse of the sentries' faces by pale rain-blurred light. Grim faces, not young; one of them drawn as though with pain. Then they were swallowed up. Into turbulent darkness beyond the lamps, Alan dropped the reins and let the alert, completely human Fancy Girl —sensing his mood, not greatly slowing—find her own way along the curve of the main road.

The rain soaked and blinded him as they moved southward, with the high stone wall of the Park of Statues curving away on the left. He should be safe enough now until he drew near the heavily guarded Field of the Balloons. Since couriers of the Guides were galloping everywhere tonight, he should be safe enough until . . .

Steady!

With the busby jolting like a cumbersome powder-keg on his head, Alan shifted in the saddle and instinctively lifted reins.

As they danced round the end of the park wall, into a long straight stretch of road with poplar trees on either side, he saw more than the glimmer of a lantern which someone was holding up about a hundred yards ahead.

Straight in the middle of the road, facing him, stood a heavy coach drawn by two dispirited horses. Round it, against the smear of yellow coach-lamps, milled a half-disintegrated platoon of Oudinot's famous grenadiers.

The yellow facings of their blue tunics were not yet altogether discoloured; they shielded their musket-locks under their armpits; and one of them, while they waited, was philosophically but vainly trying to light his pipe in the downpour. The coachman on the box, in a three-cornered hat, waved a whip and shouted. But the most uproar was being caused by the platoon's officer, who held up his lantern at the coach-window and passionately addressed some person or persons inside.

At the thudding noise of Fancy Girl's hoofs on a road grey and greasy but still hard, the officer swung round and held up the lantern.

"Hey!" he shouted to the approaching horseman, who drew rein just beyond a point where the light would have fallen on his clean-shaven face. "Hey, there! Do you speak any English?"

Alan Hepburn took one look at that coach, and guessed instantly who must be inside.

It cannot be denied that his heart jumped up in his throat, but he had to make his decision.

"Yes, I speak English very well!" he bellowed back. "Don't any of your own men understand it?"

"No, thank God, or we wouldn't be arguing here!"

"What's the matter?"

"It's the lady and gentleman in this coach. They say they're Americans named Opple."

"Well?"

"At least, that's what I think they say. They don't speak a great deal of French. I don't want to cause trouble for them if they're really staying at the Park of Statues, but they may be goddams for all I know. If you could——"

"Stand aside, all of you!" said Alan.

"You so-and-so son of a so-and-so!" screamed one of the grenadiers, who had been solacing himself with a heartening pull on a wine-bottle concealed in his shako, and was compelled to leap back with outflung arms and legs.

But Alan could risk none of them seeing his clean-shaven face. Lowering his head, touching spurs, he drove Fancy Girl like a thunderbolt straight for the side of the coach.

The grenadiers scattered before him. Their officer, the only one who wore a waterproof, hastily stood back with the lantern swinging wide. Alan drew up with a flourish at the coach-side. Turning sideways in the saddle, he thrust his head through the open window and upreared it —cumbersome busby and all—so that he was looking straight into a pair of eyes which faced him not twenty inches away.

"Eee!" said a woman's voice.

The tableau, if Alan had been in any state of mind to appreciate it, was sufficiently striking.

Both side-blinds of the coach had been drawn; only the centre glass was lowered. A reflector-lamp, with its candle, burned against the back wall.

Facing him sat a wide-eyed little woman of perhaps twenty-eight or thirty, in a pelisse of claret-coloured velvet and a bonnet with upstanding red-and-orange plumes. She was as pretty as a doll, having pink dimpled cheeks with shining black eyes under well-marked arched eyebrows, and a full smiling mouth above a round chin. But here, in a combination of demureness with vivacity, all resemblance to a doll ended.

Just beside and beyond her, astounded, sat a portly handsome man some fifteen years older. He had an orator's mouth and a ruddy complexion. His tall beaver hat was pushed to the back of his head; a five-collared cape, like his neckcloth, had been disarranged as though by his own angry fingers. Mouth open, he also looked back at Alan while the rain drummed on the coach-roof.

Then Alan spoke.

"Mrs. Hopewell," he said in English, "your obedient servant. Mr. Hopewell, yours to command. Hold hard, please; don't speak!"

Still the rain drummed.

"I will not remind you," said Alan, "of any similarity in our political sympathies. But, in memory of the many bottles I have cracked with one of you," and he looked hard at Mr. Hopewell, "and of the many anecdotes I have exchanged with the other of you," here he looked just as hard at Mrs. Hopewell, who coloured up like a peony, "I beg you to think of what I ask."

"Sir——" began Mr. Gideon Hopewell, in a bursting baritone.

But Alan rushed on.

"When you meet my wife at the Park of Statues, as you soon will, I ask you to remember that she is a single lady named Miss Lenormand; and you never saw her before. Now say something, say anything, so that I can assure the officer you are the people you claim you are."

For a few seconds, while Alan's heart stayed in his throat, it was touch and go.

But, at mention of Madeleine's name, Mr. Hopewell's expression changed too.

Whereupon Lucy Hopewell, in her best if halting accent from Miss Axminister's Academy outside Philadelphia, spoke very loudly in French for the benefit of the listening soldiers.

"And your name, my officer?" she cried.

"Marius," said Alan, giving the name of an imaginary French character whose somewhat improbable amorous adventures he had often related to Mrs. Hopewell on the sofa of a London drawing-room.

"What was that, sir?" demanded Mr. Hopewell.

The strong brandy of danger, as usual, was making Alan Hepburn drunk. He longed to call himself Captain Marius Saperpopilette. But, with the grenadiers listening, this would be sheer lunacy.

"Captain Marius Legros," he said. Whereupon, with intense significance: "Don't you remember me from Paris?"

Then, changing swiftly to English:

"For God's sake say something!" he urged. "State your name and qualifications; protest about this as loudly as you can; kick up the devil's own row."

"Sir," retorted the angry Mr. Hopewell, "your objurgations, in this instance, are scarcely necessary. As the personal representative of President Jefferson, I protest that my wife and I have been stopped on the road no less than twice tonight. We have been obliged to take a completely roundabout course on our return from Ambleteuse. Finally, as the reason for our coachman's vociferations, something has gone wrong with the coach-axle and we are unable to proceed at all. Considering all these circumstances, sir——"

Alan had heard much about the democratic temper of Oudinot's Division. With his head still inside the coach for shelter against betrayal, he called to the whole platoon instead of to the officer.

"Soldiers!" he began, like a proclamation of the Emperor.

"Hey?"

"This gentleman," said Alan, "is the personal representative of President Jefferson. If you are discourteous to Americans, who inspired your own Revolution, General

Oudinot will boil all of you for morning-soup, and well you know it. Furthermore, unless you begin at once to repair the damage to this coach——"

A concerted yell of despair went up through the rain.

"Now look, species of imbecile!" thundered a tall grenadier, "we have just come from special and unnecessary sentry-go at the Field of the Balloons, being replaced by other poor bugg—sorry, lady-in-the-coach!—being replaced, I say, by other poor swine of our own regiment. Can we stop now to repair a sacred coach-axle?"

"He's right, though!" snapped the grenadier-lieutenant. "Attention, you others, or you'll find yourselves in clink without benefit of tobacco. Attention!"

"Madame," said Alan, taking Mrs. Hopewell's hand and lifting it to his lips, "I cannot thank you enough for your generosity tonight."

Little Mrs. Hopewell, dimpling and smiling with effulgent delight, gave him such a look from under lowered eyelids that her husband made a noise like a man hit in the stomach.

"Generosity, Captain," she replied, "is a quality of which advantage may be taken in any number of ways. Do you return to the Park of Statues tonight?"

"I only conjecture so, Mrs. Hopewell.—Stand aside, grenadiers!"

Amid the outbreak of shouting and protesting, Alan snatched out his head and sent Fancy Girl forward into the dark. Some twenty yards away, beyond reach of lantern-light or coach-lamps, he pulled up and wheeled round.

"Grenadiers!" he called back. "Is there any road to the Field of the Balloons which isn't completely flooded out by the rain?"

"Aha!" thundered back the tall grenadier, in an ecstasy of pleasure. "If you turn left after you pass Condette on the right, and go up the road past the deserted forge, you'll get there well enough. But Captain Cut-throat's loose, my fine courier; they're firing at everything; and you know where you'll get a bullet, don't you?"

He stated, with relish, exactly where Alan would receive a bullet. Little Mrs. Hopewell, high-plumed bonnet and all, was leaning out of the coach-window and waving until hauled back by hands inside.

If there were any other way of entering the Forest of Boulogne, Alan thought as he let the horse carry him on blindly, he would not come within miles of their balloon-enclosure.

But, in roaring darkness, there was no other way to find the road to St. Omer and Lille save by what lights—if any remained at all—would guide him towards the Field of the Balloons itself.

A deserted forge? Vaguely he could remember some such landmark, with a gaunt ruined wall and a clump of trees, on the right of the road as their coach had gone by in the other direction towards Pont-de-Briques.

The storm, which seemed to have been dying away, was rolling back again. Lightning flickered in the direction of the sea, and a dull gathering of thunder thickened and quivered for the new assault.

Forge, or something very like it! Easy: pull up!

Alan was compelled to dismount, whispering to Fancy Girl and patting her, before he stumbled across to make sure. The narrow road up the hill, north-eastwards in what must certainly be the direction of the Forest of Boulogne, was little better than a quagmire. And not the pin-point of a light showed anywhere up ahead.

Time was crawling on; inexorably the watch ticked in his waistcoat pocket. Thinking of Madeleine, alone at the Park of Statues with menace behind two locked doors, he felt jabbed and stung by the bayonets of haste when he could make no haste.

To ride Fancy Girl up that hill was unwise if not impossible. He must lead her, and with what speed he could manage. With relief he tore off the busby, hanging it by its chin-strap from the saddle-bow and shaking his neck free at last.

There was a broken fence at one side of the road. Guiding himself with his fingertips on this, Alan pressed uphill. After a time, when the road seemed firmer, he mounted the horse and rode. Ten minutes. Fifteen minutes, twenty-five minutes: at least, to judge by the clock-beats in his brain. He carried a tinder-box, but he dared not strike a light.

Half an hour, surely? When he had promised Made-leine——

A sudden flicker of lightning, kindling everything, brought him to a stop as though he had run straight into a wall.

He was in the Forest of Boulogne. He must have been in it for several minutes.

Not any difference in rain-sound, not any sharp scent of wet foliage or earth, had warned so drenched a way-farer. Everywhere tree-trunks towered up about him under the lift of lightning admitting chinks, while Fancy Girl picked her way along a path no more than eight to ten feet wide.

Alan slipped off the horse. Groping, he led her off the path and tethered her to a smaller tree-trunk. Since the flapping cavalry-mantle would only impede him, he took it off and draped it over the mare's back.

"Steady, girl!" he muttered. "Only a few minutes to go! Only a few minutes!"

Hand out before him, he moved back in the direction of what he had determined to be the path. But he must make sure; it would guide him.

Under the branches of the tall, ghostly trees, fewer drops of rain spattered on his outstretched palm. Wiping his hands on his coat, Alan took the tinder-box out of his pocket. It scratched sharply; an oil-soaked wick sputtered and curled up into flame . . .

And instanly the challenge lashed out.

"Who goes there?"

With one movement Alan extinguished the flame and pitched straight forward, left hand holding his sword-scabbard against clanking as he flopped to earth face down. At the same instant a second voice called out, beyond and behind the first. The beam of a dark-lantern, its slide shot back, pierced out and wheeled high above Alan's head amid the trees.

"Officer of the guard, idiot!" snarled the second voice. "Did you think it was ghosts or Captain Cut-throat? Can't you see my lantern?"

"How do I know who you are? Advance, you! What's the word?"

"Yes; that's a good mama's boy! The word is 'Vienna.' And you reply?"

" 'Danube.' But look here, my officer: I'll swear I saw

a light in front of me, and somebody in a blue-and-yellow coat."

"And what the hell did you expect to see? Aren't they our own colours?"

"That may be. But I'd like to know," rose the aggrieved voice of the sentry, "why Charlot Oudinot's men, every bit as good as the Guard themselves, have to spend the night being nursemaids to a lot of balloons. We can't smoke, in case a spark touches the gas-bags. For all I know, we can't even lower our breeches and . . ."

"Listen to me, conscript," said the officer of the guard in a dangerous voice. "Are you listening?"

"Yes, my officer! Yes, sir!"

Alan also, pressed hard into the mud, listened with shaking nerves for every word.

The whole forest was alive with sentries. There must be one at every fifteen or twenty paces. Here, where Captain Cut-throat's first victim had been stabbed on the night of August 13th . . .

"Has it occurred to you, conscript, that we're not concerned with the balloons? That we're here because two-thirds of the boss's artillery passed along the forest road tonight?"

"I heard that, yes. But you can hear anything in this man's army. What good are the guns against the goddams if they're hauling them in the other direction?"

"Fool!" said the officer of the guard. "We're not using them against the goddams. We're on our way to Vienna——"

Alan heard no more, because lightning whitened above the trees and a hammer of thunder smote out the rest of the words. But he needed to hear no more.

His reading of the Emperor's design was now as certain as anything could be, apart from a public statement signed by Boney himself. But Boney could not move his whole mighty Army for another five days at least, perhaps as much as a week.

To gain this information even a few days beforehand, the men in the map-room at Whitehall would willingly give years of their lives. If he, Alan Hepburn, could send back such news by the frigate Medusa tomorrow, he would in great measure have justified his own life.

And Alan, in the devilish excitement of hearing his reasoning confirmed, made his one foolish move. He sprang to his feet.

Even then, amid the gloom and shadows of Boulogne Forest, it might not have mattered. The officer and this raw young sentry, the latter on wires of apprehension, were still engrossed in their debate. The officer, for emphasis, was swinging round his open dark-lantern.

Its thin yellow beam swayed behind him, darting through a screen of tree-trunks and touching dim shapes in a vast open space beyond the trees. It touched the wicker shapes of balloon-cars, moored on heavy ropes four feet above ground.

The wicker creaked and cracked, the ropes creaked and cracked, with troubled ship-in-a-gale noises which Alan had mistaken for a sound of tree-boughs. Above them soared incredible goblin outlines—each oil-silk surface set apart from the others because it was inflated with highly inflammable hydrogen-gas, each surface vividly painted in colours of green-and-gold—creaking with piercing notes, swaying, tuggging amid wind and rain.

Then the officer of the guard swung back.

"I tell you conscript——!" he began, and stopped with mouth open.

What happened was the thousand-to-one chance, against which you would have laid any odds. As both officer and recruit glanced round, the beam of the lantern whirled with them. It rested full on the muddy figure of Alan Hepburn, standing up and staring at the ground in front of him.

For there was a dead man lying almost at Alan's feet.

The dead man lay face downwards, against green-glimmering underbrush, in his long overcoat. He looked as shrunken and inhuman as a sack, left hand out and musket at his right side. His tall hat of black-varnished leather, with yellow brush-plume in front, had fallen off and lay front upwards to expose the brass eagle. From his rain-sodden back upreared the polished black handle of the heavy dagger driven through his heart from behind.

The piece of paper, sticking to one edge of the blood and not yet rain-soaked, bore scrawled and familiar words. Alan could make out only a few words. 'If you want to know who I am, ask Fouché' This alone he saw . . .

Then the frozen pause dissolved as both officer and sentry saw Alan.

"Christ!" screamed the pale-faced young sentry, and he whipped the musket-stock to his shoulder and fired.

The spurt of flame, the crash of the musket-shot, seemed to draw men from every tree and patch of undergrowth. Alan saw lantern-light gleam on bayonet and polished gun-barrel; that was all. Sodden bark flew from the tree-trunk beside his left cheek. Something, with a hornet-like burr, hissed and then whirred deep into earth.

Alan's horse was only a dozen feet away. He leaped for Fancy Girl's bridle, caught one of his spurs in the tangled grass, and pitched headlong with a stunning thud.

And all this time the voice of the sentry, like a madman's, went shrilling up and up through Boulogne Forest.

"Captain Cut-throat! Disguised in one of our uniforms! He's here! He's here! He's here!"

Chapter XV

Swords in a Storm

The two things that happened, in ten succeeding seconds, balanced the scale-pans equally between death and safety.

Alan, springing up, seized Fancy Girl's bridle, threw the cavalry-mantle aside, and vaulted into the saddle.

At the same moment the officer of Oudinot's Grenadiers reached out and at one stroke cuffed the gibbering recruit into silence.

Alan caught a glimpse of that officer, standing as cool as though on parade; Alan saw the long hollowed face and eagle nose, beneath the officer's own varnished helmet with brass decorations. He heard the officer's voice ring out with absolute authority.

"Listen to me, all pickets!" it said. "Here is the officer of the guard speaking. Listen to me, all pickets!"

Dead silence. Alan, quivering, also sat motionless in the saddle and had just that time to decide his course.

"Cut-throat is here," said that measured voice, "within a dozen long paces of where I stand. He has a horse, and will try to ride south down the path out of the forest. Close in on that path. Those who have lanterns, open them wide and hook them over your arms. Fire at will, but do not obstruct each other.—At the charge-step, now! Live the Emperor!"

In one vast crackling of brushes and undergrowth, the forest erupted with lights and the long flash of bayonets. Oudinot's Grenadiers, who were shortly to win Austerlitz for their Emperor, swept in at the charge.

Alan threw the dice for his gamble.

Speaking to Fancy Girl, calling to her rather than using the spur, he whirled round the dapple-grey mare and drove her at the gallop along the path. But he did not ride south, as any sane man would have expected. He rode north-east—straight towards the Field of Balloons and towards the middle of all his enemies.

154

So unexpected was the dash, and so thin the picket-line despite its great length, that he had galloped through and beyond it before the minds of men could wrench their bodies round to counter his move. Three muskets exploded. High over him sang a thin scream; a lopped branch fell as a bullet severed it amid whirling lights.

Abruptly, under Fancy Girl's flying hoofs, the spongy path opened out wide into the fifty-acre clearing of the Balloon-Field.

Out from the door of a mud-walled hut tumbled a tousleheaded drummer-boy, in his shirt, but with the big red-and-blue drum already slung from his shoulder. Its sticks whirled and fell in the furious spring-rattle call of the long roll for assembly.

More drums answered. The roll swept in increasing tempo to a throbbing rattlety-bang across the whole field. Out of other huts plunged half-dressed men with muskets. Under the noise Alan could see only their eyes and moustaches move as they called questions.

"What's wrong?"

"Head him off!"

"Live the Emperor!"

Putting Fancy Girl at a harder gallop towards the nearest of the captive balloons, Alan could never hear that sincere war-whoop in honour of the Emperor without a longing to shout back, "Hurrah for Old Q.," or "God bless the *Morning Chronicle*," or something more in keeping with his own nature, which . . .

Look out!

An engineer-officer, with a pistol, loomed up before him and fired point-blank.

Alan, whipping the sabre from his scabbard, did not even hear the shot as he fled past under the first balloon. His gamble would prove to be as insane as it first seemed unless something happened very soon, something for which he ached and prayed. There was just a chance—just a remote chance!—that somebody would be too excited to hear or obey a certain sure order from the officers.

"Don't fire in the direction of those balloons! Don't fire . . . !"

But three grenadiers did.

The first explosion, which Alan heard high above his head as he rode hard under a canopy of green-and-gold

155

shapes like a nightmare forest in the rain, was a shattering boom and a vivid white flash of violet-edged light.

But it is not the explosion of hydrogen-gas which need be feared when a musket-ball, nearly red-hot, stabs through an oil-silk envelope fully fifty feet in diameter. What must be feared is the surge of fire that follows.

Hardly had the boom and flash whacked out than a swathe of yellow flame soared up the whole side of the big balloon-envelope nearest the south-western end of the forest. Momentarily, before partly obscured in a gush of oily black smoke, that yellow glare lit the field to the smallest vein in a leaf or the dirt under someone's finger-nails.

Pictures were printed forever under the canopy of light. Alan saw a drummer-boy, petrified, his sticks half raised. He saw an engineer-officer crouching, eyeballs glistening and speculative before the officer ran forward.

Then he had to act.

His game, of course, was to wheel Fancy Girl round in her tracks; to gallop back straight in his own path; and, under the confusion caused by the burning balloon, to ride through the picket-line and gain the southern road again.

Now he wondered whether he could do it.

He was scared stiff, scared as green as the balloon-colours; his arms and legs went limp, and under him Fancy Girl shivered as he did. Burning flakes of oil-silk sailed high on a rain-stung wind. Boom went another explosion as a second balloon burst open and took fire.

The fiercely-blazing envelope of the first balloon, loud with the crackle of burning ropes and cordage and wicker, had begun to topple and shrivel up; the huge and fiery wreckage was about to collapse. But every guard would sensibly have scattered out of its way; it was his only path out of a closed trap, and he must ride under the falling island if he hoped to get out at all.

What pulled him together, steadying his nerves, was no cry of, 'Live Anybody.' It was not, regrettably, an appeal to his Deity or any inspiring thought at all. It was something insular and even unpardonable, but which has saved British colours in many a black hour: the feeling, in his stubborn Scots soul, that no damned foreigners were going to frighten him into weakening under fire.

156

And so he drove his spurs into Fancy Girl's flanks, and rode straight towards that trembling mass in the sky.

In a blur they flashed past the stakes and ropes of a still-tethered, still-undamaged balloon, while he wondered if the mare's off-fore hoof might flick against a stake and send them both rolling. The glare of the burning balloon struck him blind, as its envelope of heat shrivelled the breath in his lungs. He closed his eyes, flinched, and lay forward across the horse's back as the wreckage toppled to smother him.

"Steady, girl," he heard himself say. "Here it comes."

Fancy Girl, who had taken heart from his own surge of strength, was no longer afraid. He thought she would not make it in time. But she flew just beyond the outer edge of the flame-island, fifty feet across in its diameter, as it crashed and whoomed to earth amid a spurting geyser of sparks and a swirl of fiery particles.

The breath hurt in Alan's lungs. His eyeballs, as he lifted the lids, felt seared and scorched; he could smell the steam from his own wet coat, and a tiny burn hurt like a real wound on his cheek. Fancy Girl's hind-quarters had been stung with fire-particles; she was dancing, tossing her head, pulling at the snaffle . . .

But there was not a soul ahead of them. Not a soul.

Rat-tat-tat clamoured the drums behind them, frenziedly beating the Fire-Call. There was a noise of voices and of running feet. The sky was still painted in shifting colours of yellow-red and oily black from the light of the second burning balloon.

But grateful rain caressed his face in a green-and-black forest. There was enough light in the sky clearly to show Fancy Girl the path as she raced farther and farther southwestwards.

He was riding past the spot, now on his left hand, where the murdered grenadier lay in the undergrowth, sprawled there with his death unknown until the beam of the dark-lantern found him. Undoubtedly for some time the uneasy sentries had suspected the presence of Captain Cut-throat's killer; they had guessed at him or sensed him as men on duty will. But they had not known for certain of what had happened until Alan all but stumbled over the body.

To that list of five victims—a sentry from the engineers,

one from the 57th of the line (a regiment nicknamed "The Terrible"), a naval sentry at the quai-side, a man in the 7th Light Infantry from the Pyrenees, and a grenadier of the Imperial Marines—had now been added a victim whose name Alan did not even know. In the reports there had been little that was personal about any of them: they were young or middle-aged, experienced or inexperienced, fairly popular with their friends and tolerable soldiers though grumblers and rebels as some were: in short, only men chosen for their particular position on duty.

But why the Field of Balloons again? And why that phrase in the note: *"If you want to know who I am, ask Fouché?"*

Fouché?

No!

Alan was still willing to take his oath the Minister of Police had nothing to do with these murders. In addition to the man's caution, the latest report to British espionage mentioned a prospective peerage for the ex-republican: the title of Duc d'Otrante. It was doubtful that Fouché knew this himself; he did not know everything; but——

No, no! And stop these speculations, which were not suited to roaring through the rain. At least the sentries seemed to have been drawn away from this path . . .

Out of the gloom, from the left side of the forest-path, a loud voice struck at him.

"Halt!" it cried. "Halt, there!"

Alan did not halt; the voice must have known he wouldn't. Long ago Mercier's busby had bounced away and been lost from the saddle-bow; long ago he had lost his waterproof mantle. But he still held the drawn sabre, and swung it up.

"Halt, Cut-throat!"

No lanterns were needed. Alan's head and shoulders showed too clearly against the glare in the sky.

From the left of the path, beside a tree-trunk, he saw the first of the musket flashes. This shot gave no whistling noise of a wide miss. Like the first one fired at him by the nervous sentry, it came close enough to make him duck. Simultaneously, somebody else fired from the right of the path.

Alan, breathing with relief that both musket-balls seemed to have missed, did not look behind. At the same time, it occurred to him, he must have bruised his right arm against an overhanging branch. It was not painful; it was as though someone with bony fingers had rolled and nipped the flesh of the arm in a sharp pinch.

But he had no time for such considerations. Through Fancy Girl's haunches he could feel her slip and slither on a miry road emerging from the forest and tumbling downhill.

He need fear no further shots for a moment; it would take the sharpshooters too long to reload. But it would take them very little time to rouse the rest of the grenadiers: to tell their comrades where he had gone, and bring the whole hornet's nest streaming down the hill after him.

For many minutes he had been in no state of mind to observe either lightning or thunder; but he noticed them now. Something (perhaps it was the boom of two more explosions) made him glance back over his shoulder.

Good God, was the whole Field of the Balloons going up in a gush of flame because of one wrong shot and a high-sailing wind? The balloons had been set very far apart against just this possibility. But it was a possibility; they had always known it, even when they trained their would-be invaders in the use of a device called a parachute, which had been invented at the end of the eighteenth century.

Glancing again over his shoulder, he twisted so far round that he stumbled in the stirrup-leather.

Somebody was following him on a horse.

Somebody, riding down through open fields at much the same pace as himself, was following him with gloating intensity.

Against the burning sky and the rain was printed the outline of a high, moving busby. It was unmistakably a cavalryman's busby, though the horse seemed a post-horse and not the best in the world.

Alan knew who it was. He had known ever since he found that dead body, stabbed through the back, who it was certain to be. And there was more to it than this.

'After all,' he addressed a phantom audience composed of Madeleine, and Ida, and Mercier, 'I am no such absolute fool as not to have suspected Schneider must be following us from Paris. But I thought Schneider had been stopped. I thought he was out of the way. I thought

159

those Breastplaters must have cut his comb in the Forest of Harbelot.'

It hadn't worked, then!

To intimate he guessed the presence of Schneider, to intimate this before Fouché's men in the Room of Mirrors and especially before Mercier and Ida in the coach on their journey to Pont-de-Briques, would have been the most unwise move he could have made. So long as they believed they held a trump-card over him in Schneider's presence, it would divert their attention from his real purpose: discovering Boney's design.

And yet . . . !

At close on ten o'clock that night, in the Forest of Harbelot, their coach overtook and passed the carriage of the Foreign Minister, escorted by four troopers of the heavy cavalry.

At that time there was a chance that Schneider, a bad danger and perhaps the worst danger, might be put out of the way through no effort of Alan's own. That was why it had been worth telling Michel that Michel must on no account upset the tempers of those escorting troopers.

He had been hoping, with some fervency, for an event which actually seemed to have happened.

Schneider, galloping up behind both vehicles, would have been in no pacific mood. Schneider's cool sneer would have been at its worst as he demanded the right to pass. And this was no game Alan himself would have cared to try on the Breastplaters of Boney's heavy cavalry.

At that time, when he risked putting his head out of the coach-window for a quick look behind, he thought he had heard noises of trouble and the clash of steel. But he could not be sure. And now it was evident that Schneider —the indomitable Prussian, the best swordsman in the Grand Army—had somehow triumphed over the Breastplaters and was following his enemy with a personal hatred and concentration which nothing could shake off or deviate.

Still looking back over his shoulder, as the lightning lifted and the thunder smashed hard, Alan saw not only his enemy. He saw Schneider dressed and bedaubed like a figure in a bad dream.

The man's busby had already been dark, and his boots were black. His flapping cavalry-mantle, tightly fastened

160

about his neck but rising and falling in sodden weight to the gallop, was black, too. And, to make him invisible when he stabbed his latest victim, he had heavily smeared his face with soot.

The Breastplaters had mauled him, true enough. One edge of the busby was shorn away by a sabre-cut. Schneider's right arm, as he held his drawn sword stiffly, had received some wound whether light or severe. But it showed only the triumph of his bony jaw, the cold certainty of his own invincibility, as he swept down hard for the kill.

'By God,' thought Alan, in a sweetness of hatred, 'are we going to have this out at last?'

He shifted his wet grasp on the hilt of his own sabre, and partly lifted it. And a stab of pain, astonishing him, twisted up all the way from his elbow to his right forearm.

The pain was so unexpected that he started to open his fingers, and just saved himself from dropping the blade. Come to think of it, his whole right sleeve felt heavy and sticky and moving with what could only be blood.

That marksman, to the right of the forest-road, had not missed after all. The bone in his arm was not broken, or he could not have moved it; apparently no artery was severed either. Yet before long, when he began to lose too much blood . . .

But Schneider was wounded too, and in his sword-arm as well; and it did not stop the unbeatable Schneider.

Nearer and nearer Alan was coming to the hard, well-surfaced main road, on which he could turn right towards the Park of Statues and the waiting Madeleine. He had a far better horse than Schneider's; he knew it.

And the two sides of his nature warred within him as they always did.

'You promised to meet their champion on a fair field. Are you going to run like a scared rabbit now? Turn and fight, blast you! Turn and fight!'

That was one side. Back to him, with cool derision, came the other side.

'Tonight, you know, you have indulged in quite enough useless heroics. A minute more and you will be on a good road; you can give Fancy Girl her head and leave Schneider nowhere. Once you have Madeleine at your side, you

161

can both disappear into the darkness on foot. Uncle Pierre and Aunt Angèle, at the Sign of the Sleeping Cat, will hide you against pursuit. Is your God-damned pride more important than sending the message by *Medusa* tomorrow? Forget Schneider and ride on!'

Alan rode on.

With belated caution he remembered the quagmire in the patch of side-road between the abandoned forge and the clump of trees. Just saving himself from a fatal tumble there, he gained the main road and whispered to Fancy Girl for every ounce of her speed.

Save for the wetness of the road, there was no need to ride carefully. Behind him, north-eastwards and along the entire length of the ridge two miles away, the glare in the sky was so high and intense that its shimmer flickered through the poplar trees on the road here.

The blaze had leaped out of control. Fifty acres of oil-silk balloons were afire, with their flames perhaps spreading to the surrounding woods as well. The alarm would have gone north to the Boulogne Camp by this time, rousing everybody.

Alan's arm throbbed with an intenser pain; it seemed to be swelling up. With an effort he lifted the swaying sabre-blade; he stabbed again and again, with angry concentration, to get its point into the slot of the scabbard; and he felt his body sway in the saddle, surprisingly, as the blade dropped home.

What ailed him was increasing giddiness from loss of blood. But he did not know this and did not care, because he was in the final stretch.

He tore past the village of Condette: where, on the left as you rode in this direction, a narrow lane led seawards towards the Inn of the Sleeping Cat. He passed the spot where, in some previous age, Mr. and Mrs. Hopewell's coach had been stranded.

Whatever repairs might have been necessary to the coach-axle, they must long ago have been completed by the platoon of grenadiers; the road lay empty and clear.

Shortly, on Alan's right, towered up the wall round the large grounds which enclosed the Park of Statues. Its curve as yet hid the gates from his sight. But he was so near home at last that . . .

162

With added speed he rounded this curve. He galloped into sight of the gate-posts and the lights atop them under which two sentries should have been standing, before he suddenly remembered—too late—the absence of Mercier's busby and of the disguising cavalry-mantle.

But that was not all he saw, as he drew rein and clattered to a halt.

The Hopewells' coach had again been stopped, this time facing the gate. It was still surrounded by a gesticulating platoon of men, of whom three or four had removed tunics and waistcoats. The officer was there, lantern in hand.

In front of the coach, with musket levelled and bear-skin cap stark against the light, stood the burlier of the two sentries on duty. His white-gaitered legs were planted a little apart. The bayonet on the musket was pointed at Mr. Gideon Hopewell, in many-collared cape and beaver hat, who stood in front of him while Mrs. Hopewell leaned out of the coach window.

"Confound it, my friend!" Mr. Hopewell was roaring to the sentry, in English. "How many times are we to be stopped tonight? Don't you recognize me?"

Conscious that the sentry did not understand a word, he appealed to the officer.

"If you will ask this gentleman here . . ."

"Now listen!" the sentry said to Mr. Hopewell in French. "I am Jules Dupont, a grenadier of the Imperial Guard, and I am carrying——"

"But——!"

"——I am carrying a sacred knapsack over a broken collar-bone where I got a bullet. I don't say that to brag; I say it because I've been three and a half days in sick-bay, and I only took English-leave from the hospital because there's a parade of veterans tomorrow. As Lieutenant Ravelle claims," and he jerked the bayonet towards the officer of Oudinot's Grenadiers, "you may have been staying at the Park of Statues for two days. But I can't identify you, and my pal is a blue who's new to this beat. However——"

"If you will examine my credentials——"

"However!" roared Dupont of the Guard. "I have sent him to the house for someone who can identify you. If you will be patient, sir——"

163

Lieutenant Ravelle, the officer of Oudinot's Grenadiers, had caught the clatter of Fancy Girl's hoofs even after the sound had ceased, and had already swung round with the lantern held up.

"Wait a minute!" he said. "Look ahead, there, down the road! I know that dapple-grey horse, don't I?"

And disaster, fine and full, smote Alan Hepburn just when he had believed himself well out of it. He was about forty feet beyond full reach of the lantern-light.

"That's the officer of the Guides, Captain Somebody, who knows these Americans personally—Hoy there, Captain! Ride forward!"

Alan could not ride forward. The lights on top of the gate-posts, to say nothing of the coach-lamps and the officer's lantern, would disclose with deadly clarity a clean-shaven horseman in civilian's clothes.

Lieutenant Ravelle strode towards him, lifting up the lantern.

"Hoy there, Captain!" he repeated impatiently. "I know who you are, right enough! What's the matter with you? Why don't you speak up?"

"Sacred name!" burst out a tall grenadier. "Would you look at the sky, over the Field of the Balloons? It was bad enough a few minutes ago, but look at it now! Has some English spy been setting fire to the place?"

"Spy?" echoed another. "You mean Captain Cut-throat?"

At the touch of that devilish name, by instinct and without knowing why, the men began to spread out across the road and look to the locks of their muskets.

Alan, breathing harder yet and with harsher effort, heard a new sound grow and gather along the road at his back.

It was the hoof-beats of Lieutenant Schneider's horse, always there with its rider as inexorable as fate, riding up to block his path in that direction, too.

"You know," cried an ecstatic voice, "ever since that reward-offer was posted, ever since eight-o'clock soup-time on Monday night, I've been dreaming . . . !"

"God, so have I," said another. "A hundred gold-pieces and all the booze you can drink. I'd rather have that, almost, than sleep with Pauline Bonaparte. If we could——"

"Hold on, there!" shouted the tall grenadier. "That fellow on the grey horse! He said he was carrying a despatch to the Field of the Balloons. You don't suppose . . . ?"

Lieutenant Ravelle was striding closer with the lantern.

Alan knew he must act, and act at once. He tried to flog his tiring brain; he tried to think of something such as always, before this, had saved him.

But he was held in a kind of paralysis. He was conscious of all things through a blur of dimming senses in the rain-misty light: of Mr. Hopewell turning round, of Mrs. Hopewell leaning out of the coach-window, of the click of cocking flint-locks and of Oudinot's Grenadiers slowly raising their muskets to aim . . .

Lieutenant Ravelle, standing in front of him, swung up the lantern so that its glow illuminated his mud-smeared features and mud-black clothes. At the same moment, beyond its dazzle, Alan saw the other sentry of the Imperial Guard emerge from between the gate-posts. Madeleine was with the sentry, and he saw Madeleine's stricken face.

"You're no cavalryman!" shouted Lieutenant Ravelle. "Who are you?"

Round spun Alan on Fancy Girl, with the spell shattered at last, and drove in the spurs as he had used them under the burning balloon. Hardly had the mare settled herself to gallop in the other direction than Lieutenant Ravelle dropped flat in the road to avoid the bullets of his own men.

"Fire!" he said.

All that saved Alan from being shot to death, when he had completely failed in that emergency, was something the grenadiers should have foreseen themselves.

Released from duty for so long a time, they had been too careless about guarding their musket-locks against damp. Ten triggers were pulled; only two gun-barrels fired a bullet at the retreating horseman. One bullet grazed the hind-quarters of the dauntless Fancy Girl; the other struck and ricocheted with a wiry whing from the surface of the stone wall.

Along the road, round the curve of the park-wall, Alan rode as hard towards the approaching Schneider as Fancy Girl could carry him. There was no dodging or avoiding Schneider now. Whether he liked it or not, he must face their best swordsman tonight.

There was something else, too, which he saw as soon as he rode into the straight of the road and caught sight of Schneider coming on towards him.

The pursuit of him was on the view-halloo from the Field of the Balloons. Though it was a long distance away, nobody could fail to make out that mass of men with weapons struggling down from the ridge under the eerie-lit sky. There were horsemen with torches far in front of them.

Alan pulled up his horse. So did Schneider.

They were about a hundred yards apart: on a straight stretch of road, between tall and thin poplar trees, lighted like a subterranean cavern by the pink glare of the sky. The road's surface, ordinarily white, stretched away grey and greasy under the rain; its puddles glimmered pink, and swift water ran in the ditches on either side.

Patting Fancy Girl's neck, speaking to her with words he never afterwards remembered, Alan settled himself in the saddle and with an effort managed to draw the sabre from its scabbard.

Schneider stood between him and the side-road which led to the Inn of the Sleeping Cat. So it was kill or be killed: if he could defeat Boney's champion and silence him, there would be just time to reach the inn before both sides of the pursuit converged against him.

If, if, if!

Up there, a hundred yards ahead, Schneider also was settling himself. He was unbuckling the heavy cavalry-mantle, throwing it off to get room for his sword-arm. An encounter like this was as much a test of horsemanship as of skill with the sword: one slip on that greasy surface, one miscalculation, and the chop or stab of your opponent's blade had finished you. Schneider, for some reason, did not appear to be so sure of himself on horseback. But that may have been illusion; that may have been . . .

They did not speak or call out; there was no need to do so.

At the same moment and with the same instinct, hatred of each other and all the other stood for, they both set spur to charge. Sabres back, tautened to jockey for position, they rode at each other under the burning sky.

Chapter XVI

"At the Side of My Fair One . . ."

Madeleine Hepburn opened her eyes.

She was lying in bed—or, to be exact, on the bed—in the same blue-and-white bedroom she had been supposed to occupy.

This, in her still-drowsy state, was the first fact she could grasp. Since the heavy velvet curtains had been drawn on the two tall windows facing front, the room was in darkness except for a few odd chinks where glimmers penetrated and showed clear daylight.

Daylight. Madeleine, in a rush of horror, sat up straight.

Realizing that she was still fully dressed, but under the weight of sleep and exhaustion only partly conscious of other things, she slid off the bed. She ran to the left-hand window. Its gold-bordered blue curtains clashed on their rings as she threw them back; she turned the knob of the window-catch and pushed both its leaves wide to a fresh, clean, sweet-scented morning after rain.

It must be many hours after sunrise. The pink softness of the sky was fading into a hot, hard bluish-white; but fragrance lingered on drenched grass and trees, and a hint of the sea was in it. There was not a sound from the house. Most of the world seemed still to lie in a hollow of sleep . . .

Feeling grubby and dishevelled, Madeleine looked down at herself. She was wearing stout shoes, and a day-dress of white sprigged muslin, very high-waisted, its puffed shoulders much crumpled. She had changed into that dress because Alan said——

Full realization came to her.

Alan.

Last night . . .

The infantry-officer, in the road in front of this house, holding up a lantern into Alan's face. Alan, so covered

167

with mud that few but herself would have recognized him, riding away into the dark and rain while the musket-shots exploded after him . . .

Madeleine glanced quickly round the bedroom, whose luxury by daylight appeared tawdry and spotted. In the bed in the alcove, under the coverlet, Ida de Sainte-Elme lay motionless.

Motionless? Poisoned and dead, instead of merely drugged?

Madeleine flew to the alcove. She could not tell about such matters, but Ida seemed to be breathing naturally; her pulse was steady, if rather slow and thin. On the other hand, when that woman woke up——

Madeleine waited for a time, listening to the whisper of the throaty little marble clock without ever thinking to look at it, while her own pulse-beats slowed down. Then the rattle and probe of a key, in the lock of the door to the corridor, had the same effect on her nerves as the probing of a surgeon's knife when she had once been strapped down for a small operation.

Locked in? She had been locked in! And where were the two brass keys entrusted to her care?

The door opened. Mrs. Lucy Hopewell, after a conspiratorial look round the corridor, slipped in carrying a tray with a steaming pitcher and cup of hot chocolate, a plate of crescent-rolls with much butter, and a dish of marmalade. Hastily putting down the tray on the little table beside the door, she snatched the key from outside, relocked the door on the inside, and put a finger to her lips.

"Sh-h!" said Mrs. Hopewell. "Eat this, my dear, and pray don't argufy. I mean to smuggle you out very soon, and there should be no danger as early as this. Notwithstanding, if I am to assist you properly . . ."

"Assist me?" cried Madeleine. "But—you can't! I mean . . ."

Mrs. Hopewell's vivacious eagerness and the sparkling light in her bright black eyes gave her the look of a child on Christmas morning. This was a little belied by her full, knowing lips and other evidences of maturity in her small figure, adorned by a morning-gown of yellow satin, which was cut much like Madeleine's except higher in the waist

168

and lower at the bust. Her black hair had been arranged in the Paris style of the latest month: not in top-curls, but close to her head in waves with one flat curl plastered to the centre of her forehead.

Even the slight look of haste and strain round her eyes did not mar the relish with which she spoke.

"My dear," crowed Mrs. Hopewell, dimpling and shivering with pleasure. "I have seldom enjoyed myself so much in my life. My poor husband, I am obliged to warn you, is in a state which approaches the gibbering. But truly, madam, you must not mind Mr. Hopewell."

Momentarily she grew very grave.

"Mr. Hopewell," she said, "has no love for intrigue, which seems to me a most discouraging trait in a diplomat——"

"But I thought he said——!"

"Yes, yes, my dear, I know! But then, though Mr. Hopewell talks a great deal about neutrality and maintaining his status-something, what really signifies is that he does not like the English. There is a very good reason why most Americans do not and cannot like the English; it will take a hundred years and lots of wars with other people to repair the damage. On the other hand, he does very much like you. Just as, in all frankness to tell you, I simply love your husband——"

Seeing Madeleine's face, Mrs. Hopewell was deeply and honestly stricken. Uttering cries, she ran forward and seized Madeleine's hands.

"Oh, dear, I do manage to put my foot in it! Now listen! He is safe. That is what I must tell you first of all, and you must remember it. He is safe."

For some seconds Madeleine did not speak. Then she could not control her voice.

"Are you sure? How do you know?"

"Sh-h-h! For heaven's sake!"

"I'm s-sorry! I'm not quite myself. And I am terribly, terribly grateful. But——"

"Of course you're upset! And, oh, dear, I've ever such a lot to tell you; and I must choose the most important things first. But wait," continued Mrs. Hopewell, with dreamy delight in her Christmas-morning eyes, "wait until you hear everything he did to Boney last night. What a man!" said Mrs. Hopewell, in a tone perhaps not quite suitable for a diplomat's wife. "Land sakes alive, what a man!"

"Yes! That's just it! I'm—I'm rather fond of him . . ."

"Rather fond of him? Land sakes alive, don't you make any more fuss over the man than that?"

"You see," replied the fiercely stammering Madeleine, in such relief that she could not talk straight, "you see, I've been married to Alan since three years last June, and I'm only beginning to understand what he's like. As for Alan, he—he doesn't understand himself at all. He honestly thinks he's a coward."

"Yes, I know," said Mrs. Hopewell. "We have American cowards like that. They were the ones who saved us with bayonets, under General Washington, when the Continental Congress wasn't worth a continental damn."

Suddenly and inexplicably, Lucy Hopewell herself seemed near tears.

"My husband was one of those same cowards," she said. "He went through the worst of it, beginning when he was a boy at Valley Forge in '77. I like to remember that, you know, if ever he seems a little pompous."

Whereupon she again ran forward and seized Madeleine's hands.

"And I'm not really a fool and a rattle, you must understand; I have only been going on like this because I think it will cheer you, and I am sure it will. Just remember that: Mr. Hepburn is safe."

"Where is he?" cried Madeleine. "He is at an inn, isn't he? An inn called the Sleeping Cat?"

"Yes! How did you know that?"

"And he isn't dead," said Madeleine. "I think I should have known if—if that had happened. But he is wounded, isn't he? Badly?"

"No! Not in the least seriously, though he lost a good deal of blood from a wound in his right arm . . ."

"A sword-wound! I knew it! He met a man named——"

"No, no, no!" soothed Mrs. Hopewell. "You must not disturb yourself with fancies. It was the crease of a bullet-wound, and not dangerous at all."

Madeleine shut her eyes, and tried to reach the right state of calmness.

"I'm afraid," she said, "you will have to tell me what

happened, because I don't remember." Horror seized her again. "I didn't faint, did I? If there is anything in this world I detest," she said passionately, "it is a fainting woman."

"Between ourselves, so do I," confessed Mrs. Hopewell. "But, la, now! I daresay we must do what the men expect of us, or how would the world go on at all? Tell me, my dear: have you been losing a great deal of sleep, or else going through a whole lot of unpleasant experiences one after the other?"

"Well—yes. I have."

"Hah, I thought so! And last night, when you came out to identify us . . . How on earth, my dear, was it you who came out to identify us?"

Under that sprightly and beaming presence, now dancing about excitedly despite her formal yellow-satin gown and her formal hair-style, Madeleine was partly regaining her own cheerfulness.

"Well," Madeleine admitted, "I daresn't let anyone else answer the door when the sentry knocked. He wanted to wake up a servant named Victor, the only one here who speaks English. So I confessed I spoke English, and hoped to brazen it out. But you seemed to know everything already . . ."

"I did. Ho, didn't I?"

"And then——"

"My dear," said Mrs. Hopewell, doing another dance-step, "you were calm as a Quaker meeting, even when they began shooting at your husband. You were perfectly calm until about twenty minutes later, here in the house, while Mr. Hopewell was preaching a sermon about what he could or could not do as a neutral. All of a sudden you tumbled over unconscious, and I made Mr. Hopewell carry you up here. You see, there were two keys in your hand . . ."

"Keys!" said Madeleine. "Those keys! I lost them——"

Over Mrs. Hopewell's face went a look of modest pride, as one who should say "Hem!" And she stopped dancing and drew herself up with dignity.

"My dear," she said, "if you are troubling your head about a bedroom in which there is a cavalry-officer unconscious and smelling of laudanum, and a powdered servant tied up and asleep, pray banish those fears, too.

171

The men have not been discovered; and they won't be discovered just yet. I made Mr. Hopewell spend the night in there."

"You . . . what?"

Mrs. Hopewell shook her head.

"Poor Gideon," she said wistfully. "It is very wrong of me to laugh at him, I know, because truly I love him. But—ee! I have never seen him in such a state since the damn Federalists called him a drunkard and a bigamist."

After brooding over this for a moment, while Madeleine remained speechless with affection and admiration, Lucy Hopewell dismissed her own fears.

"Then," she went on, "about an hour after that, when I could not sleep for the life of me because I was so excited over this, there was someone prowling about the house. I woke up Mr. Hopewell, which he positively resented, but no one saw us go downstairs. It was a woman called Aunt Angèle—"

"Aunt Angèle? Who's that?"

"My dear, she is the wife of the man who keeps the Sleeping Cat Inn. It is difficult to make people understand my French, which infuriates me, but I understand almost everything that's said to me. Aunt Angèle had a message for you, and I persuaded her to tell me instead. That is how I know . . ."

Abruptly a shade of uncertainty, even of apprehension, sprang so clearly into Mrs. Hopewell's face that Madeleine could not help seeing it. New traps were ahead; other fangs waited to strike.

"What is it, Mrs. Hopewell?" she asked quickly. "Is there something you haven't told me?"

"No, no, no, to be sure there isn't!" retorted Mrs. Hopewell, firmly but not altogether convincingly. "Yet your own position is not safe; and we must lose no time if we are to smuggle you out of the house! I pray you and pray you to drink the chocolate before it grows cold. Eat something, anything, against morning humours. Please do: there's a dear! At any time we may be interrupted——"

They were interrupted, in fact, by a light but long and complicated series of knocks at the door to the corridor.

At the first rap of the knocking, Lucy Hopewell jumped and squeaked like a doll. Afterwards, reassured by the elaborate signal, she hastened to unlock the door. She assumed

172

a suitable air of wide-eyed meekness as her husband came in; then she quickly locked the door again.

Mr. Hopewell, a stranger would have decided, had judged the real and crowding danger of the situation rather more accurately than his wife. He was freshly shaven, and with the whitest of muslin neckcloths and linen collars; his portly figure was set off by a high-collared bottle-green coat and the new-style white trousers.

But his ruddy face appeared less ruddy, and by some illusion there even seemed to be more grey in his hair. He was biting his lip as he bowed to Madeleine, whose knees trembled as she returned the greeting with a curtsey.

"Mrs. Hepburn, your servant," he said formally. A little of his sternness gave way, but exasperation returned when he looked at his wife.

The latter tried to forestall him.

"Now, Mr. Hopewell——!" she warned, lifting an admonitory forefinger.

"As you please, madam," said her husband. "But, if you must give way to a childish and unbecoming taste for intrigue, will you at least try not to conduct all things after the manner of a Restoration play?" He indicated the door behind him. "Three long knocks, three short knocks, then a combination of long and short knocks! You would have us all in vizard-masks, I'll be sworn, if any masks were available."

"Now, Gideon! *Please*, my love!"

"Never mind, never mind!" He looked at Madeleine. "Next, Mrs. Hepburn, with regard to the immediate future . . ."

Madeleine was no coquette; on the contrary, she despised the arts of coquetry too much for her own good.

"Mr. Hopewell," she said, "you and your wife have stood our friends at a time when few others would have dared to do it: the Emperor has frightened everyone. I can't thank you properly, because I lack the gift of expression." She ran to him and gripped the lapels of his coat. "But please believe that I love both of you, and it's not a figure of speech and I mean it!"

"Well," said Mr. Hopewell, and glared at the floor. "Well."

After a pause, gingerly, he disengaged Madeleine's hands and stepped back and cleared his throat.

"Mrs. Hepburn, I can't pretend I like what is happening here. I am in a position more devilish awkward than you know. Only two days ago I was paid a personal call by the Emperor himself——"

"Of course you were," said his wife scornfully. "He was trying to impress you. You didn't let Boney pull the wool over your eyes, did you?"

Gideon Hopewell, who had strode across to open the curtains on the second window, threw them back on their rings and turned round with the strengthening sunlight on his face.

"As the wife of a diplomat, my love, will you oblige me by not referring publicly to the Emperor of the French as 'Boney'?"

"Just as you say, Mr. Hopewell. But I still ask——"

"Furthermore," her husband was continuing, when he caught sight of Ida de Sainte-Elme in the alcove, and all his sense of propriety rose in outrage. "Good God, is that woman still in bed? We cannot stay here, Lucy. Hadn't we better go downstairs at once?"

"Gideon, my love, we can't go downstairs or anywhere else; we must be as quiet as quiet, until that carriage from the inn arrives to take Mrs. Hepburn away. People in the house may be about at any moment and find the servant who isn't drugged!" She broke off, watching him. "Very well, very well; just a moment!"

Picking up her heavy satin skirts, Mrs. Hopewell scurried across to the alcove, where she drew shut its blue-and-gold curtains.

"There!" she said triumphantly. "If that surly-looking wench is out of sight, she won't offend your Presbyterian conscience. But you were saying, about the Emperor?"

Mr. Hopewell, with a troubled forehead, was again gnawing at his under-lip.

"There is something about the man," he confessed. "I detest his tyranny and militarism as much as Mr. Jefferson does. But—there is something about the man."

"Naturally he has a way with him," retorted Mrs. Hopewell, "or he wouldn't be Emperor at all. And he has fine eyes. But do you know what I think?"

"You are prejudiced against the Emperor, my love, because he believes woman to be an inferior creature who should be seen and not heard . . ."

174

"Eef" said Mrs. Hopewell, jumping up and down with her small fists clenched.

"Mrs. Hopewell, madam, I implore you to remember yourself!"

"I think," cried Mrs. Hopewell, "he's an odious little man who's acting and acting and acting!"

"Acting?"

"Yes! All the time!"

"Much as I may dislike his principles, Lucy, at least I can credit him with sincerity in them. He is devoted to his own people, and in particular to his Grand Army, who strike me as being—well! a tolerably fine lot of men."

"Yes!" cried Mrs. Hopewell. "Those men are too good for him, because most of them worship him. But heaven help that little tin god if they ever discover he doesn't care a rap for anybody except himself and his own precious relatives! However, Gideon, since you seem to be won over to his side . . ."

"Won over to——?" echoed Mr. Hopewell; and the change in the atmosphere was almost terrifying.

He was standing by the far window, one hand raised to the curtain; and most of the colour had drained out of his face. Madeleine, watching and listening with a quick-beating heart, was conscious of forces whose nature she had not guessed. It was towards Madeleine that he turned.

"Mrs. Hepburn," he said quietly, "do you know why I was sent to Boulogne to see the Emperor? No? Do you, Lucy?"

"No, of course I don't! You're always so secretive that . . ."

"Mrs. Hepburn," continued the American envoy, "early this month our Secretary of State, Mr. Madison, received a message from President Jefferson. The substance of that message I was required to communicate to the Emperor in person. The message, and I quote word for word, was this. 'Considering the character of Bonaparte, I think it material at once to let him see that we are not of the powers who will receive his orders.'"

Gideon Hopewell moistened his lips.

"We are a small nation, Mrs. Hepburn, though one day we may stand on equal terms with the lords of the earth. Until such time, I fear, we are thinly populated and not

175

very strong. But Mr. Jefferson's meaning was a simple one. 'Let us have no threats, sir; attack us if you dare.' That is the substance of the message I was obliged to deliver to the head of the mightiest military power in the world; and one, I might add, which I was very pleased to deliver to his face."

In the dead silence which followed, Madeleine again ran forward.

"You mustn't involve yourselves in this! You mustn't; I won't allow it! I'll go away from here immediately, or you can go yourselves! So long as you don't betray Alan so that they'll kill him——"

Gideon Hopewell's face went from white to red again.

"My God, madam," he shouted, "did you ever seriously think I would? Am I so much of a Judas, or even so little of a gentleman, as to betray any man at whose table I have dined? I would only desire you to understand that my position *is* difficult; and my wife to understand that I, who still carry scars from the War of Independence, am not likely to be 'won over' by a usurper and a tyrant."

Lucy Hopewell turned away abruptly.

"Madeleine, my dear!"

"Yes?"

"You're right to be proud of your husband. But don't you think I'm right to be proud of mine?—Gideon, dear, I'm sorry!"

"Now enough of this nonsense," roared the red-faced Mr. Hopewell, as though they had been doing all the talking and not he. "Relations between the Emperor and myself cannot be called cordial; you will guess why he wanted me to inspect some new guns which, incredible as it would appear, can fire a projectile for a distance of over five miles. But matters have not come to so sad a pass, Mrs. Hepburn, as you seem to think. Let us consider what is best to be done."

More uneasy than he had been when he spoke of his own concerns, Mr. Hopewell looked at Madeleine and hesitated.

"My dear lady," he continued, "I don't know what Hepburn means to do this morning, and I prefer not to know. Except, if my wife correctly translated a long and most incoherent narrative from an innkeeper's wife——"

176

"Gideon, I am perfectly certain I understood most of it!"

"Except, then, that he means to go straight into the camp and carry out his original plan. My life on it, Mrs. Hepburn: I would not stand in your husband's shoes for a million dollars!"

"Gideon!" his wife said warningly. But Mr. Hopewell was too harassed to consider his own personal diplomacy.

"According to reports from the sentries at the gate this morning, his exploits last night were far from soothing. He——"

"Gideon!"

"He stabbed and killed a sentry; he deliberately set fire to the Field of the Balloons; he insulted and humiliated the Emperor's best troops. He himself is Captain Cutthroat. And all this, for some reason, was inspired by the Minister of Police."

"Mr. Hopewell, you don't believe that!" said Madeleine. "You can't believe Alan is Captain Cut-throat!"

"No, madam; I don't believe any of it. I am merely quoting the story. But the Boulogne Camp is in a state of wrath bordering on delirium. If Hepburn insists on venturing there in spite of everything——"

Mr. Hopewell, nodding to himself, paced up and down with one hand under his coat-tails and the other lifted to mark points in the air.

"In that event, let us consider the things in his favour. Fortunately, no one has yet identified our fugitive with the 'Vicomte de Bergerac' who is staying here. Had anyone so identified him, you would be under arrest now. My wife and I might be in some trouble as well."

"Listen to me!" pleaded Madeleine. "Will you please let me go away before they do identify him and compromise you both? It's not far to that inn; Alan said I could get there easily on foot."

"And risk being stopped and questioned?" enquired Mrs. Hopewell. "A carriage will be here at any moment; I propose to accompany you; and two women in a carriage will go unnoticed. No, no, no!" said Mrs. Hopewell, stamping her foot and really vexed. "I won't hear of your going alone, that's all! But what I can't understand, Gideon, is how the Minister of Police comes to figure in

177

all this. Didn't you meet him once in Paris? A red-haired man with a queer, dusty little wife to whom he was deeply attached?"

"That is the man. And I can only assume, Lucy, the story has become garbled as such stories usually are. But while I am speaking, my love, will you oblige me by refraining from interrupting any more than is necessary?"

"I am so sorry, Gideon my dear. Pray do continue!"

"Well!" said the orator, resuming his pacing. "First, the fugitive has not been identified. Second, nobody can recognize his face again; it was covered with mud. Third, he is believed to be disguised in the uniform of Oudinot's Grenadiers.

"All this will cause confusion and assist him. Further, I seem to remember there is to be a grand review of the Emperor's Army-of-Italy veterans, with a number of brass-bands: which should draw a great concourse and help in obscuring him. If only Hepburn, as a civilian, has some excuse for his presence there when he is stopped and questioned . . . !"

"But he has!" exclaimed Madeleine. "There is no time to explain; but Alan is still carrying a pass, signed by General Savary, which allows him to go anywhere in the camp during the day."

Lucy Hopewell beamed with delight.

"There, you see?" she crowed, as though this disposed of all difficulties. "He'll beat them yet; and you are not to worry!"

Madeleine threw out her arms.

"Mrs. Hopewell, I can't help worrying! Last night, when Alan said he meant to stand on the cliff near the Emperor's pavilion, in full sight of the whole army——"

"I beg your pardon?" exclaimed the American envoy.

"That was what terrified me most of all; and the question of Schneider!" Madeleine looked at Lucy. "And yet, you know, you're quite right. I have a mad and wild and silly kind of certainty that Alan can outwit and outmanoeuvre the whole lot of them, if only he has his health and strength! What reassured me most was your telling me he was safe, without any sword-wounds. I was afraid he might have met Lieutenant Schneider, and there might have been a fight as there nearly was in the Room of Mirrors . . ."

178

Gideon Hopewell stopped short in his pacing, and wheeled round.

"Lieutenant Schneider?" he repeated. "Lucy! Is that 'the officer with the German name' the innkeeper's wife mentioned?"

"I—I think so, yes."

"Lucy! Haven't you told her?"

"Told me what?" said Madeleine.

"Gideon, my love, the girl has not had a mouthful of food or a sip of that chocolate, which is as cold as charity now! She is in no fit condition . . ."

"Told me what?" repeated Madeleine, near hysteria.

Mr. Hopewell looked grim. "Your husband, madam, did meet Schneider."

"They met and fought, then? And it's all over?"

"They met, yes; but they did not fight and it is not even settled yet."

"What on earth do you mean?"

"This Lieutenant Schneider, it appears, is a holy terror. Earlier in the evening he attacked four heavily armed Breastplaters. He killed one, disabled another, and escaped the other two in order to follow Hepburn.—Lucy! What was the rest of it?"

"Well, you see," replied the now-nervous Mrs. Hopewell, "he had been wounded too, like your husband, only several hours earlier; and he disregarded it; and . . . Oh, Gideon, it's not my story!"

Mr. Hopewell was pacing rapidly again.

"Apparently," he said, "Hepburn noticed something strange about the other fellow's seat in the saddle, but never guessed what it was until they galloped at each other and Schneider collapsed off his horse."

"And Alan didn't——?" Madeleine knew the answer even before she spoke.

"No! Instead of running a sabre through him, as any sane man would have done, this lunatic husband of yours left him in the road and escaped to the inn before pursuit closed on both sides. If Hepburn can be up and about this morning, perhaps the other fellow can do as much. To my mind, madam, it is among the least of your worries; they are beating the whole countryside for Hepburn. I mention it only because this Aunt Angèle seemed so much exercised.

179

"Confound it, ladies!" added Mr. Hopewell, giving vent to his need for action by flinging open both leaves of the second window. "Why should this trouble you so much? Are there not more serious things to worry about?"

"I am not worrying about anything!" retorted Mrs. Hopewell: "Mr. Hepburn will beat Boney; you see if he doesn't; if only Madeleine will eat something!"

Her husband looked at her, and then mopped his forehead with a handkerchief.

"Fortunately," he said, "it is still early; and Hepburn will not venture near the camp until that review of veterans begins at half-past nine. Meanwhile, Mrs. Hepburn, your vital necessity——"

"It is——" Lucy began vehemently.

"No, my love: permit me to correct you: it is not to eat anything. Her necessity is to leave here before Schneider tells his story and the legions descend on this house. That carriage! What in thunderation is delaying the carriage?"

Leaning out of the long window with its little iron balcony, he peered left and right across the statues, across the gravel drive, across intense green under the hot, ever-strengthening sun.

"The carriage," said Mr. Hopewell, "is another instance of the unpunctuality and inefficiency I have found everywhere abroad. We should be able to see it, or at least to hear it. Listen!"

After a pause Mrs. Hopewell scurried to the other window.

"No. Gideon, you listen! Don't you hear band-music?"

It was true. Though the noise was far away and not loud, a soft wind blew steadily inshore and carried it clearly: the swinging, rollicking beat of massed bands.

"I know that tune," said the startled Lucy Hopewell. "It's called, 'Auprès de ma Blonde,' 'At the Side of My Fair One.' Why in heaven's name should they be playing a nursery . . ."

"Nursery?" exclaimed her husband, mopping his forehead again. "That, my love, is the celebrated marching-song which the Emperor's Army of Italy brought back from the scene of his first great triumphs in '96."

"But it can't be as late as nine-thirty yet! We've been too careful of the time! It can't be . . ."

180

With one instinct they all swung round to look at the busy little clock, which in their preoccupation had gone on unobserved and even unheard. Its hands stood at twenty minutes to ten.

"Ten o'clock!" said Madeleine. But she did not say it loudly, and no one else heard her: she remembered too vividly it was between ten o'clock and noon that the forty-four-gun frigate *Medusa* sailed at the shore-batteries without firing a shot, if the ship appeared at all.

"Now you're not to become excited, either of you!" cried Mrs. Hopewell, who was again jumping up and down. "I informed you that all would be safe and secure; and, truly, so it is. The carriage is here now: listen!"

Both Mr. and Mrs. Hopewell drew a breath of relief and crowded to the window. Madeleine, her eyes still fixed on the clock, was so concerned with Alan that she did not particularly care whether a carriage came for her or not.

The ship, of course, might not appear in the morning: which would only, sickeningly, protract the torture of wondering how Alan fared and even where he was. Listening to the whir and tick of the clock, she heard under the surface of her mind the noise of wheels and hoofs on gravel, the creaking and swaying of springs . . .

And a sense of wrongness obtruded into Madeleine's mind just before Lucy Hopewell spoke.

"Gideon!" she said. "That doesn't look like any sort of carriage an inn would send! It's a heavy travelling-coach, all covered with dust as though it had come a very long distance."

Madeleine's gaze left the clock.

The feeling of dread which struck her, like a prevision, was one of those inspired guesses which can fly at once to the heart of truth. She ran to the window beside Lucy Hopewell just as the coach swept into the grass courtyard of the fountain, and swung round beside the front door below.

Mrs. Hopewell, her lips and eyebrows framing a wordless question, was pointing and pointing again, still without speaking, at the figure of a man emerging from the coach. Madeleine nodded. Only too well she recognized the withered face under the high chimney-pot hat.

"Yes," replied Madeleine in a steady voice. "That's the

181

Minister of Police. That's Fouché himself."

As she said it, there occurred what had been ready for them for some time.

With a sharp rattle and clash of brass rings, one of the heavy velvet curtains closing off the bed in the alcove was pushed and then hurled aside. Words in French, stinging with hatred and determination, made them all turn at the same time.

"You are right," said the voice of Ida de Sainte-Elme. "I have been awake for more than a little quarter of an hour. Alan can tell you, my precious boarding-school miss, I understand English fairly well."

With one arm out where she had thrown back the left-hand curtain, and holding tightly to the other blue-and-gold curtain for support on her tottering knees, Ida knelt at the foot of the bed.

With her hair wildly dishevelled, the gauzy yellow gown all but torn off her, and her breathing so shallow and harsh she could barely speak, she was less like the beauty of last night than like a woman in a madhouse.

"Then he will be on the cliff by the pavilion, eh? To signal a ship, I imagine? Thunder of God! We shall see!"

Ida flung herself backwards. She staggered to her feet on the floor, seized the bell-rope hanging beside the head of the bed, and yanked it again and again to summon help as the band-music in the distance, with the strains of 'At the Side of My Fair One,' swelled high from the Field of Mars.

Chapter XVII

The Most Famous Hat

On the parade ground at the Boulogne Camp, under a hot sun which was rapidly drying its bare-trampled earth, the review had not yet begun.

At intervals round that immense field stood tall white flag-staffs, gilded and crowned, from each of which fluttered a silk pennon inscribed with the name of one of the Emperor's victories in his first Italian campaign of '96. Even from a distance you would have seen 'Mentenotte,' 'Millesimo,' 'Dego,' 'Ceva,' 'Mondovi,' 'Lodi,' 'Castiglione,' 'Bassano,' 'Arcola,' 'Rivoli' among the names which curled out in gold letters and floated up with the out-flowing breeze.

Beyond the flag-staffs, round three sides of a hollow oblong, were drawn up the younger foot-regiments: their colours dark-blue faced with red or yellow or orange, under a glitter of bayonets as vast as light-points on the sea, with their drums in front of them. But no drums had as yet rolled, no muskets were at salute, no concentrated cheers had gone up from the onlookers thronging beyond.

Only the massed bands were first parading. There were twenty of them, the chosen of Boney's hundred regimental bands, though they looked small in that field.

But patriotic emotions had already begun to quiver in scattered shouts. The moving brass instruments flashed back the fiery sun; cymbals smote hard on the opening bar, and the swinging march smashed across the camp from twenty bands at once.

> At the side of my fair one
> How sweet it is, how sweet it is——!

Alan Hepburn, sitting a slow and heavy-bodied black horse on a hill some two hundred yards away from the southern edge of the parade-ground, found his own heart stirring and swinging to the intoxication of the music, as his eye was caught and intoxicated by the stimulation of Boney's colour and pageantry.

If this was the effect on him, who hated the conqueror and all his works, what must it be on those young Frenchmen to whom Boney held out such an appeal?

"Soldiers!" the Emperor had cried in his emotional fashion, at the beginning of the Italian campaign which was being celebrated today. "You are naked and ill-fed; I will lead you into the most fruitful plains in the world. Rich provinces, great cities, will be in your hands. There you will find honour and fame and wealth."

And those words had been the key to the Emperor's whole policy for nearly ten years.

At the side of my fair one
How sweet it is to sleep!——

To Alan, weak from loss of blood and light-headed under the hot sun, it seemed that he had seen nothing but movement and pageantry—yes, and eerie dreams, too —ever since last night he rode out into battle with Fancy Girl.

He shut his eyes, and his mind moved back to it.

To a burning sky, and to Schneider's black-daubed face (incredulous, stricken) when Schneider unexpectedly collapsed off his horse just as Alan flung a sabre-cut at his head and Schneider parried it. One cut and parry; that was all.

The torches of pursuit, in the hands of soldiers, were clear along the road behind and in front when Alan had galloped down that side road to the Inn of the Sleeping Cat beside the water.

Himself giddy and bleeding like a stuck pig, he had knocked at the door of the low, sinister-looking building, and given the arranged password to the man who opened it.

He could not understand who stayed at the inn, or even who drank there. He could see nobody in the place except the so-called Uncle Pierre, a massive sombre man with a pock-marked face and a broken nose, and the so-called Aunt Angèle, who was also massive but very handsome in her own none-too-clean way, as excitable as her husband was grim and sombre.

In the low inn-parlour, while the sea crashed against beach and jetty outside, and a dim light glimmered from a floating wick in a bowl of fish-oil, he still bled all over the place until Pierre twisted a turncot tightly round his right arm, and Angèle bathed and bandaged the wound while Alan told his story.

There was not even any ornament in the stuffy room except a big steel engraving of Georges Jacques Danton, already yellowed against the damp wall. It may have been only to Alan's heated and tiring imagination that the heavy pock-marked features of Danton, the lion of the French Revolution, dead and guillotined these eleven years, came to look exactly like the features of the middle-aged Pierre bending over him.

Alan's first attempt, once his reeling head steadied, was to go back again to the Park of Statues for Madeleine.

"No," said the heavy-voiced Pierre.

"But I can't leave her there!"

The fish-oil lamp glimmered weirdly; the sea charged the beach as an army might have charged it; the handsome if overblown Angèle, surname unknown, brought him steaming broth which Alan drank gratefully.

"Look out of the window," said Pierre. "The roads and even the fields are full of soldiers with torches. You would not get twenty metres alive. Your government pays me well to take these risks. And there are other reasons." He glanced at the face in the steel engraving. "But no man sells his neck. If you will look at those people searching for you——"

"I know that! They had already found Schneider when I left. But——"

"This Schneider. Was he badly wounded?"

"I couldn't tell, but I don't think so."

"Then, when he recovers, he will tell them who you really are and what you look like?"

"No, he will not!" said Alan with some violence. "I will gamble any odds that is what he will not do."

The pock-marked face, with its broken nose and hairy nostrils, loomed over him like a goblin.

"You seem very sure," said the heavy voice. "Why?"

"It is too much a question of a personal grudge; he
185

cherishes it like a maniac. Schneider will not breathe a word to anyone until he is sure he can't find me and kill me himself."

"Well! It may be so. He is not a man to trifle with; one of those Breastplaters, in the troop escorting Talleyrand, told my friend Legrand at Pont-de-Briques how he killed their leader with a single cut through the neck. However: it may be so."

"I will take my oath on it!"

"As for your woman," said Pierre, glancing at his own woman, "she cannot come to you for the same reason you cannot go to her. She is safe enough where she is at the moment. They are looking for Captain Cut-throat," a strange contortion twisted his features as again he peered at Danton's picture, "in someone who has been here-abouts for a long time; not in an arrival at the Park of Statues tonight. Twenty persons, you say, saw you ride away from there not long ago?"

"Yes!"

"Then the soldiers will not search there. But, in five minutes, they *will* search here. We must get you into the concealed cellar at once."

"But——"

"Attend to me!" said the heavy voice.

Momentarily, while the sea thundered outside, Alan wondered in a dull way what the history of this smuggler, Pierre Somebody, had been. For all his appearance he spoke like a man of culture and education.

"I know exactly what you mean to do tomorrow, if you are strong enough. And you must be strong enough! Your eyes are turning up now: can you hear me?"

"Yes! The devil take Boney!"

"Tomorrow morning you shall have a different horse; that grey one in the stable would be suspected. You must wear the blue-and-buff clothes; the bloodstains are the worst to conceal, but my wife shall try to clean and dry them as well as possible, and the rest you must risk. You cannot ride armed with a sabre into that camp, but I will give you a pistol you can hide under your coat. Even one shot may on occasion be useful. In the meantime, I counsel you, remember your mission and forget this woman of yours at the Park of Statues——"

186

Middle-aged Angèle, who had been looking at Alan, spoke for the first time.

"I will take a message to his woman," she said.

"Fool!" said her husband curtly.

"I will take a message to his woman," said Angèle, "and you shall not stop me. I am well known here; would any suspect me on the road? Am I not acquainted with the secret gate in the wall where the Emperor's distinguished guests," and she sneered, "may bring in their little friends of the opera or the ballet unknown to the sentries at the Park of Statues? I will carry a message; yes!"

Pierre, his hairy hands on his knees, jerked his head towards the window.

"Whatever you do," he snapped, "this young man goes at once into the cellar. If you listen, you will hear them coming along the road to find him now."

That night, in a damp cave of a cellar where the sea-noises had a hollow boom, Alan at first could not sleep at all. He had a touch of fever; images, pain-and-fever-inspired, thronged incessantly behind his eyelids.

He was safe enough there, even when feet trampled above and musket-butts banged the stone roof above his head. He lay in the dark, wrapped in a thick bedgown belonging to Pierre. His watch was so soaked that at first he feared mud or grit had got into its works; but its ticking seemed still to go on reassuringly when, about two in the morning, lantern-light burnt his eyes and he saw Angèle. Her brown hair was drenched and her wet dress plastered to her.

"I have been there. All is well."

"You saw her?"

"All is well," insisted Angèle, kneeling beside him and putting her hand on his forehead. "She had been through much, and they let her sleep. But I spoke to an English lady——"

"An English lady? You mean Lucy Hopewell?"

"To be sure she is English, or I would not have trusted her! I could not understand her well. But in the eyes, in the eyes, you can tell always if they understand you; and she understood. They had a hackney coach, but they sent it away before they knew they would have need of it. Never mind! We have a carriage here. We have not used

187

it in some time; God, what need have we for a carriage here? But tomorrow, when it is safe, it goes to fetch your woman to the Sleeping Cat."

"I can't thank you . . ."

"It is nothing. Now kiss me; I am not young, but kiss me—again!—and sleep until I call you. To defeat your enemies but still to spare them: that is good. Now sleep."

He whirled out into darkness with the words, "Captain Cut-throat," "Captain Cut-throat," "Captain Cut-throat," "Captain Cut-throat" ringing in his head like the sea-noises outside. And he did not open his eyes until the lantern-light blinded him once more as Angèle touched his shoulder.

"It is seven o'clock," she whispered, "and a fine morning. Breakfast is waiting; there is hot water if you would bathe; your clothes are not good, but they will do. There is a test before you today. Make haste!"

That was how, reasonably in his right mind, on a green and fresh-scented and heartening day, he set forth again with a slow but reliable black horse called Gladiator.

It was no doubt during unconsciousness, from that part of the brain which tells us by instinct what is true or false, that Alan knew he had been wrong in his interpretation of those events at the Field of the Balloons: wrong about the murder of the last sentry, wrong about the last and too-garrulous note left behind at the order of Captain Cut-throat.

Wrong, wrong, wrong!

There was something he should have seen about the motives of Joseph Fouché . . .

Never mind!

The strangest and in a way most vaguely disquieting part of the whole three-mile journey, from Pont-de-Briques to the centre of the Boulogne Camp, was that not a soul asked to see his papers or even stopped and questioned him.

In his breast pocket, with a loaded pistol bulging uncomfortably between coat and waistband, he carried the pass signed by General Savary. The map retrieved from Mercier, after memorizing it as well as he could, he had destroyed.

He passed the Park of Statues: where two sentries, different ones from last night, scarcely glanced at him. A little farther on he passed the château of Pont-de-Briques, a grey building looking very much like the Park of Statues. In the courtyard stood a still-beautiful woman who could only be the Empress herself, golden of skin, with heavy-lidded blue eyes and the devil in them, wearing a long gown of white cambric, and laughing amid a group of giggling girls.

The whole place was a-swarm with sentries of the Guard. Sentries were everywhere farther on. But, even when he had taken up a position on rising ground two hundred yards south of the vast parade-ground, with the camp spread out before him and the waters of the Channel glistening beyond the brown line of the cliff-edges straight ahead, there was still no question and no challenge.

Trouble lurking ahead? Disaster waiting in ambush?

The hot blue sky, the accursed breeze blowing steadily seawards—which would only delay the frigate *Medusa* if she appeared this morning—were omens he did not like.

He had no wish to go too close to the parade-ground. This city built on the downs above the Channel, this city of little thatched-roofed houses with street-signs painted up on boards, was divided into streets and avenues; he could shut his eyes and see the map.

Just on his left, as he sat in the saddle on Gladiator's back, the Avenue de la Fédération curved ahead and should eventually come out in an open space beside the Emperor's pavilion. He could see the Emperor's pavilion, about a quarter of a mile ahead. On one side of it rose a gigantic flag-staff for signals to the ships, with no flags on it now; at the other side of the pavilion was a battery of monster mortars—sweet 'uns, the gunners called them—which had their counterparts at Ambleteuse and, according to British information, could carry shells nearly five miles out to sea.

When the proper time came, he could ride along the Avenue de la Fédération to take up his position at the cliff-edge near the pavilion.

That is, if nothing happened.

Meanwhile, this lack of interest in a wandering and hatless civilian might only mean that they were more lax

189

here than they would have been in an English camp. Civilians did often visit the Boulogne arsenal, of course. Or it might mean that all interest had become centred on the review about to begin in splendour on the pennon-decorated Field of Mars.

Certainly most men not on duty of some kind, in this one of the four camps at least, seemed to have gathered round the thick-ranked, motionless regiments into whose hollow oblong—waiting there expectantly—would soon march or ride or haul guns all the triumphant men of Boney's old Italian campaign.

Craning round, Alan could see in the distance a troop of Horse Grenadiers trotting along some unknown street. On the battery of monster guns above the harbour he could see artillery-men, as small as blue-clad ants, lounging as they smoked their pipes and looked back at the parade-ground.

But these were exceptions.

Everywhere about him it was hot and quiet and empty. The Avenue de la Fédération, which according to the notes on Fouché's map, (Fouché, Fouché!) quartered the Emperor's veterans of the Imperial Guard, was as deserted as a street in the ruins of Rome.

There was nothing wrong here! Those veterans of the Guard would be taking part in the parade. They would be . . .

Crash! went the shattering bang of the cymbals, on the first bar of the great marching-song; the pennons streamed out their gold letters; the blue regiments were statues beneath gathering and growing shouts; and the unsteady Alan, despite himself, found his blood beating and his imagination going like a drum as the twenty bands moved and wheeled across his vision.

Yes: Boney knew how to manage it. "You will find honour and fame and glory." That was the lure for all men, amid the band-music and the rainbow dazzle of uniforms, to bear his eagles unflinching from the Baltic to the Nile.

> *At the side of my fair one*
> *How sweet it is to sleep!*

Hullo!
Alan, his head swimming and a throb in his swollen and
190

intensely painful right arm, stood up in the stirrups and blinked to clear his eyesight.

The bands had ceased playing in a sudden dead silence from all onlookers. The bands themselves were wheeling again in a glare of brass, but dissolving so as to clear the open side of the huge hollow oblong. Then it began.

The drums leaped to life with a low, quick rattle, gradually thickening and deepening. First it was a single shout, bursting out. Next, as shakos and bearskins sprang up to twirl round and round in the air on the points of lifted bayonets, the whole mass was split with yelling mouths in one mighty war-whoop that shook the sky above the downs:

"Live the Emperor!"

At the same instant, by a concerted signal, twenty bands crashed out together.

> Come now, ye children of the fatherland:
> The day of glory now is here!
> Against us——

Into the open side of the oblong cantered a small group of horsemen, all wearing cocked hats, and all but one with gold oak-leaves sewn along the seams of their tunics. The single exception rode just ahead of them, in a much smaller cocked hat and a grey coat.

By God, it was Boney himself!

Afterwards Alan Hepburn was amazed at his own amazement. Though he had never seen Boney in person, this was the place of all places, and on this occasion, when he could expect to see the great man. But, in the welter of band-music and colour and emotion, he had forgotten this as much as it had been forgotten by heavily-moustached men, the queues of their hair flapping and gaitered legs a-dance, in a frenzy and delirium of worship.

Even now Alan was too far away to get anything like a good view of him, though the Emperor seemed stouter than he looked in his portraits. You only fancied the flash of the celebrated eyes as the grey-coated little figure rode slowly along the ranks, looking at them before he and his marshals took up their position to review the troops who should march in.

He was riding a white horse: a very tractable one, unlike

191

the horse he rode in pictures, because the Emperor was known as an indifferent horseman and it would never do to have him fall off. At this distance Alan could not even recognize any of the marshals, except Soult by his curved Oriental sword and Ney by his red head.

If only he had——

Sanity, penetrating through the screen of a swimming head and the agony of the stiff right arm, struck Alan awake with the recollection, like physical nausea, of the one obvious thing he had forgotten.

He had forgotten to bring a telescope. He had brought a telescope from Paris in his luggage. Even when he was compelled to leave the Park of Statues, there would still have been time: a seaside inn like the Sleeping Cat would have been certain to have one.

He must have a telescope, to make sure his message was received when the frigate Medusa stood in under all the guns. Even though he had very long eyesight, he could not be certain without that glass.

But he had forgotten it. And there was no time to return for one now. Medusa might even be here this morning; and, though it was not time for her to be sighted just yet, still he could not desert . . .

Here, automatically, he raised his eyes towards the sea ahead.

What he saw, or thought he saw, he at first refused to believe.

It must be his blurred vision, or sun-dazzle on water; in either event, it could only be some distant image which had deceived him. It could not be the English frigate herself: beating to windward slowly, it was true, and yet coming in steadily out towards his left.

But it was.

Pain wrenched his arm again, as his hand flew to the left-hand pocket of his waistcoat, and to the heavy watch with the jewelled fob. His stiff fingers bumped the pistol which was jammed into the left-hand side of the waistband, groping again before they could fix on the watch.

Last night he had hoped, and believed, that rain or mud had not got inside the watchcase and made it go wrong . . .

Its hands pointed to ten minutes past nine, the same as the last occasion on which he had looked at it. The watch had stopped. He had no notion what the real time was.

But he was a quarter of a mile away from the cliff-edge near the Emperor's pavilion, on a horse whose best speed was an indifferent trot; and the ship was standing in closer at every moment.

Chapter XVIII

How an English Ship Broke Out Her Colors

Trying and trying without success to spur Gladiator to a faster pace, riding north along the Avenue de la Fédération towards the cliff-edge and the Emperor's pavilion, Alan found another question vivid in his mind.

What was delaying Boney's artillery in firing at that ship?

As he understood it, Medusa had no sooner to show her figurehead than every gun within reach cut loose at once. And the ship's commander, the irate Captain Bull, who was never told why he must take such punishment without returning it, could only grit his teeth on the quarter-deck.

And yet, except for the continuous cheering and band-music rising up from the (now-hidden) parade-ground towards his right, there was no other sound at all. Not one of the coastal guns had come into action.

He ought to have been glad of it, no doubt. And yet any unknown factor, in a situation bristling with doubts and uncertainties . . .

Ahead of him, in its dust, the Avenue de la Fédération stretched out completely deserted under sun-glare between lines of thatched-roofed houses. Clearly this was a street occupied by old, experienced troops, who liked to make themselves at home wherever they went. The little front-gardens were bright with carefully tended flower-beds. The sanded paths leading to every front door, beyond a knee-high wooden fence to protect the flower-beds, had been decorated with patterns of white sea-shells.

But why no guns?

Since he had ridden down off the hill, Alan could no longer see anything over the roofs except the gigantic flag-staff on the cliff-edge by the pavilion. Then, as the annoyed or stimulated Gladiator suddenly broke into a brisker trot and lifted Alan's hopes, he glanced up at the flag-staff—and understood.

Hitherto that flag-staff, by which the French admiral-in-command sent signals to his own ships, had been completely bare. Now ropes stirred; coloured flags were climbing the staff and cracking out in the breeze.

Ships! And warships at that!

It was no wonder the coastal-batteries were silent. Boney, or his admiral, meant to use warships against an English frigate standing in as close as possible with her guns silent.

But this, surely, could not be possible? Every one of Boney's warships was blockaded somewhere in port or else fleeing from Nelson down the coast of Spain. The British Admiralty knew that; they would permit *Medusa* to flirt with the shore-batteries, where she had at least a chance of escaping, but they would never allow a frigate to sail silent against an approaching warship and certain suicide.

Then what . . . ?

It was a certain remark made by Victor—Victor, the footman at the Park of Statues; Victor, Joseph Fouché's agent—which returned forcibly to Alan now.

"Depend on it, my lord viscount, they will deal with the English ship! . . . If M. Decres cannot spare ships of the line, at least there are enough Imperial gunboats."

Imperial gunboats. That was it.

Ordinarily, of course, no gunboat or even a swarm of them would venture against a heavy frigate: the frigate would blow them out of the water. Yet those gunboats, though small, were very fast and they carried heavy metal: they mounted three twenty-four-pounder guns, as well as two bow-chasers and a stern-chaser. Determinedly used, they could play the devil.

And the French were furious. The French were tired of being insulted. The French Jack Tar, whatever his shortcomings as a seaman, had all the guts of the army. Worse still, so far as Alan's mission was concerned, a sea-fight off Boulogne would raise such a fog of gunsmoke that no message from the cliff could be seen.

From somewhere far ahead of Alan, as he fought against time along the Avenue de la Fédération, echoed out the unmistakable boom of a heavy gun over water, and a cheer which was not among the cheers from the parade-ground.

He could not swear it was the boom of a twenty-four pounder—the frigate mounted only eighteen-pounders—but it was a heavy gun. It did not sound like a shore-gun. If he heard any more . . .

What he did hear, rising up behind his back, was a gallop of hoofs in the dust instead of Gladiator's jog-trotting hoofs, and the calling of a voice through the hot, silent avenue.

"I have got you now, I think," said Lieutenant Hans Schneider.

Flying up at the gallop, between the little houses with their sanded paths and sea-shells, no longer was Schneider the dark-daubed nightmare he had been under the pink-lit sky. He wore a resplendent uniform, a dress uniform as always, and his chestnut-coloured horse was as curried and glossy as though on parade.

But his bony face was pale, he carried his right arm in a sling, and he did not even try to draw the sabre that bumped against the horse's flank. His left hand, lightly carrying the reins, was otherwise empty. What he meant to do, as he touched spurs and came thundering up . . .

"Stand!" yelled Schneider.

Then things happened too fast for the action of Alan's conscious will.

As Schneider raced up and overtook him, sweeping the mare in a curve to avoid Alan and get ahead of him, Alan saw the man's left hand drop the reins and dart across to his right side.

Out from the right-hand saddle holster Schneider brought up his long flintlock pistol. Catching the reins again deftly in the same hand, he wheeled round his horse in a cloud of brownish-white dust. He came face to face with Alan, some twenty feet ahead, as his reins dropped again and Schneider lifted the pistol in his left hand.

Alan's stiff fingers fumbled, but brought his own pistol wrenching out of the waistband just in time. Both weapons whipped up together, their barrels gleaming, some twenty feet apart. Alan, covering his enemy's heart at a point under the silver-braided blue dolman ahead of him, sat stock-still and pulled the trigger.

The lock snapped—and the pistol missed fire with a harmless clack and powder-sputter.

That was all.

196

Then, while Schneider still did not fire, but held his own pistol levelled with a slight triumphant smile spreading across his bony face, the cheers and the band-music grew even louder from the Field of Mars.

(*He is holding that weapon in his left hand, and he may miss even at this distance. Ride straight at him and chance it. Ride——*)

"That was very foolish," rose Schneider's clear, arrogant voice.

(*No! Better still, swing off the horse and charge him on foot. If you can pull him out of the saddle——*)

"Did I say I wished to kill you?" asked Schneider, lifting his blonde eyebrows. "I do not wish even to harm you. Not now."

The words, starkly incredible as they seemed, made Alan stop with all his muscles tense.

"If you mean that . . ." he began.

"I mean it," replied Schneider. "For some time I have been following you, and waving away those who would have stopped or challenged you. An escort, I! Would I have done that, eh, if I meant you harm?"

"I can't tell what you're playing at. But, if that's true, lower your pistol and stand aside!"

"No," said Schneider, with his tightened little complacence. "Not until you make me a promise."

Medusa must be getting closer. Again Alan heard the distant boom of a heavy gun from the sea.

"What promise?"

"Refuge," said Schneider.

"What?"

"Refuge. I cannot say too much, even in an empty street. But, if you go to England," said Schneider, "then *I* go to England in safety. Understood?"

Schneider's rush ahead had carried him over to the side of the little street on Alan's right. Schneider sat erect in the saddle, outwardly unperturbed. And yet Alan's scalp crawled with the verification of what he realized last night must be true.

"So that's it!" he said. "So that's it!"

"Take care!" said Schneider, his face beginning to change and his trigger-finger tightening.

"You are Captain Cut-throat's killer," said Alan. "Two night ago, in all sincerity, I told some friends of mine you

197

were ready to commit more murders at Captain Cut-throat's order. I was wrong: he gave you no such order this time. Last night you killed another sentry on your own account, and deliberately you tried to involve Joseph Fouché. Now you've stopped to wonder what Captain Cut-throat thinks of it; you're frightened to the living soul of you at what he'll do in revenge; and you want refuge in England!"

"Take care, I say!" shouted Schneider. "It was in this street I shot a fool of a guardsman for his insolence to me. You'll get the same if you are insolent. Do I have your promise, or not?"

"No, you bastard!" said Alan, completely losing his head. "You'll get no refuge in England or anywhere else!"

The report of the gunshot, though it would have gone unheard to anyone else under the renewed cheering and band-music, sounded deafening in Alan's ears.

Instinctively he had tightened his body to meet a bullet at twenty feet; instinctively he had flinched and closed his eyes. But his eyes automatically opened; and he saw that Schneider had not even pulled the trigger.

The hammer of the pistol was still back, reared up like a fang; no smoke came from the glistening muzzle. On Schneider's face, under the high dark busby, the look of arrogance was sagging into one of rather stupid astonishment.

There was much strength in the man. Even when the pistol dropped out of his hand, jarred off and exploded in the road so that his horse's legs shivered, he remained steady in the saddle.

Using his good left hand on the saddle-bow he swung slowly down from the horse at the side of the dusty little street. He took a couple of meaningless steps, a magnificent figure in light-blue and silver and red trouser-stripe above the polished boots. But he stumbled against the knee-high wooden fence round one of the little front-gardens. He reeled, swung round, and pitched straight over backwards into a trim bright flower-bed.

Not until then, as Alan himself dismounted and ran over to the garden with its sanded path and sea-shells, did he see—or at least observe—the blood on Schneider's light-blue dolman and tunic.

Ever since Monday night he and Schneider had been seeking each other to settle their differences with sabres. They had exchanged one cut-and-parry. They would never exchange another; Schneider lay on his back, shot dead through the heart in an apparently empty street, by some musket Alan had not even seen.

No movement stirred in the Avenue de la Fédération except some domestic washing, hung out on a line and swaying in the breeze. A little distance away from Schneider's body, in a sanded path, stood a watering-pot painted bright blue.

Then, as Alan looked down at him, the same breeze rolled from the distance a noise of firing: light and heavy guns rumbling over the sea.

The ship, you fool! The ship!

Wake up, wake up, wake . . .

How Alan coaxed the speed he managed from Gladiator, who almost galloped, it is not possible to say. But he measured time less by distance than by the decreasing sound of parade-cheers and band-music from behind him, and the increasing sound of jubilant cheers from in front.

Here it was: pull up!

The large open space round the Emperor's pavilion was totally deserted except for four sentries of the Marine Guard, oblivious to anything except their duties, pacing inside the head-high palings of the pavilion-fence.

Alan, pulling up Gladiator, looked round quickly. He had expected to see naval officers at the foot of the giant flag-staff. But the signals had been hoisted; whoever hoisted them had hurried away to Admiral Bruix's smaller pavilion towards the right. Telescopes bristled there; men gesticulated. But nobody glanced at the newcomer.

Alan dismounted and ran to the edge of the cliff, with the wind singing behind him. Above the roar of cheering from the beaches below, he could hear voices from the direction of the admiral's pavilion.

"Remark it, now! Remark how close the little gunboats go!"

"It is magnificent, that!"

"Magnificent, yes! But why don't the goddams fire?"

Fully twelve Imperial gunboats, well spaced out behind each other, with the wind behind them and slightly on their port quarter, were swooping down on the frigate and pouring fire at her before veering off and coming round in a slow circle to do it again.

As Alan watched, the leading gunboat let drive with her first bow-chaser, then the second; going round to starboard, she brought to bear one of her big twenty-four pounders. The heavy gun-shock blended with a concussion like the flat smack of an enormous palm against water. *Medusa* took the round-shot full across her forward bulwarks. But not once did she falter, or cease to come in slowly and doggedly against the wind.

That wind had delayed her just long enough. Within half a minute she would be close enough for a man with a telescope, on her deck, to see Alan's signals from the cliff. If the smoke were not too thick, if the smoke . . . !

Whack! and *whack!* went the bow-chasers of another gunboat; then the hollower boom of the twenty-four pounder. *Medusa*, her crew piped to battle-stations but still showing no colours, took all three shots in her hull and steadily came on.

The sun danced through a smoke-haze which blew and lifted over grey-green water. Alan raced along the edge of the cliff until he had his back towards the seaward side of the fence round the pavilion. There, where his blue coat and buff waistcoat would show up most conspicuously, he could not raise his arms or he would have been a conspicuous target at once. But he lifted the stiff fingers of his right hand as high as he dared.

And it was worth the try, though he could hear a sentry of the Marine Guard pacing inside the fence within a dozen feet of him. He was almost sure he caught the sun-flash of three telescopes aboard *Medusa*, just as she staggered before another blast of fire.

One single letter, now . . .

The letter X if Boney would invade Britain, the letter Y if he had abandoned the project.

And the letter Y was the most conspicuous of them all. Right hand uplifted, three fingers folded under, thumb and little finger up, Alan gave the signal with the right hand, with the left, with the right again.

"Are they insane, these goddams? Or have they no powder or shot?"

"She is holed again; I think she is listing!"

"If the little boats could elevate their guns to smash her masts——"

BONEY IS——

No, thought Alan desperately as his fingers flew; that was not compressed enough for what he had to say. He must do it in three words before the thickening smoke . . .

BONEY COUNTERMARCHING AUSTRIA.

"Grand God, she is not still coming on?"

"There is something strange about this! I tell you there is! If you ask me——"

BONEY COUNTERMARCHING AUSTRIA. BONEY COUNTERMARCHING AUSTRIA. BONEY——

Alan, even as his fingers obeyed him in repeating those letters over and over, found his whole body trembling like that of a man with malaria. He had practised the alphabet so much that the letters formed themselves with automatic motion. Glancing to his left, he saw the blue-uniformed artillerymen on the battery of monster guns yelling at each other as they pointed towards Medusa. Glancing to the right, he saw the wink of brass telescopes also concentrated on the struggling frigate.

Incredible as it seemed, nobody had observed him.

BONEY COUNTERMARCHING AUSTRIA. BONEY——

But had the ship received his message? That was what he could not tell, if he sent it a hundred times. With his own folly to blame, in not remembering a telescope, he would still live hours, days, perhaps all the short time he had to live, without ever learning . . .

Then Alan stood rigid, and his hands dropped amid the blowing gunsmoke and the howling voices from shore. Medusa was going about on her course.

And signal-flags broke from her; and Alan, cursing his own stupidity again for failing to remember something in his favour instead of against him, read the clear news they carried to him over the grey-green water.

MESSAGE RECEIVED.

Then Medusa had done it. She had stood in, against every obstacle and every ill-star of bad luck, and had won after all.

'Now clear out!' he was silently urging her. 'Get away, you ruddy fools, while still there is time. Those gunboats are coming in again . . .'

'She is on fire!'

"No!"

"I tell you, she is on fire! Look through this glass! It is not a bad blaze, but it is there!"

No, Alan thought, it was not a bad blaze. She could still get away; she ought to get away; she must with any sense in her head get away.

But, even as he thought so, more than the news sent by the signal-flags occurred to him. Only Medusa's captain could give him a message with naval signals. This time the captain knew his mission; he knew, now, it had been fulfilled; and he knew his time of punishment was over.

'Get away, you fools!' cried Alan's silent voice. 'You're in no fit state to——'

He could not hope to hear the boatswain's pipe. But even at that distance, across water, he could hear her crew begin to cheer. Her colours climbed and broke out. Above the smoke flew the Cross of St. George. And Medusa—listing, crippled, and on fire—wheeled in her tracks to fight.

Many of her guns were out of action, their crews dead or helpless. But, as the ragged crash of her first broadside reverberated out over the water, a split-second after the blossoming of gunsmoke and gun-flashes, the tone and tempo of the yells from shore abruptly altered. Even that ragged broadside caught the gunboats racing in.

The cries from shore became howls of another kind. All the attackers veered off, except two determined gunboats which still charged at her like hounds at a boar. Round swung Medusa, to give them the weight of her other broadside—just as a last wild twenty-four-pounder shot opened her hull at the water-line. The other broadside smashed out; smoke extinguished everything; one of the gunboats blew up; and presently, as the haze began to lift, they could see the other gunboat as only wreckage. Medusa, with the smoke-foam round her jaws, hung there waiting.

Still she waited in challenge, firing no shot, until the heaving water was empty except for wreckage, and not a sail stirred out against her. Then, with the wind at her back, she shouldered round painfully and stood out to sea while nearly every coastal gun opened fire after her.

The din of the firing deafened hearing and deadened senses. In the low-town, spread out like a map, you could

202

barely distinguish the four forts for the gusts of their own batteries.

But the cannonade did not go on for many minutes. First at intervals, then abruptly, it died away to dead silence.

In a clear sea stung with light-points, *Medusa* was sinking. Rescue-boats from the shore were already putting out to pick up survivors.

And Alan, sick at heart, stood on the cliff with his head down.

He could not, he discovered, move the fingers of his right hand or even his arm. But this did not trouble him.

"Why didn't you get away?" he cried. "You had time to get away! That message will never be delivered. It was all for nothing."

He did not know that he had spoken aloud, bitterly and in French, until another voice struck at him from not far away on his right.

"Yes," said this new voice with a thin, savage harshness, "it has all been for nothing. And that was because it is war."

Alan looked round.

On the eight-foot-wide path, between the edge of the cliff and the palings of the pavilion, stood Joseph Fouché. In his rusty black coat with the pewter buttons, in the pepper-and-salt trousers as usual, he loomed up lean and frail under a high chimney-pot hat with a badly brushed nap; and his snuff-box was in his hand.

A little distance behind him, near the edge of the cliff where the track descended to the low-town, was drawn up an open carriage whose green-and-gold panel on this side bore a flaming letter N. Ida de Sainte-Elme, in cloak and bonnet, was climbing down out of the carriage and following the Minister of Police.

Contempt for himself was printed on Fouché's withered face.

"Dull-wit that I am!" he said, and rapped his knuckles against the lid of the snuff-box. "To have had the evidence before me, in the record I read out to your wife on Monday night, and yet never to have suspected the sign-language until Madame de Sainte-Elme told me you would try to signal a ship! Dull-wit that I am!"

"I have been expecting you," said Alan.

Again the Minister of Police struck the lid of the snuff-box.

"That is just as well," he said. "The game is finished, M. Hepburn. Your course is run."

Chapter XIX

The Craft of the Serpent

And yet still, ironically, Alan's presence on the edge of the cliff had attracted nobody's attention.

Perhaps it was not so strange as he thought. Though few persons in the Grand Army knew the Minister of Police by sight, the presence of an Imperial carriage near the pavilion was reassurance enough when one of the carriage's occupants—in this case, Fouché himself—approached and spoke with apparent casualness to a hatless stranger looking out over the sea.

Alan, now that the whole game had ended, was in the dull state of mind wherein the attention will occupy itself with trifles.

Behind him he heard the steady, inexorable footfalls of a Marine guardsman, in dark blue with orange facings and trouser-stripes under the bearskin cap, going past and fading away. There reared up the narrow side of the high, grey-painted pavilion itself. Two of its corners, on this side, were enclosed in glass so that the Emperor could look out over the camps or over the sea.

The glass corners, he noted with great and detached care, were heavily muffled in curtains. Ah, yes! On this occasion Boney had been staying at Pont-de-Briques; he had not visited the pavilion at all. And Alan's mind, like a fly, buzzed slowly and heavily round this point—as though it mattered.

But, if he was in a detached state, Joseph Fouché was not.

"God strike me dead," muttered the atheist Minister of Police. "God strike me dead!"

Ida de Sainte-Elme, in a long-sided bonnet with upstanding scarlet plumes and a long-sleeved flapping pelisse whose red-and-black velvet reached to her ankles, braved the whirling wind to hurry and stand at Fouché's side.

205

"Don't blame Alan!" Ida burst out. "Blame that damned wife of his, who deliberately drugged me! Or blame those Americans, now that you've got them all under guard at the Park of Statues. Didn't you know he would try to communicate with the English?"

"I knew he might try," said Fouché. "I did not think he could succeed."

Again Ida, with vehemence, wagged the blowing plumes of her bonnet towards Alan.

"But he has not succeeded!" she said. "He has most miserably failed!"

"He has failed, dear lady, through no fault or planning of his own."

"What is the matter with you? I have seen you angry before, but never have I seen you so angry as this! What is the matter?"

"You do not know?" enquired the Minister of Police. "You do not know?"

Then, controlling himself with the usual bloodless impression he gave, and with his face withering and sharpening to a set, sardonic expression, he surveyed Alan from head to foot.

"Well, M. Hepburn!"

Alan tried hard to summon up a sardonic grin in reply, but he felt too sick and exhausted; he could not manage it.

"Well, M. Fouché!" he said.

"Then from the beginning," snapped the Minister of Police, "you never intended to find Captain Cut-throat at all!"

"Come, dear sir!" said Alan. "This is no time for rogues like ourselves to fall out. You never intended from the beginning that I should find him. Your game was, and still is, to have me caught by yourself and executed as Captain Cut-throat, to resound in praise of your cleverness and ability as supreme police-chief."

Fouché's red-rimmed eyes narrowed.

"You knew that?" he asked softly. "How did you know it?"

"Well, my friend! You have an excellent espionage-service. Don't underestimate ours."

Rap went the bony knuckles on the snuff-box.

"Be good enough to answer me!" said Fouché, thrusting

forward his long and snake-like neck so that the tall hat wagged. "I do not ask you to betray any accomplices. Your position cannot be worse, I solemnly assure you, than it is now. So it can do no harm to tell me. How did you know?"

Alan pressed his left hand over his eyes.

"At a time like this——!" he protested. "What's the good of——?"

"*How?*"

"For months and months," replied Alan, "you have been saying a certain thing, not in jest but in sober earnest, to the one person on earth you really trust. If you ever put hands on this unknown X, this spy who had been troubling you and Talleyrand for so long, you said you would employ him somehow in your own service."

There was a curious expression on Fouché's face, but he did not comment.

Alan looked wryly at the smouldering eyes of Ida de Sainte-Elme.

"Long before the question of Captain Cut-throat ever came up," he said, "I had certain instructions. During a happy night of love with a charmer who shall be nameless . . . Oh, what difference does it make now?"

It was Ida, her nostrils distended, who spoke then. "Continue!" she said.

"Well! I was told to leave my despatch-box unlocked. Then I was told to go away and keep myself out of sight, as though I had taken fright and gone into hiding. When I returned, they told me, I should be arrested and called on to enter your service."

Fouché looked as withered as an idol.

"All this is nothing!" he said. "I was asking you——"

"Very well!" Alan retorted. "During the week I was in hiding, the Captain Cut-throat murders began. From the very first it was rumoured—ask anyone here at Boulogne! —that you would be called in to investigate. You heard that. So did our agents. You insist on knowing this?"

"Yes!"

"While I was in hiding," said Alan, "you were already looking for me to arrest me. Our people told me that very possibly, when I went back to have myself arrested, I might be called on for a different role. Originally the game had only been to have one of our men as an agent in the enemy's camp. Now I might find myself in the enemy's camp in a quite literal and far more important sense. And you insist on hearing how they knew I might be sent to find Captain Cut-throat? It was because, to this one person on earth you really trust, you had already confided a beautiful plan."

Now that it was no longer of any use to the frigate *Medusa*, the wind had begun to change.

It whipped and blew round the corner of the cliff-edge, fluttering out Ida's plumes and her red-and-black pelisse. It stirred even the badly brushed nap of Fouché's hat. But both of them stood rigid, and neither noticed.

The Minister of Police did not speak; it almost seemed that he could not.

"The one person he trusts?" cried Ida, with contemptuous amazement. "*This* inhuman vulture trusts anybody? To whom did he tell it, then? In whom did he confide? From whom did your own accursed secret-agents learn it?"

Alan looked at Fouché.

"I would not have told you," he said quietly, "if you had not guessed before you asked me. Yes. It was your wife, the lady you call Bonne Jeanne."

The Minister of Police did not move or even blink. He stood rigidly, holding the snuff-box. But out from behind the red-rimmed eyes, for a disturbing instant, peered a stricken human being.

And Alan saw it.

"Reassure yourself," Alan said with curt bitterness. "The lady is quite virtuous; and she would never think of telling your secrets to anyone. But she has a passion for cream-ices and gossip with female friends. She did not think this plan of yours was at all important; and, originally, it wasn't. Reassure yourself, then!"

Joseph Fouché looked down at the snuff-box. Carefully, with his long corpse-like fingers, he put away the box in the tail-pocket of his coat.

"M. Hepburn," he said, after a pause, "I thank you."

But Alan, out of pain and weariness, only snarled at him.

"Thank you for nothing!" he said. "Your plan very soon became important, didn't it? I went back to Paris and was arrested on the night of the 20th. The very same night, you received the message you expected from the Emperor; but

208

a far more difficult order than you ever expected. 'Find Captain Cut-throat in seven days.'

"You knew that was virtually impossible. But the Emperor expects to be obeyed; it would go very badly with you if you failed him. It never mattered to you one sou who Captain Cut-throat really was. All you wanted was a scapegoat, somebody who could be proved to everybody's satisfaction as an English agent stabbing sentries in the pay of Pitt. And you could produce the victim instantly, as evidence of your great acuteness. Isn't that true?"

"Yes," said the Minister of Police calmly.

Alan, now, was pouring out words before he could stop himself.

"The mouse," he said, "was in your hands. You could let him run a little way, just a little way, before the cat jumped. 'See!' you could then say. 'I suspected all the time this Vicomte de Bergerac was Captain Cut-throat; I gave him the chance to betray himself, so heavily guarded he could never hurt us in the least; and now, behold, he *has* betrayed himself. Kill him; give me the credit!'—Isn't that true?"

"Yes," said the Minister of Police calmly.

"Never mind!" said Alan. "Because what difference does it make? The full details I don't know and never knew ..."

"No," observed the Minister of Police, pursing his lips. "You have not fathomed them all. I flatter myself," and his eyes opened wide, "they were more effective than you think. Except for an indiscretion of my wife——!"

Ida de Sainte-Elme began to laugh.

"Your wife!" she said. "The master of destinies, who uses all other people's women to suit his own ends——!"

Now Fouché did move. He spoke softly and even agreeably, but his voice choked off Ida's laughter in mid-burst.

"I invite you, dear lady, to have a care."

"But it *is* comical, don't you think?"

"No," said the Minister of Police.

"I'm sorry!" said Alan, who had now gained control of himself and felt hot with shame. "I shouldn't have burst out like that, Minister. I walked into your trap with my eyes open; there's no complaint about what happened. Now let's get this over with!—and I'll try to be a good loser."

Wind whistled round the cliff. Fouché, high-shouldered, regarded him with steady and curious red-rimmed eyes. Fouché spoke all in one inflection.

"A good loser," he said. "The English. God strike me dead."

"Well, what do you want me to say?" demanded Alan. "Is there any reason why you and I should hold anything against each other?"

"Alan, *I* hold nothing against you!" Ida said impulsively. She hesitated, she even softened, when her enemy was white-faced and defeated. "If there is anything *I* can do——?"

"Yes! If they'll let me see Madeleine before——"

"You want to see her, do you?" screamed Ida.

"Oh, God," said Alan, "why can't we all behave as we should behave, instead of acting like a lot of children as soon as our pride is touched? And you, Minister of Police! Now that I seem to be again in your loving care, what will happen? Where are you taking me?"

"We are going to the pavilion," said Fouché imperturbably.

"What pavilion?"

"The Emperor's pavilion," replied Fouché, raising his eyebrows, "which not surprisingly you will see just behind you. Very shortly, dear sir, you will meet the man you are pleased to call 'Boney.' Calling him 'Boney' is not a liberty I myself should care to take with the Emperor. Still!——"

Alan's head was swimming once more.

"Look here, need there be all this mummery? You've got me; but need you parade your captive in chains like a prisoner in a Roman triumph?"

"Yes," Fouché said very sharply. "Yes, I must! I have promised the Emperor that this morning, without fail, I will introduce him to Captain Cut-throat. His Majesty will be surprised, I feel, when he learns who has really been trying to destroy his Grand Army. Nevertheless, I must——"

"No!" said Alan. "And I'm damned if I submit to it. I am guilty of espionage; I have never denied that. But I am not Captain Cut-throat. You know I'm not. If you think you are going to show off, as usual, by airily exhibiting me as the victim of your bow and spear . . ."

The Minister of Police looked straight at him.

"How do you know what I am going to do?" he asked.

Fouché did not shout these words, of course. With his weak throat, he would have been incapable of shouting anything.

And yet, as he drew himself up with wide open eyes and the frozen-blooded expression which could make even Ida de Sainte-Elme shiver, the effect was just as though he had shouted.

This game was not finished. Something else—not worse, of course; it could not be worse than what had happened already—but something lurked round the corner or waited to spring from ambush. The Minister of Police would still take his pleasure in another ace-up-the-sleeve.

The wind whooped at his seedy clothes and his broken-down hat. As though conscious for the first time that they were standing in a somewhat breezy spot, as perhaps he was conscious of it for the first time, the Minister of Police looked round testily and touched Ida's arm.

"You, dear lady, shall go with us."

"I?" exclaimed Ida, evidently astonished. "To the pavilion?"

"Come, dear lady. It will not be the first time that a person of the female persuasion has visited the pavilion in secret. And this sudden maidenly modesty, I feel, sits most strangely on your bonnet. Accompany me, if you please!"

He was already impelling her back along the path towards the open space, and the stunned Alan could only follow.

"But the pavilion is closed!" Ida was protesting. "The Emperor is at some review or other (I can hear the music now, can't you?); and those reviews always go on for hours!"

"Dear lady, this matter is of such importance that to find Captain Cut-throat, and end the threat to his Army, the Emperor would leave the side of military glory itself. He has promised to leave the end of the review to—well, no, not to his Commander-in-Chief, but to his friend Marshal Berthier. You enjoy conflict, I believe?"

"Conflict?"

"The lust of battle," said Fouché, with benevolent tenderness, "is never very far from your eyes? Be of good cheer, then! Very shortly, madame, I promise you such

211

a scene of conflict as you are unlikely to view very often! Ah, here we are!"

They had emerged into the open space, and turned right towards the open gate in the fence round the pavilion. Just outside the gate ran a long wooden hitching-rail to which was tethered a horse with a very plain saddle. Inside the gate, talking to a Marine sentry, was an unobtrusive-looking man in fine but very sober dark clothes with white wrist-ruffles.

"Sir," he addressed the Minister of Police, with an uneasy eye and a worried forehead, "I have the Emperor's order that you are to be permitted inside, and His Majesty will join you presently. But there is no one in the pavilion to receive you; the curtains have not even been drawn back on the windows, and——"

"My dear M. de Meneval," said Fouché at his most courteous, "that will do admirably! We want as little attention attracted as possible and no crowd round us. Let the curtains stay closed, by all means. There are lights?"

"Yes, yes, I left a candelabrum burning in the foyer. But I am riding out to the parade-ground now," the man addressed as M. de Meneval nodded towards the horse, "and where shall I tell His Majesty he will find you?"

"The council-room will be best suited to the matter, I think. I have the honour, sir, to present you to Madame Ida de Sainte-Elme and my lord the Vicomte de Bergerac."

"Enchanted, enchanted! But, sir, sir, precisely what is happening here?"

Fouché turned to Ida and Alan.

"Precede me," he invited.

The Marine sentry saluted. As they went up a gravelled path to a door in the long side of the pavilion, Alan had time only to see past the cook-house and the fence a small ornamental lake on which floated two black swans. Then they were inside, and Fouché had closed the door behind them.

The tall, gaudy foyer, dark except for a branch of five candles burning on a table, smelt heavily stuffy and musty. Picking up the candelabrum, Fouché led the way with echoing footsteps towards a door of a room which, if its curtains were opened, would have faced out on the sea and, from one angle, towards the cliffs of Dover in the distance.

212

"That," explained the Minister of Police, closing the door of this room behind them, "was the Emperor's private secretary as opposed to his official secretary, General Duroc. He is discreet; but we do not want him now."

Neither Ida nor Alan paid attention. They were in the eagle-eyrie of the Emperor.

The large, lofty room, which dwarfed the light of the five candles, was as full of the Emperor's presence as though he had already arrived.

Its walls, papered in silver-grey, had no ornament except a big red-coloured map of the English ports and the French ports on either side of the Channel. But the painted ceiling created a somewhat spectacular effect: against an azure sky, an eagle in clouds of authentic gold-leaf represented the Emperor being directed by his star to hurl a thunderbolt at England.

"Now!" said Joseph Fouché.

He went to a large oval table, its top covered in green baize. Aside from one plain chair, upholstered with green morocco and set against the table, it was the only piece of furniture here.

"Now!" repeated the Minister of Police, putting down the jumpy lights on the table and removing his tall hat, which he placed beside the candelabrum. "Now at last I can do what I have promised myself. I can give myself the luxury, for once, of speaking freely and honestly."

Ida was looking more and more uneasily round the room of threat and power.

"But what," she challenged him, "is there to speak freely and honestly about? Even if the serpent wishes to do so?"

"The serpent does indeed wish to do so." Fouché, pushing the chair to one side and standing at one end of the green-covered oval table, looked at Alan. "In much of what you said a while ago, concerning the design to convict you as Captain Cut-throat——"

"Are you telling me I was wrong?"

"Not at all. You were right. But I do not think," said Fouché, rubbing the palms of his hands together with a dry rustling noise, "you appreciate how complete was the case against you. You are an Englishman, the best choice for the role. Since my own agents had been looking for you without success during the week of August 13th to

213

19th inclusive, you could have had a perfectly fair trial without being able to prove you were not at Boulogne stabbing sentries."

"I understand that, thanks!"

"Do you?" enquired Fouché. "Everything, I wonder? As exhibits in the affair, I presented you with one of the daggers and one of the notes signed by Captain Cut-throat. Those meant nothing, nor did the pass I was obliged to give you. But this was only to conceal something else I gave you."

"If you mean——"

"I mean a complete map of this camp. As a British agent, you would have tried to make use of it. You would never have mentioned to anyone that you had it. Found in your pocket, as it was meant to be found, it would have damned you past hope. It is probably in your pocket at this minute——"

"That's where you're wrong!" said Alan. "Was I gull enough not to suspect that map? I invented an excuse to produce it so that Mercier could take it away from me. When I got it back, because I had to have it, I destroyed it as soon as I'd memorized it. But what's the good of repeating all this, I keep telling you? You've caught your mouse. Why do you keep prolonging the torture? I knew I couldn't hope to counter every move you made: very well! Let it go at that. If you'll just accept my assurance that Madeleine is innocent, then bring on your guard and execute me before I lose my nerve!"

The Minister of Police raised his red eyebrows.

"And who," he enquired, "who said you were going to be executed at all?"

Ida's gasp, as she backed away from the table went unheard by Alan.

Alan, about to demand what sort of new cat-and-mouse tactics were being employed, saw that Fouché was in earnest and meant what he said. Alan saw it, but he could not believe it.

"You and your wife,"—the bloodless lips were moving with precision,—"had intended to take a boat which puts in at the coast tonight. That is so, is it not?"

"Yes! But . . ."

"You are assisted by Pierre de Lautrec, a professor of philosophy at the Sorbonne during the days of the Revolution, once an acquaintance of mine and now the keeper of an inn near Condette. Am I, Joseph Fouché, completely ignorant of what goes on in these dominions under my very nose? You and your wife, I say, had intended to take that boat tonight. Very well! You shall take the boat as you intended; and whoever attempts to stop you will do so at his cost. I have said it."

Alan's first impression was that exhaustion, and the pain of his wounded arm, might have touched his brain or turned his senses. His gaze went up to the eagle and the thunderbolt against the azure ceiling. He looked down again at the withered, malignant face, hung there over the candle-flames with long neck extended, as though the Minister of Polce were condemning him to death instead of . . .

Instead of . . .

"You are giving me my life?" Alan shouted. "You are setting Madeleine free, too?"

"Have I not said it?"

"But what's the reason for this generosity?"

"Generosity?" repeated Fouché, with contempt. "Dear sir, I cannot afford generosity. It comes too expensive. If I do this, believe me, I have motives of my own."

"Anyway, how can you do it? Won't the Emperor himself be here at any minute?"

"He will."

"Then how can you explain everything that's happened, especially with me here? Haven't you promised to produce the real Captain Cut-throat?"

"I have."

"And can you produce Captain Cut-throat?"

"Of course."

"Thunder of God!" said Ida de Sainte-Elme. As though to get rid of a weight stifling her, she unfastened and took off her elaborate bonnet. Off came the pelisse as well, showing her in a red-and-black day-dress which seemed to heighten the tawny flush on her cheek-bones. Bonnet and pelisse were flung on the table.

"Thunder of God!" said Ida. "I counted myself equal to most occasions; but you, dear Minister, will remain double-faced and unpredictable until Judgment Day. Whatever trick you are planning here . . ."

"If I let this man go, Madame de Sainte-Elme," said

215

Fouché softly, "have you any cause to speak of it afterwards?"

"I—I have nothing against Alan, now that he has so miserably failed in his mission! I have never wanted to see him shot! But what I have to tell the Emperor about that woman, which I will do as soon as he gets here . . ."

Fouché smiled, showing his bad teeth.

"Dear lady," he said, still softly, "you will tell the Emperor nothing about her. Considering what I know of your past, are you in any position to dictate terms to me?"

"No, perhaps not!"

"Ah."

"And yet Alan is right in one thing! What do you propose to say to the Emperor? You must find explanations for him. What can you tell him?"

"The truth," said Fouché, looking at her curiously.

"Truth, truth, truth!"

"You would speak of jesting Pilate?"

"I am more likely to speak of jesting Judas, dear Minister, who is nobody but yourself! Why do you set these people free? What is your motive?"

"Ah, yes. My motive."

The Minister of Police's tone remained agreeable. His nostrils were pinched as Alan had seen them before. Slowly, very slowly, he reached to the back of his coat and took out the snuff-box, which he weighed in his left hand.

"There is much," he said, "that I consider only a part of life. There is much I can watch with indifference if not positive amusement. There are, however, certain things which annoy one of even my philosophical temper, and which I do not permit at all. I will not have my intelligence mocked. Nor will I have all my best efforts met only with betrayal.

"Various persons, in this affair, have made various blunders. But the greatest blunder of all was made by the so-called Captain Cut-throat. It was very fortunate last night that I was well on my way to Boulogne when I received a semaphore-message at Amiens. I was on my way, of course——"

Here the red-rimmed eyes moved to Alan.

"I was on my way, of course," said Fouché, "to expose you as Captain Cut-throat before you could do any great harm. The message I received, from one of my agents in

216

this camp, caused me to continue my journey all night in a state of annoyance which I shall not attempt to describe. Do you begin to understand, M. Hepburn?"

"No!"

"You do not?" asked Fouché, raising his eyebrows. "And yet last night, at the Field of the Balloons, another murder was committed. Let it be so: I am not disturbed at that. But, when he caused this last murder to be committed, Captain Cut-throat was guilty of a truly memorable error. Captain Cut-throat allowed a paid agent to leave a note implicating me. And that, dear sir, is not done with impunity."

Ida was frantic.

"But in what way," she screamed, "does this affect what you have to tell the Emperor? Why should he care whether Captain Cut-throat tried to implicate you?"

The Minister of Police rapped his knuckles on the snuff-box.

"Because the Emperor himself is Captain Cut-throat," he said. "And I am prepared to prove it before the whole Grand Army."

Chapter XX

The Justice of the Emperor

During a long silence, while the candle-flames shone steadily on silver-grey walls in a curtained, airless room, the only person who seemed unmoved was the malignant Fouché.

"This affair," he went on, taking snuff, "presents a curious problem in ethics. How far is the head of an auto-cratic state justified in doing technical evil if he really thinks good will come of it? How far may he go in cynically ordering the deaths of a few men for what he believes is to the benefit of his whole people?

"It is true, since he believes himself inspired by his star or his destiny to rule the world, he need not hesitate or blame himself. It is further undeniable, in this case at least, that the Emperor has technical right on his side: he could say with truth that he was justified; and, in fact, was only administering justice.

"Every one of five sentries, those who died between the 13th and the 19th August, was a malcontent and a trouble-maker, a danger to the Army, possibly even a member of the Olympian Society. By strict letter of military law, they could have been tried and condemned to death: that was why they were chosen as victims. In any court of all Christendom, if any court existed to try him, His Majesty could arise with truth and passion and prove himself free of all blood-guilt. Nevertheless, I feel, it does not quite solve the problem presented by . . ."

Here Fouché broke off, regarding the others in some impatience.

"Come!" he added. "Come, M. Hepburn! Surely you suspected that the Emperor himself was Captain Cut-throat?"

"No! I did not!"

"Tchaa," said the Minister of Police. "You disappoint me. Now I suspected it almost from the beginning."

"But——"

"I had formed a higher opinion of your intelligence, M. Hepburn. In the Room of Mirrors, indeed, there was one point when you said you knew where to find the assassin; for an instant I thought you might have discovered the whole design, and I feared my face had betrayed me. Then I saw you must suspect only Schneider, the obvious agent, and not the less obvious employer behind him. So I was content to let you imagine you were still outwitting me."

The Minister of Police frowned.

"It is true," he conceded, "that in the matter of the sign-language you did outwit me. You very nearly succeeded in that, and I ought to make you pay dearly for it. However! I overlook it because you failed to see the identity of the real Captain Cut-throat . . ."

"But the Emperor," said Alan, "was the one person who had no reason to be Captain Cut-throat!"

"On the contrary," replied Fouché, "he was the one person who had every reason to be Captain Cut-throat, if we disregard the cloak with which his dramatic gestures and his theatrical skill surround everything he does."

"Listen!" said Alan. "This revolutionary secret-society! In England we had good evidence that the society called the Olympians really existed ..."

"And so it does," said Fouché, sharply rapping the lid of the snuff-box. "It very much exists, as I assured your wife. That was why our gracious Emperor was compelled to invent 'Captain Cut-throat' at a critical time. Would you care to hear the points you seem to have missed?"

"Wait! Wait! Wait!" gabbled Ida de Sainte-Elme.

Ida, again like a madwoman, was alternately peering round the lofty room with its thunderbolt painted on the ceiling, and then over her shoulder at the door to the foyer.

"Do you realize," said Ida, striking her fist on the green-covered table, "that the Emperor himself will enter by that door at any moment now?"

"And how else should he enter, dear lady?"

"You propose to tell him all this?"

Fouché bared his bad teeth.

"It will please me much to do so," he answered. "You must forgive me if, a while ago in the hearing of a Marine Guard sentry behind the pavilion-fence, I was obliged to deceive both of you about the identity of Captain Cut-throat. However! I promised you a scene of conflict; and, believe me, you shall have one."

"Oh, thunder of God!" breathed Ida—not as a curse, but almost as a prayer. "You can't do it!" she cried. "You mustn't! You daren't!"

"Indeed, dear lady? And what is it that I, Joseph Fouché, dare not do?"

He looked at her steadily, lifting the red eyebrows as he again opened the lid of the snuff-box, and his mouth twisted. The diamond letter "N" glittered against his grubby shirt-front. Then, controlling himself, he glanced at Alan.

"I do not think, dear sir," he went on in a conversational tone, "you quite understand the character of His Most Gracious Majesty. In his own way, I suppose we must admit, he is a great man. He is not even, in his heart, what the world would call a bad man. But he is guided by his

219

star, by his Corsican impulses, and by a certain bad taste. He does things which are worse than crimes; they are blunders.

"One of these things, last year, was his treatment of the young Duc d'Enghien. This hapless and indeed not over-bright youth had committed no crime and was not plotting anything. The young Duc d'Enghien was not even living in France. His only offence lay in being an aristocrat, representing the old Bourbon monarchy. And so, to set an example in case the royalists should go on plotting against the new régime, our Emperor had this young man kidnapped across the French border, summarily tried at night, and shot in a ditch at Vincennes."

Again taking snuff, coldly and implacably when he spoke of any blunder, the Minister of Police made a grimace.

"As it occurred with the royalists last year," he said, "so it occurred with the republicans this year. The Emperor, here at Boulogne and obsessed with his plan for invading England, found himself opposed by strong elements of republicanism among his marshals and generals. They were not murderers, it is true; but they were men of dangerous influence. Marshal Augereau, who nine years ago saved His Majesty's reputation when the Emperor's courage failed him before the battle of Castiglione! General Oudinot, who should have been made a marshal but for some reason has been overlooked! I spare you the whole list. Nevertheless, as I pointed out to Madame Hepburn, this agitation against the Empire reached its height not over a fortnight ago—well before the middle of August.

"Now then! Since your expression appears strange, dear sir, shall I be definite? Shall I tell you why, when the full evidence came into my hands on August 21st, I knew Captain Cut-throat could be nobody but the Emperor?"

"Yes!" said Alan.

"No!" said Ida. "Listen!" she added, wringing her hands. "Don't you hear horses approaching this pavilion now?"

"You hear only the wind, madame. It will be ten minutes at least before His Majesty can . . ."

"But when I think of his face coming in at that door——!"

"Endeavour to be tranquil, dear lady; you enjoy conflict, I think?"

220

With great nicety Fouché closed the lid of the snuff-box and addressed Alan.

"Two things, from the beginning," he pursued, "seemed to me completely incredible. Thus. Five murders had been committed in seven nights; three daggers and five scraps of paper, signed as by 'Captain Cut-throat,' had been left behind as very clumsy evidence—apparently it did not deceive you, so I need not repeat it—that the murderer must be an Englishman. The Emperor, presumably with no time to trouble about this, turned it all over to me.

"Now there is one habit of His Majesty as notorious as his habit of wearing a cocked hat or indulging in dramatic gestures. It is this: he cannot keep his own hands off anything. He must see all, know all, direct all, from the placing of the guns in a battery to the kind of pictures that are painted on a corridor-wall at the Park of Statues."

Once more the Minister of Police's anger simmered, as his face hung above the candle-flames in the curtained and airless room which might have been his own office.

"Yet I was asked to believe," he said, "that for a whole week, while sentries were being killed and notes and daggers were accumulating, the Emperor never once looked at the daggers or applied his own acumen to the notes. Never once! I was asked to believe he left all this to the faithful but not-very-competent Savary; and, at the end of the week when the most fantastic 'ghost-murder' had taken place, he then turned it all over to me without further concern.

"Tchaa!" said Fouché, making a sudden movement which completely terrified Ida. "Am I a babe in arms, then, to be deceived by this?

"One other thing I was also asked to believe. Somebody—and none could tell where or how the rumour began—had started one of those camp-rumours which can run like fire. This rumour said that 'Captain Cut-throat's activities might incite mutiny against the Emperor. Our troops did not give themselves pause to think. They simply repeated the news, as people in crowds will do.

"But where was there any evidence of mutiny? Had there been a single act of it? There had not. You, Madame de Sainte-Elme, were present when I stressed this fact. The Emperor sent me an excited despatch about a riot at the

221

men's theatre and two duels among officers. Yet there was no mutiny in any of it, as I told you.

"Indeed, why should the acts of Captain Cut-throat in stabbing the Emperor's soldiers turn those men against the Emperor himself? In logic's name, why? Was it not more likely to bind them closer in loyalty to him against a common enemy, as in fact it did?

"This rumour of mutiny because of Captain Cut-throat's murders was all a sham, and it took no subtle intellect to see why.

"The Emperor, I repeat, was already being plagued by republican elements; and also, for some reason I could not and still cannot fathom, was delaying his invasion of England for so long that it was rousing great impatience. Some measure had to be taken at once. Now His Majesty's invariable stratagem, when he is in difficulties, is to distract people's attention: to create a diversion, and give them something else to talk and think about. That is how he wins victories in the field, and . . ."

Here Fouché broke off sharply.

"Did you speak, M. Hepburn?"

"No!" said Alan. "That is, not exactly. I was only thinking that I said the same thing myself, in different circumstances. Boney's Corsican blood was up, I take it? And he devised as theatrical a series of events as his coronation or his reviews, with Schneider as his agent and reflector-lamps as stage-properties for his most spectacular effect? Or had you seen the secret of the reflector-lamps?"

"And again," snarled the Minister of Police, "do you take me for a babe in arms? Yes; I did. However. If what he wished to do was distract people's attention, this had been done with a vengeance. You agree?"

"Most heartily!" said Alan. "Most heartily!"

"Nobody in the Grand Army," said Fouché, "could talk of anything but Captain Cut-throat. In their thirst to have the blood of this assassin, they had all but forgotten their wish to plunder London and to ask why they were still kept inactive. Furthermore, in their concern about a sham mutiny, they were not likely to be lured into a real mutiny. All this was characteristic of His Majesty; it could have been inspired by nobody else.

"Nevertheless, dear sir! The errors made by the Emperor, much worse than crimes, were also characteristic.

He, or so he believed, could not reveal the meaning of the sham evidence he had created himself. *He* could not show that Captain Cut-throat was a devilish Englishman. He must remain aloof, a god on Olympus. Someone else must do the menial work of discovering it. I was the obvious choice to do it—and mark this! I did not object!"

Rap went the Minister of Police's knuckles on the snuff-box for emphasis. His long neck thrust out snake-like until the candle-flames stung him, and he drew back.

"Whether he expected me to be deceived by his scheme, I cannot say. Perhaps he did. He knew at least I would read the evidence as he wanted it read, and that I would play his game. He was right. I was willing to serve him, and serve him well, because it suited my interest to do so.

"But His Majesty should not have been so carried away by impatience. Early on the morning of August 22nd I despatched a courier from Paris to Boulogne, with a long report telling him my evidence for believing Captain Cut-throat was an English agent. The courier with my report arrived at Boulogne at ten o'clock that night. Yet the Emperor could not restrain that impatience of his. He knew by semaphore-message that a courier was on the way. And at eight o'clock soup-time on the same night, two hours before anyone could have known what was in my report, he issued a public proclamation that the assassin had been proved to be a disguised Englishman and offered a hundred gold napoleons for the villain's capture."

Automatically Alan Hepburn attempted to snap the fingers of his right hand. Again, vaguely surprised, he found the arm useless.

"Minister," he exclaimed, "you are telling no word of a lie now. I have heard both those same statements made: one of them by Victor at the Park of Statues, and the other by a grenadier of Oudinot's Division. But——"

"But what, dear sir?"

Alan, now almost as uneasy as Ida, himself looked towards the door of the foyer.

"You are not going to expose this publicly?" he demanded. "You can't risk telling the Grand Army that the man they worship has been having them stabbed in the back to suit his higher purposes?"

The Minister of Police looked him full in the eyes. And Fouché smiled a wicked smile.

223

"Perhaps not," he answered. "But at least I am going to threaten it, and see what the Emperor says. It is time this strutting Corsican had a lesson. Believe me, dear sir, I am acquainted with so many secrets of his—in documentary evidence which can be opened should misfortune befall me—that he will not have me arrested or shot."

"No!" cried the stricken Ida, hammering her hands on the table. "You can protect yourself. But the rest of us can't. Thunder of God, we shall all be under arrest within the next twenty minutes! Have you no more consideration for your faithful servants than that?"

Fouché took more snuff.

"How unfortunate for you, dear lady!" he said. "Since you have assisted me so much by losing me the services of the best secretary I ever had, Raoul Levasseur, how very unfortunate for you!" The withered face changed. "I said before, and I say again, that I would have served the Emperor well so long as he served me well. He does not like me; that is of no consequence. Nevertheless! When through some whim or caprice of his southern blood he chooses to involve me in his ridiculous stage-effects, and have his agent Schneider leave a note accusing me of complicity in murder, my well-known loyalty suffers a change."

"But he didn't——" Alan began.

"Didn't what?" enquired the Minister of Police.

Alan checked himself just in time. And the whole hazard unrolled before him in a flash, worse than it had ever been before.

He and Madeleine were not saved: they were lost. Unless . . .

Fouché's offer to free them, though quite genuine, had been inspired by spite against the Emperor when the Minister of Police's own pride was hurt.

Schneider, Alan was willing to swear, had never been told by the Emperor to kill that sentry last night or to leave a very un-characteristic message accusing Fouché of complicity. Very shortly Boney himself would come storming in and say so. What was worse, as soon as the Minister of Police recovered from his wrath—and that could not take long—then Fouché must very quickly guess this fact for himself.

His offer would be withdrawn. The boat to England was a mirage; Alan and Madeleine were done. Unless . . .

224

There was one more move to be made in this battle of wits against the formidable Minister of Police: the last, the trickiest of all. If it succeeded, he and Madeleine would still go free. If it failed . . .

Throw the dice, now! Have a go!

"Minister," Alan said in a voice which sounded strange and hoarse even to himself, "there is a reason why you must not tell the Emperor anything when he arrives."

"Tchaa!" said the Minister of Police.

"There is a reason!" Alan insisted. "Merely as a courtesy to an enemy you have defeated, will you hear it?"

"As a courtesy, dear sir——! Well!"

"Let us suppose, for the sake of argument, that you decided not to tell the Emperor anything. No, no; you like philosophical debate; only suppose that! If you made that decision, could this whole affair be kept a close secret?"

Fouché was looking at him curiously.

"In what way?" he asked.

"Well! Ida and I, God knows, would be silent. Captain Mercier would be silent about all that has happened, so as not to imperil his career; he knows nothing of the real Captain Cut-throat anyway. But I meant silence as to everything. What about Victor?"

"If you refer," Fouché said contemptuously, "to the footman at the Park of Statues, he is a relation of my wife, and he knows more of my affairs than I like. I was obliged to take him into my service as a family responsibility. However, I could guarantee his silence if it were necessary. But, since I see no reason why I should not administer a lesson to the Emperor——"

"Wait, wait! What about the Hopewells? They leave very soon, I know. All the same, Ida said you had them 'under guard.' You haven't had them arrested, have you?"

"Dear sir!" exclaimed the exasperated Minister of Police, "am I likely to 'arrest' the diplomatic representative of a neutral power with whom the Emperor still wishes to keep up friendly relations until he uses Louisiana or Canada as a pretext for invading them? I requested them, as a courtesy, not to leave the Park of Statues until they heard from me; that is all. What, precisely, have you to say to me?"

Alan swallowed the lump in his throat.

"It concerns Lieutenant Schneider," he answered.

225

"That murderous lout? I requested the Emperor to send me his best swordsman. And what must he do, as a spy on me, but send me the fool he was using as Captain Cutthroat's agent? You saw, I hope, that Schneider must be under the protection of some authority far higher than his colonel or even than Marshal Soult? Otherwise he could hardly have attacked whom he liked and even killed whom he killed without punishment or so much as a reprimand. Yes; he was under august protection. But what of Schneider?"

"Schneider is dead," said Alan.

For a second or two, before the stark fact of death, silence held the airless council-room in the eagle-eyrie above the Channel.

"Dead?" echoed Fouché.

"I was there when he died. Somebody, whom I never saw, shot him down with a musket in the Avenue de la Fédération."

"Well! I am not surprised." Fouché's eyes narrowed. "The Avenue de la Fédération? Come! It was of interest to learn everything about this Schneider. Last Saturday, I hear, he tried to kill but did not manage to kill a guardsman named Jules Dupont in that same street. Immediately afterwards, Dupont's younger brother ran out into the street and tried to kill Schneider with a musket. He did not succeed; but I dare say he has succeeded now." Fouché lifted his shoulder. "My dear sir! If you are afraid Schneider has told the Emperor you are a British spy, and that you are given away, be reassured. Nobody has had time to see the Emperor today——"

"I was fairly sure of that. But it was not what I wanted to tell you in persuading you we must all be silent."

"If you have anything that can persuade him," burst out Ida, "for God's sake say it! I know I can hear horses now!"

It was true. A clatter of hoof-beats, many horses, drew closer to the pavilion.

"Very well!" said Alan. "You are misjudging the Emperor. He never told Schneider to implicate you in this affair. Schneider did that on his own; and, if he had lived, he would have heard a thing or two about it."

The Minister of Police stood motionless, corpse-like

thumb and forefinger poised over the snuff-box. His eyes widened, and then narrowed.

"It's true!" insisted Alan. "If you reflect, you will know it's true. You humiliated Schneider in the Room of Mirrors; you threatened to have him reduced to the ranks. It was the kind of act he couldn't and wouldn't forgive. He could not openly attack you, so on his own initiative he killed that sentry and left the note to implicate you. This morning he realized what he had done, and what the Emperor would do to him. Only that would have frightened the man as much as it did!"

The clatter of hoof-beats had come nearer and drawn up before the pavilion.

Sweat was running into Alan's eyes.

"As for the Emperor," continued Alan, "he has the very highest respect for your ability whether he likes you or not. Shall I prove that? Let me ask you a question, M. Fouché. You are very fond of your wife and children?"

"Take care, sir!" said the Minister of Police, stiffening in all his joints. "So far you have been most courteous with regard to Bonne Jeanne. But if now you dare to make any——"

"And she, I imagine, will enjoy being a duchess?"

Again, while you might have counted five or six, Fouché did not speak. He began to do so, but he kept silent as a kind of lean question-mark in himself.

"You yourself," said Alan, "though you care nothing or profess to care nothing for such guards, will enjoy seeing your eldest son a duke if the Empire survives?"

"And precisely what——" Fouché was crying out, when Alan cut him off.

"No, Minister, you do not know everything! The Emperor means to raise you to the peerage with the title of Duc d'Otrante. Look at me! You know men; you will know whether or not I am telling the truth. I say this is true; and you must be willing to risk your judgment that it is."

Now it was Alan's turn to stare at Fouché over the candle-flames.

"If you administer a lesson to the Emperor, you will soothe your pride and vanity. He can't shoot or imprison you. But, if you tell him you know he is Captain Cut-throat—if you provoke him to the wildest burst of rage he will ever show in all his life—then your Bonne Jeanne will never find her name in the peerage and neither will any of your children."

Quick footsteps crunched on the gravel of the path leading to the pavilion's front door. The steps halted, while a voice gave instructions to others. In the council-room they could not hear what was said; it was something to the effect that the man who spoke would go alone into the pavilion. But it was the quick, harsh, impatient voice of the Emperor.

Most of all, as the thick air pressed against him, Alan was conscious of Ida's startled face turned round.

"Alan!" she said. "You have signed your own death-warrant!"

"No!" said Alan—who was again riding straight towards his enemies in the hope of escaping them.

"Your own death-warrant!" insisted Ida. "Sometimes you are so insane that I stop wondering about you and almost wish you to have that woman you are so fond of. Look at our Minister of Police! He has no generosity; he said it himself. If the Emperor did not try to trick him, if the Emperor has a high opinion of his talents, you are as good as dead from now on. He will never let you get away to England and tell everybody this story about Captain Cut-throat!"

Joseph Fouché's red-rimmed eyes, briefly, seemed remote and far away, fixed on other places and other persons.

"Duchesse d'Otrante," he murmured. "Duchesse d'Otrante!"

Then, carefully replacing his snuff-box in the tail-pocket of his coat, he straightened up and became his cold, formal, bloodless self.

"M. Hepburn," he said, "it is not often, in this game of ours, that I meet an enemy who treats me with any degree of fairness or honour. I appreciate yours, as I think you know. But it cannot alter matters in the least."

"You see?" cried Ida.

"It is true," the icy voice continued, "that in my justifiable wrath against the Emperor I was anxious only for his victim, yourself, to escape him. That has changed. There is much in what Madame de Sainte-Elme says: you cannot be permitted to go away knowing this story. The

228

Emperor still believes you to be the Vicomte de Bergerac, my investigator. I think I will enlighten him at once . . ."

(Now! Hit him!)

"And I," said Alan, "don't think you will."

"No, M. Hepburn?"

"No!" said Alan. "Decency and fairness be hanged! I am out to keep Madeleine now, as you cherish your Bonne Jeanne and your children; and every bit of fair play goes overboard at this minute."

"Meaning what?"

"In the first place," said Alan, "I can never tell this story in England because nobody in authority would believe me. You don't understand how stuffy and dignified and thick-headed the government of His Britannic Majesty can be. You and Ida and I know Boney played this trick for perfectly good and logical reasons to gain his ends; it was even his own idea of justice; but they would only say it was beneath the dignity of any ruler, and shut me up in a madhouse for blackening his character. Unless you appreciate the nature of the British, you'll never know how true that is!

"In the second place, if you arrest me the Emperor hears this whole story at once. He's always glad to see a condemned prisoner. He'll have me shot very quickly, yes; but you'll tumble from your high place and you will never climb back again."

Fouché stood rigid.

"Since he is Captain Cut-throat," said Alan, "and since he doesn't even mean to invade England now—no, don't look surprised!—he will be only too gratified if you say Captain Cut-throat has been too clever for us, and it would be useless to investigate further. Tell him that, here and now, and the whole affair is kept silent. Tell him anything else, Minister, and I blow the gaff myself!"

"Dear sir," said Fouché, "are you threatening me?"

"Yes!" said Alan. "I am threatening you, as you have threatened so many others. There it is, Minister, and the choice is yours."

They faced each other across the table, their glances locked.

Outside the pavilion, the short, quick footsteps strode up to the front door. The outer door opened and closed with a hollow bang and slam which went vibrating through the council-room itself. A voice, harsh as a crow's, called impatiently in the foyer for somebody to fetch lights.

Still Fouché and Alan stared at each other, both of them trembling. Ida de Sainte-Elme, with a little moan, sat down in the one chair and put her head in her hands.

Then, not troubling further about lights, the impatient footsteps strode across the foyer.

The door of the council-room was flung open. Ida sprang up from her chair and swept a deep curtsey in the direction of the doorway.

Joseph Fouché also turned round, very slowly.

"Sire!" he said.

Then, once again, his tone became cold and poised and emotionless.

"I take the liberty, Sire," he continued, "of making you acquainted with Madame Ida de Sainte-Elme, a great admirer of yours; and with the Vicomte de Bergerac, who has been assisting me in my investigation. It is with sorrow, Sire, that I must report our complete failure to find this mysterious Englishman. I can only state my regret at my failure; and express the hope that at some future day, not too far distant, I may serve your Majesty as your Majesty really ought to be served."

And so, with the stateliness of an old-time courtier, the Minister of Police bowed very gravely to the man in the doorway.